Mr. Theodore Mundstock

Mr. Theodore Mundstock

By Ladslav Fuks

FOUR WALLS EIGHT WINDOWS

NEW YORK

Published by:
Four Walls Eight Windows
PO Box 548
Village Station
New York, N.Y. 10014

First Edition.
First Printing   August 1991.

Library of Congress Cataloging-in-Publication Data:

Fuks, Ladislav.
[Pan Theodor Mundstock. English]
Mr. Theodore Mundstock / by Ladislav Fuks. — 1st ed.
p.   cm. Translation of: Pan Theodor Mundstock.
I. Title.   II. Title: Mister Theodore Mundstock.
PG5039.16.U38P3513   1991
891.8'635—dc20   91–2988
CIP
Printed in the U.S.A.

A rabbi
once asked
his disciples
this question:
"What should a man value most in life?"
The first disciple answered: "Good eyesight."
The second said: "Good friends."
The third declared: "Good neighbors."
The fourth replied: "The vision of things to come."
The fifth: "A good heart."
The rabbi agreed
with the last speaker,
for what he said
embraced all that had been said before.

Talmud, Pirke Abot, 10

MR. THEODORE MUNDSTOCK

CHAPTER I

It was almost dark when he got back with his shopping, and so he switched on the light in the hall. His shadow appeared, and before he could summon up courage to turn round and look at the door, his shadow rushed at the letter box and back into the room.

His shadow touched the lamp switch, tore open the envelope, and flitted over the first and last lines.

He sank into his desk chair, staring at Columbus's ship on the pale lampshade.

"My nerves have all gone to pieces, Mon," he said to his shadow and went on staring at the ship. "The minute I see something white in the letter box I'm dead certain its my summons and, just look, there isn't even an official heading on the envelope." And he thought to himself, my nerves have all gone to pieces but it's time my shadow Mon went away.

His shadow moved away and the pale lamplight fell on his face and chest. "Thank God for that," he whispered, stroking the creature he found at his feet. The creature seemed to have a speckled body, bright red eyes and a yellow beak; it was looking up at him happily because he'd got back safely with the shopping.

[1]

"I've got back safely with the shopping, chicky, but my nerves have all gone to pieces," he told the creature sadly. "It's just an ordinary letter and there am I, thinking it's my summons. I just can't bring myself even to look at that letter box." And shaking his head he picked up the letter and read:

Dear Mr. Mundstock,

You take care of all kinds of creatures walking the earth, but you've forgotten there are any such people as the Sterns. It's six months since we saw you last. It's autumn and you really ought to dress properly. You'd no overcoat on when Simon met you in Havel Street, in the wind and the rain. He raised his cap but you didn't notice him and so he didn't like to stop and speak. He wants you to come and see us. So does the poor old lady, you know what she's after—fortunetelling. So does Freda, but you'll be surprised how poorly she looks. I'm afraid it's on account of her engineer breaking it off. A most unfortunate business you haven't heard about yet. Poor girl, there's nobody she can turn to, you know what Otto's like, he just shrugs his shoulders—you've known him thirty years. It's no good talking to the old lady unless you talk in riddles, and Dr. Propper's had a stroke, may the Lord have mercy on him. You are my only hope. We'll expect you early one evening, when we're still allowed out; that's the time we sit in the dining room. You can drop us a line if you like, to make a real evening of it, Otto says it would be better but you needn't bother, the things he says don't make sense any more. Best wishes from us all,

K. Stern

P.S. Mr. Mundstock, I'm crying all the time, wherever I go, though I don't let myself think of the horrors ahead of us. I don't even dare to remember there is anything of the sort. Have you got any reliable news? Do come soon, please. K. S.

[2]

"So it's from Mrs. Stern, chicky," he put the letter down, touched, and stroked the creature's back. "I was there yesterday, and here they are, asking me again. Freda's engagement's broken off, that's a sad thing. Simon . . ."

He jerked his hand up and sat stock still. Had he really met the boy and failed to see him? In Havel Street? Ha-vel Street? He held his head in his hand. When was he last in the Old Town, in heaven's name? He thought back desperately. It must have been the day the Backers told him Steiner and Knapp had got away to Slovakia to join the partisans, but it was Balthazar Street they lived in. He had gone down Armourers Lane, past the druggist's on the corner, and on to the bank to pay the rent, but by way of Soap Street. It could only have been the day he went to see old Moyshe Haus in Benedict Street, where he used to have his second-hand stores, but that day he'd hurried down Maisel Street not to be noticed. It must be three years since he'd been in Havel Street at all, in fact he hadn't been there since the Germans had come, as sure as his name was Theodore. It must have been somebody else Simon met, and now the boy was thinking he'd passed him by . . . A wave of sudden pity came over him, and he had to lift his head from his hand and smile wanly at the creature by his foot.

"You know, chicky," he said, staring into space, "for years I used to cut the stamps off old letters in Havel Street, and bring them home for him to stick in a book; how could I possibly pass him by and not notice him? At Purim I used to take him to the zoo; the monkeys and the elephants were his favorites, and of course all the hens, chicky." He stroked the creature's neck as it delightedly rubbed his cheek, and he suddenly remembered Simon standing in front of the monkeys' cage clutching a bag of peanuts he'd given him, and not knowing what to do with them. The boy watched the monkeys skillfully shelling the nuts and objected piteously: "I can do that too, and I can jump and swing, I'm clever as they are, I am, aren't I? Only I haven't got a cage, that's all." And he had smiled and

[3]

patted him and said: "Much cleverer, you're a human being, you see, and they're only monkeys," and he was so happy . . . "And when Hanukkah came round I used to take him to a puppet show," he whispered with his eyes fixed on Columbus's ship, remembering the time he'd taken Simon to see *Sleeping Beauty*. Everything about the play was light, rose-pink and fragile as china, even the dresses and the faces of the puppets. Punchinello came on and planted a rose in the garden; he was afraid it would fade, and Simon was afraid too, and whispered: "What's going to become of the rose?" And he had laughed and comforted him: "It'll grow, the same as you." Then the witch came and put a spell on the rose, and Beauty pricked her finger on one of the thorns and fell into a deep sleep. When Punchinello broke the spell and woke the Sleeping Beauty up, the rose grew bigger and more beautiful, and he had said to Simon: "There you are, you see all the spells are broken," and Simon had clapped with joy because it had all come right in the end, yes, he recalled it clearly, that was what it was like when he took him to see the puppet show during Hanukkah . . . And then he remembered, heaven help him, the puppet show during Hanukkah, but there was somebody else in Havel Street and he mistook him for me. He snatched his hand back and his neck felt stiff. The creature flapped its wings in fright and the Cizeks' clock next door started to strike.

"It's time to get supper, chicky," he pulled himself together, "I know you're hungry, aren't you, so come along . . ." and leaning on the arms of his chair and with his mind full of somber thoughts he got to his feet and went into the hall to put away his shopping, the two white paper bags he had dropped on the basket chair by the door when he turned to look at the letter box.

In a flurry he picked up the paper bags and took them behind the curtain that hid a pretense as a kitchenette, thinking what a good thing it was that Mon had made so little trouble by going away, at least he wasn't going to bother him,

[4]

but then he saw him standing a little way off. He hasn't gone far, he thought, he wants to vex me. And he pretended not to notice.

"We'll cook something for supper," he nodded at the creature with its inquisitive eyes on his, "we'll have a real feast tonight," and he showed it the paper bags. The creature rubbed against his leg and then retreated, wisely. It didn't want to be snapped at for getting underfoot while he was cooking. He found an onion and a bit of fat and was just looking round for the rest when Mon spoke.

"Funny thing, asking him round again when he says he was there yesterday," Mon whispered and fell silent.

It's started! he sighed and began looking for something under the table. He had explained why. Because of Simon. And because they wanted to ask his advice about Freda. She said so in the letter, quite clearly. And to tell the poor old lady's fortune. And hers as well, Mrs. Stern's, he thought to himself, hers above all, for heaven's sake, they want me to go round because of the fortunetelling . . .

"It's only foolishness," he waved in the direction of the creature's blinking eyes, "a gipsy woman taught me how to read the cards one summer, when I got lost in the Vah valley. I gave her some money and a clothesline . . ." He realized there was nothing under the table and that he'd forgotten to buy any bread, but it was too late then. Never mind, we won't need bread tonight with a feast like this, he thought, and said out loud:

"She taught me to read the cards properly, though; it always comes out for the Sterns."

"Except for the sad things he doesn't bother to mention," said Mon, "so why do they ask him round?"

The creature pecked at his shoe and he remembered he would need the pale blue dish. Then he caught sight of a ring on the stool where a mug had stood, and picked up a dishcloth because he liked everything neat and tidy in his modest kitchen.

[5]

"Why?" said Mon.

For heaven's sake, he thought to himself, because they'd seen better times! On Sunday mornings with the window wide open and Mrs. Stern frying veal cutlets. She busied herself at the stove, stirring, adding flour, adding stock, adding salt, tipping the pale blue dish, chopping onion on a board and scraping it off with the back of a knife, and in ten minutes they'd eaten it up and there was nothing left, though they had enjoyed while it lasted. He enjoyed it, too; the Sterns used to ask him round to dinner on a Sunday. And when she cleared the table she took the dishcloth, damped it, dipped it in the bag of soda she kept on the stove and wiped it back and forth over the table until it shone. She liked everything neat and tidy in her kitchen. The last time had been three years ago, though, and now what were things like? Oh, dear me, now it was all she could do to wipe the ring off where the mug had stood, and cook something a hen might condescend to eat if it had to.

"I'll be as quick as I can," he comforted the creature pecking at the floor, and damping the dishcloth he dipped it in the bag of soda behind the burner and wiped it back and forth over the stool until it shone. A good thing I learned to cook properly, he said, I wonder where I picked it up . . .

"Why do they ask him round?" Mon insisted.

He found the dish and put it near the burner. "That's one thing," he said.

"Why?" Mon shouted.

"I still haven't found the matches," he said to the creature with a sigh, and as he looked for them he thought how Otto used to sit by the kitchen table while Mrs. Stern was cooking the dinner, and ask him the news from Havel Street, although nothing had ever happened all the thirty years he'd been working there, so that he didn't really ask him anything at all and just sat quiet, lifting his hand and letting it fall now and again. Otto never quarreled with anybody, though he had a cloth business in the Green Market and two children to think of! He'd lost the shop now, anyway, and so really Otto'd been the wisest of them all in those days. And their eighty-year-old grandmother in her lace cap and her plush armchair, who could read Hebrew and was so highly thought of. She used to say she was going to the Jewish cemetery in the evening to look for her grave, the only light shining in this valley of darkness and bitter woe. She'd been looking for it all the thirty years he'd been going to see them, that was when Mr. Klein was the porter there, before he died of old age. From thinking of the grandmother his thoughts passed to the slender, pretty, dark-eyed girl with the full breasts and flowing locks smelling of mignonette, poor Freda who pretended she was too shy to get married but who blushed whenever her engineer's name was mentioned, three years ago, and then he thought of Simon again, the lovely clever boy so like his sister in looks. He used to kneel on the floor gluing the stamps from Havel Street into his book and Mrs. Stern snapped at him not to get underfoot while she was cooking . . . His neck felt stiff again, but luckily he recognized the flapping wings on the floor and the gas escaping from the burner, and so he hastily struck a match and set to work.

There was millet in the one bag. Heaven only knows where Pazourek the baker had got hold of it now, in wartime, but there was no doubt he had slipped it across to him in the shop, so he could make some porridge. The baker had a fine face and well-kept hands and refined manners. He held the door open for his customers and called the ladies "Madam" and could speak German. He often gave Mr. Mundstock a bit over the ration. In the other bag there was a very special treat: blancmange powder. Mr. Mundstock never made blancmange, especially in wartime, but the baker had told him just to mix it into hot milk. And he'd whispered that you could just as well mix it into hot water. Finding that he'd got an onion and a bit of fat ready by the burner he decided to make porridge and leave the special treat for the first holiday to come round, not to let it spoil. In less than two months it would be Hanukkah . . .

"As if that was why they asked him round," Mon interrupted him; "it's no time for that."

Oh dear, oh dear, he hasn't gone away, he can see it all; all right, then perhaps they ask me round because of what I know. Because I know the latest news about the transports from poor old Moyshe Haus in Benedict Street, who's communing with spirits these days and has the latest news straight from the Jewish Community Office. Because I know the first transports left for Lodz not long ago, and they're going to be leaving all the time now. Every one of us can expect the summons any day, only there's no need to be afraid, they say once you get to the concentration camp you get dulled to it and don't even feel the horrors. That's why they ask me round, in fact she says so in her letter . . .

"That's not why!" Mon screamed. "He was there six months ago and the first transports have only just gone. Why tell lies? It's because he doesn't tell them that, just because he tells them the exact opposite. Because he'll tell them there aren't any transports going to Lodz and aren't going to be any, that's why they ask him round. Because he'll say it's all imagination, expecting the summons. Even if the Germans are still advancing it'll all be over soon, that's why they ask him round. Because he's a liar and a cheat!"

His hands fell to his sides.

The world reeled round him.

Because I'm a liar and a cheat, a liar and a cheat!

"Chicky," he called out to the little eyes blinking at the blue tongues of flame, "because the man making porridge for you on this burner is a liar and a cheat . . . Chicky," he suddenly became earnest and tears welled up in his eyes, "the worst thing of all is to lose hope. To lose hope is the worst that can happen to anyone. Even a rich man is a beggar if he has no hope, and

[8]

what would become of us miserable creatures with our Star of David? Do you know what the grave is, chicky?

"If I knew a way out of the horror, chicky, if only I knew," he whispered. "There are my books in the room behind us, books I've collected over thirty years, a sofa I turned into a bed at night so I can lie there and sleep, and a door, but the door opens here into the hall, and you can't escape from the concentration camp that way. A lamp, with a ship moving over an endless sea, endless because it goes round and round—can I hop on board and sail away, on a lampshade? Or should I start trying to talk to the spirits, like old Haus—is that the way out? The mirror, yes there's a mirror in there too, but all I can see in that is myself. And the window, the light comes in through it as long as it isn't blacked out, the fourth floor window . . . If only I knew a way out I'd tell everybody, I'd help everybody whether they wear the Star of David or not, they're just as badly off as we are, or just a bit better off because they've got a tiny bit more hope than we have, but I'd help them all. Only I don't know how. I don't know a thing . . ." he was whispering now, "the valley of darkness and bitter woe, that's what Mrs. Stern called it; I wonder if she's found that grave?" Sadly he raised his eyes from the creature with its bright beady eyes, but halfway up he stiffened; over the burner hung a calendar with a picture of a chimney sweep riding a lucky pig and the words "Alois Klokocnik, Butcher and Delicatessen, 1941". . . He remembered that next day he wanted to venture to Haus's place, not for news from the Community Office, but because Haus was an unhappy man whose nerves had given way and so he'd started communing with the spirits, so it would have to be the day after tomorrow for the Sterns. Half-blinded he felt for a pencil and made a cross by the day after tomorrow, with a capital S. Then he wiped the tears from his eyes, picked up the onion and started chopping it on the board . . .

Somebody knocked at the door.

The knife dropped from his fingers.

[9]

The creature spread its wings and stretched its neck and fled, fled in terror as fast as its thin legs would go, into the room.

"There's nothing to be afraid of," he called after it, "it's not a summons, it's only the Cizeks, they always knock instead of ringing. Oh dear, my nerves have all gone to pieces, a good thing I know how to cook, at least." He wiped his hands and went to open the door.

On the landing stood Mrs. Cizek with a plate in her hand.

"Just a bite, Mr. Mundstock."

Then she looked at him anxiously.

"You haven't got a visitor, have you?"

Good, kind Mrs. Cizek with her worried look and anxious face.

He did not know how to thank her properly. He felt so much happier all of a sudden.

"Come along," he called joyfully into the room as he shut the door, "Mrs. Cizek's brought us some buns, she must have had a baking day, look." And as the creature pattered tentatively back he said:

"D'you know what, chicky? We'll save the buns for Friday evening, for the Sabbath. We're not going to eat them today when we're cooking a real feast. Then on Friday we'll get out the best plates and put the buns on them and sprinkle them with sugar, and put a cloth on the table, and for once the table will be set properly. . . ." All at once he narrowed his eyes, staring into space, and said: "I'll sit in the armchair and you can perch on the arm, and I shall imagine we are at the Seder feast. There will be candles lit and the *Shulhan Aruk* lying in front of us. I will open it and read you something nice, perhaps the piece that says we must love our neighbors or see that the little birds fallen from the nest don't freeze to death, or the piece about trusting. The buns won't be stale by then. Not today, oh dear, no," he said, covering the buns with a dish and putting them away under the stool, "we won't need them today."

"I'm not going to give you hot porridge, though," he said when he'd closed the cupboard door, "you'd burn yourself. You shall peck your fill when it's cooled." He wanted to bend down and stroke the creature again, but he realized he hadn't really begun to cook the supper at all, yet, and when the creature pecked happily at his shoe he hastily plunged his fingers into the bag to sprinkle the millet into the pan with the fat. A good thing that Mon had gone, he thought.

"What about the others, though," Mon spoke up a little way off, "the Sterns aren't the only ones to invite him, are they? Do the others invite him because he makes everything sound so good? Do they?"

Oh dear, he's still here, he thought to himself as he bent over the burner where the margarine was turning into yellow water, it's true that there are others who invite me. And he raised his head resignedly and replied:

"That's because I used to go out a lot before the war . . ."

"I must tell you something about those days, chicky," he turned to look below the burner, "quick, before our good supper's ready. Before the war I used to get about a lot, in Gentile society as well as Jewish. I used to go to the Hlavovka Café, on the corner of the Square. There were great big mirrors on the walls, and that made the place seem twice as big, and there were glass bead lampshades and chairs and tables and leather-covered wall seats and iron Musgrave stoves in the corners for heating when it was snowing outside. The gentlemen who used to gather there in the evenings used to invite me to join them, and so I used to go too. For a cup of coffee, or a glass of red wine on a Friday, before the Sabbath. Nobody went there on Saturdays, but they closed the place on a Saturday, anyway . . ."

"It'd make more sense if he stirred that pan," said Mon, "and took care not to burn it."

He picked up a spoon and started stirring.

". . . and for a game of billiards, too. That's a long stick, chicky, and you hit two white balls and one red one with the end of the stick, but the most important thing is the blue chalk you rub on the tip of the stick. The chalk has to lie on the edge of the table, on the rim, but only a tiny scrap. The gentlemen used to play bridge too, but I never got the hang of it . . ."

"He'd do better to put more millet in and a pinch of salt," Mon hissed, "and some more water and shake the pan a bit. . ."

He added more millet and a pinch of salt, poured on some water and shook the pan and went on in a whisper:

"The real reason the gentlemen used to ask me to join them, though, chicky, was to talk about world affairs and keep abreast of politics. It was Fuchs who told me that, he used to smoke cigars and always ordered export quality beer. There were lots of newspapers hanging on frames on the wall, and the *Tagblatt* of course. The gentlemen used to read it every day, and so did I, but we didn't speak German in the Hlavovka. That was where the people who spoke Czech used to meet. Jan Ervin Mangel the journalist from the *Hlasatel*, Hugo Kraus the chairman of the Educational Publishers, Dr. Lechner from Moravia Street, who never took money from poor patients, Muneles the senior physician at the Sisters of Mercy, Reich had a carriers' business, Fleissig a leather-goods shop, Wolf had a daughter who studied skin diseases, he used to take the *Tagblatt* at home and then one day he came and said he'd stopped taking it. His daughter married Maur, the man who blew his brains out when he lost his money . . . Fuchs owned a cheese factory and once he gave Kraus a donation of a quarter of a million to build a Czech school in Rumburk. That upset the German M.P., he was a Jew too, but only half, and after that he wouldn't buy Fuchs's cheese and said the ones with the fox and the crow on them were poor quality. What's become of them all now, I wonder . . ." Then he said: "But to finish what I was saying. The Germans used to meet somewhere else, I didn't go there, but I went to the Hlavovka Café every day with the other gentlemen, for a chat

[12]

and to read the papers and play those billiards I was telling you about . . . And that's why the others still invite me, I suppose, because I used to go out a lot . . ."

"Suppose," shrieked Mon, "suppose he put the onion in since he bothered to chop it up?"

Oh dear, the onion, the onion. He hastily seized the board and scraped it off with the back of the knife.

"What's the matter with that bird, or whatever it is," Mon snapped, "isn't it hungry?"

The little creature was hopping about underneath the burner, its eyes gleaming.

"It's hungry, poor thing, but supper's nearly ready, now."

"Heavens above, hasn't he cooked the stuff yet?"

It isn't quite ready, but it will be in a minute. He stirred and added salt and water, shook the pan, and even skipped round a bit himself, to hurry it up.

"How come," Mon asked, "that he learned to be *such* a good cook?"

"Well, now," he sighed as he looked at the pale blue dish, and then had to smile even against his will, "that's just the way life worked out . . ."

"I think it's done," he said, turning off the gas, and the creature flapped its wings happily and nearly twisted its head off, but he soothed it: "Just wait till it cools a bit, but it'll be so good, you've never eaten anything so good. No buns for us today, we're going to have a real feast!"

He carried the dish from the kitchenette into the room with the creature delightedly trotting behind him. He sat down and got ready to eat, and the creature came close to his chair and waited patiently for him to tell it to eat, too. Then he caught sight of Mon.

"Oh, heavens, he's still here, he'll drive me mad—and I thought we'd finished . . ."

"So there are others who invite him, are there?" asked Mon. "Who, for instance? Let him just try and remember their names . . ."

[13]

His tired mind began to chase names.

The Backers. To ask whether they ought to hide their things if they were sent away. Pictures and the fur coat she got as a wedding present and can't bear to part from. The Radnitzers, did he think they'd be sent away? He used to be a bank clerk. Kolb, what was he to do with the twenty thousand he'd saved for a rainy day? Haus, what did he think about the spirits? He lived in his old second-hand shop in Benedict Street now. Mrs. Heksch the house owner—he was so upset he felt choked— what did he cook for supper so as not to spend too many ration tickets at once? "For heaven's sake," he shouted out, getting to his feet abruptly, "this is what I make for supper, this stuff on my plate, but tonight's an exception, madam, I've made millet porridge today," he said warningly and was forced to grab at the table and sink back into his chair as things began to reel and he realized that the only one who never asked anything was Mr. Vorjarhen and . . . the names had put him in such a fever of excitement that he felt on fire: neither did unhappy Ruth Kraus.

It began to seem strange, incomprehensible that all these people wanted to see him, it made him uneasy, he felt as though fire was eating into him, as though he was smoldering, something pecked at him under the table, something cold, he jumped to his feet and that moment he seemed to burst into flames, everything went black and he paled . . .

"The Lord have mercy on his soul!" he heard the cry, and the shadow coming between him and the pale light of the lamp fell on his face and chest, what was he eating, what on earth was he eating? Porridge? Thunder and lightning! He was eating blancmange and onion!

With a least effort, from beneath his own shadow, he remembered the bag he dipped the dishcloth into on the stool, and realized he was eating soda and onions in margarine.

"A good job he didn't give it to that hen to eat," said Mon and disappeared.

With an empty stomach but not the slightest urge to eat he

crept into the hall and behind the curtain. He reached for the plate of buns. The creature watched what he was doing, its head sadly drawn back between its shoulders. "Here you are, chicky," he offered it a bun, "the porridge was nice, but I forgot millet is runny and you can't have runny food at night. Peck at this, it'd only get stale . . ." And the creature jerked its head forward, pecked once, twice, and then again and again, until it came to the jam inside, then it wiped its beak on its breast feathers or a leg, and he stroked it and nodded, and the creature knew supper was over and it was time to go to bed. It pecked at his shoe, bent low, then fled up onto the basket chair by the front door, the beady red eyes blinked once more and then it slept. Speckled, with such yellow legs and beak that it would need the most precious cadmium yellow to do them justice in paint . . . Then he put the rest of the buns away and said there'd be no *Shulhan Aruk* on Friday, but at least they'd had a bite to eat that day . . . And he went to get ready for bed.

On the table in the room he caught sight of the Sterns' letter again, and there rose in his tortured mind the thought of their only hope. The hope that was all in all to them now. His thought of hope tasted strongly of soda, but they probably felt even worse. He did not know what was right; if he did not go and see them, would it be letting them down, or would it be the right thing to do? He did not know the answer, and yet his own honesty depended on it. He thought of them with the taste of soda in his mouth, as he turned his sofa into a bed. He thought of Mrs. Stern, Otto Stern, the poor old lady, Freda, and very, very much of Simon. And he was still thinking of them with the taste of soda in his mouth when he put the light out and lay down.

Then something very strange seemed to begin.

As though something began to sprout from the fierce questions that were tearing at his mind that day. As though through the everlasting fear of getting a summons, of the way to the mustering point for the transport, of everything that tormented him day and night and bore him to the ground, through it all something green was pushing up into his aching consciousness. He had no idea what it was, he simply felt it had something to do with him, just as a man's eyes, appearance, life, have something to do with him, and it was something to do with a lot of other people, too, like the Sterns. As if in that hopeless horror from which there was no way out a tiny ray began to appear, a ray hidden from him before, but the longer he lay awake the clearer he began to feel it was the only hope of salvation . . .

He was a long time getting to sleep. The soda burned his gullet and he heard the Cizeks' clock strike midnight and half past twelve and half past one. Every now and again he heard a soft croaking from the hall and wondered if the creature was hungry, and he could hear Mon walking about the room and coming to stand close to his bed, and he whispered to himself that if it hadn't been for him he would certainly never have made such a mess of the supper. At these moments he stared into the darkness as though he wanted to catch sight of him, he desperately wanted to catch sight of Mon, at least his outline, at least the shadow he cast, but it was hopeless and in vain. All around him hung the thick darkness no light could penetrate. Outside in the street everything was plunged in the safe darkness of air-raid precautions and the window of his little room was carefully blacked out.

CHAPTER 2

There are thoughts that crush. There is desperation heavy as the blocks piled up into the pyramids of Egypt. Near the park someone fell to the ground; a policeman's helmet gleamed among the crowd that gathered. The man with the star was going that way, too, but he had no right to notice what happened in the street, and so he turned round and went *the other way.*

A summons to join a transport, his visit to the Sterns, the concentration camp. The feeling that had come to him the evening before, as he tried to go to sleep. Thoughts that crush.

He suddenly heard his name.

His shoulders drooped and he clutched his bag to his star. His eyes came to rest on the tower beyond the park. But what he saw at his side was a ghost.

A face in a black kerchief.

It was one of the women who used to beg in the park, she had known him when he was better off. He looked across the street, he'd better get to the other side. But she stretched out a hand to touch him. And he smiled . . .

"Mr. Mundstock, it's really you . . ."

He had a vague feeling she wasn't a beggar after all. He did not know the woman. He wanted to say "How d'you do" and cross over to the Blue Lily passage.

"Mr. Mundstock, I'm trembling all the time. The master may fall down in the street any minute. Please, Mr. Mundstock, you don't happen to know whether he's been to see a doctor?"

The street was empty by the approach to the passage. He wanted to say goodbye and get away.

"I'll tell you all about it, Mr. Mundstock . . ."

"For heaven's sake," he pulled himself together, "whatever are you thinking of? They'll put you in prison! You must leave me at once!"

Perhaps she was a brave woman, perhaps she thought she was so old, she'd be safe. As she pointed towards the park, towards the one empty path covered with dead leaves, he felt sorry for her. She was old and wrinkled in her black kerchief. From childhood he had learned kindness to others. He resisted, caught in a trap. Standing in the street with her was worse than walking along by her side. They had to move, it did not matter where. They had to . . . He had to go with this unknown woman into the park, along the path covered with dead leaves . . .

"Mr. Mundstock, the master used his food ration tickets to get extra cigarettes. The master smokes and sits up with the light on till two in the morning, and when I go in to clean up in the morning . . . The master has ten ashtrays in his room . . ."

His mind was half on what she was saying, half wondering who she was. And why he was walking along with her. If he hadn't turned round and gone the other way he wouldn't have met her. He was a target woven of straw, with a six-pointed star in the middle, and his bag. The bag did not cover the star. That was a trick they soon saw through. Anybody seeing a man clutching his bag to him on the street could ask what he'd got to hide on his breast. If he happened to be an informer he would call the police. The summons would come all the quicker, the way to the mustering point for the transport.

He was in terrible danger walking along with this old woman, and he didn't even know who she was . . . Simon had met him in Havel Street although he hadn't gone that way at all. And if somebody met him now he was going this way . . . ? Fear whirled round in his head and suddenly became like lead.

The park!

They had reached it safely.

"Mr. Mundstock," he heard his name again, this time under the black boughs of the trees. "My master. . ."

Who was it, whoever was it? Mrs. Schleim? Why did she call her husband "master"? Rebecca talked like that, at the well, and so did Judith, but surely not Mrs. Schleim? He stared at the dead leaves on the path they had reached, as yellow as the star on his coat. The Sterns! Saturday would come round, but he could not face the question of how the visit would turn out. He looked straight ahead and saw there was nobody going their way. The people hurrying across the park went down the main avenue. This side path was only for the desperate. The lead that filled his head flowed over the Stern family and the fear of meeting the desperate. Heavens, it couldn't be her. Anny Schleim was an actress in the German Theatre and her husband was a dentist. What was all that about ten ashtrays? What did they matter? Who was she talking about?

"The master said he'd have to leave the light on and smoke, didn't I know he was making his will?"

There are people who make wills, almost everybody was doing it. Mrs. Heksch had her house to leave and Haus of Benedict Street had something to pass on, too, he'd had that second-hand shop. The Sterns? Wouldn't it be better to have a meal before he went there? His eyes staring, he wondered if he'd made a mistake. There were no desperate people on that path. The only one about was himself. He was meeting himself. That was why there was a spy round every corner, on the faded grass, in the blackened bushes, at the turn of the path.

Parks were supposed to give people pleasure! Havel Street! Not to be there and then to meet him was terrible. To go along and not meet him was good luck. The best luck a man in his position could meet with, anyway. But he hadn't met with it, alas. . .

"One day the master said he couldn't be sure he'd ever come back from the concentration camp and he wanted to have a clear conscience. So he was leaving me his house and twenty thousand."

Heavens above, wasn't it Mrs. Weber? But who on earth would be leaving her a house and twenty thousand? The Streckers? They didn't even know her. She was talking like Judith but she wasn't wearing the Jewish star. Surely, in God's name, she hadn't taken it off? That wild idea had occurred to only two people he knew, Steiner and Knapp, when they got away to Slovakia. Could it be the janitor's wife? What an idea, Mrs. Civrna wasn't more than fifty . . . His lead-filled head was swelling. He knew he'd have to have a meal before he went to the Sterns, he'd have to take something, anyway. His eyes fell on her shoes as she trod the dead leaves, and although he still didn't know who she was he found himself thinking she wouldn't be badly off with a house and twenty thousand.

". . . and said that if he did come back after all he'd take me to his country place in Klanovice, and he said he'd take my sister and brother-in-law and their children as well, and give us a good time, and he'd make me the manager."

He was in despair. Mrs. Jarna came from Mokropsy. Quite apart from the fact—he pulled himself up horrified—that Mrs. Jarna had been dead these fifteen years . . . He looked at her shoes and saw they were black and very worn.

Suddenly he wanted to cry out.

He had recognized her.

Lifting his eyes from her poor shoes he saw a little way off on the grass the statue of a poor old woman in a black kerchief and black shoes. That was her.

My nerves have all gone to pieces, he thought as they went in the direction of the statue. Mrs. Schleim, Mrs. Jarna fifteen years dead! Whatever made me think of such a thing? He cast a grateful glance at the statue of the poor creature standing on the grass with clipped bushes round it, and noticed she was holding a bag. The woman by his side had a bag too, in the hand further away from him. Now that they were passing the statue he saw it wasn't a bag she was holding, it was a book. A book. She was an old writer! He leaned forward in desperation to see if the woman by his side had a book too. She was carrying a bag. His knees buckled under him with horror. It was somebody else. . .

He had not time to get himself in hand. Beneath his feet he saw the leaves thinning and the black ground showing through. Feeling that their side path was coming to an end he lifted his eyes and could not see . . . The avenue ahead of them seemed to have no end.

There were fewer leaves on the ground in the avenue, but the crowds of people! Perhaps it was because they had reached the avenue so suddenly that his mouth would not form a word of protest that they had got there before they really got there and that it was too late not to be there. And with somebody he didn't even know a thing about. His little room with the hen running about and waiting for him to come back at any moment. His sofa, his lamp with the ship on it. He was hurrying back there, and where had he landed instead? Where had this face in the black kerchief led him? To the cemetery? They passed a clump of weeping willows. Underneath the trees there were little piles of dry earth, graves. A stork standing on one leg between them. No, it was a cross. No, a bird-table, with a leaf blown by the wind sticking out from under the shelter. That was another illusion, like the statue. It was a fat sleek cat looking out from under the shelter and at that moment he realized he would never get to the end of that avenue. He would collapse and that would be the end. The most miserable end he had ever imagined. The idea that even in his coffin he would be a miserable creature made him feel faint. No, that wasn't possible, he protested, he would take something! Why, he'd got three sedatives at home, prewar Swiss tablets. Where had he got hold of them? He had never taken the things. Not that it mattered. They were precious jewels. Better go to the transport mustering point without them, they couldn't save him then, but before he went to the Sterns. . .

They passed the bird-table, and the black boughs of the trees made a network overhead sprinkled with hundreds of red and yellow scraps of confetti, and the crackling and rustling of his name came from it. Cats were dashing about overhead talking about the summons. Similar cats were running in and out of the black bushes alongside the avenue under the trees, and every step they took was a step in the direction of the mustering place. Every second he spent in the company of this face in its black kerchief was one second nearer death.

At the far end of the avenue that seemed to have no end two men in gray leather coats and green hats with the brim turned down appeared and came slowly nearer with markedly military tread . . .

The last spark of life fled from his eyes and his leaden head sank. There was somebody walking by his side and talking and talking, but whether it was Mrs. Schleim or Mrs. Jarna it was all the same. The two men were nearer now and their steely eyes were looking at the head on his chest. When they got within twenty paces he would shout. It's not me, it's somebody else . . . but their gray eyes had already penetrated his bag, which was quite empty, anyway. That's not a star I'm wearing, oh dear no, can't you see it's only a yellow leaf fallen on my coat? He felt himself reddening, he had denied himself but it was no good. The cats in the bushes squealed and his head on his shoulders was a solid lump of lead. He saw the two men through a mist, seven, six, five paces away, by his side somebody's face in a kerchief, a face that kept on talking and talking and then came the moment when it all died out. All he was aware of was the leaden head.

Then the miracle happened.

One of the men in the leather coats turned round to see who was coming behind him, and then he said something to the other. Then they passed on and did not even notice him.

"To tell you the truth, Mr. Mundstock," he heard the voice lamenting by his side, "my master has been making his will for weeks and he's gone and given himself nicotine poisoning."

"Lord, what was this thing . . ." he realized he had lost consciousness for a moment, although he had seen everything that went on . . . "Heavens above, what a strange thing . . ."

"Yes indeed," the lament went on, "and his dead brother prophesied it all before it happened. You must have known him, he bore the same name as the master, except that he was Rudolph, and he lived in Vinohrady. The master's hands turned all blue and his fingers were swollen, like worms they looked, and in the end he went to see the doctor. It must have been about a month ago . . ."

He could not help turning round.

Two backs in leather coats were disappearing at the other end of the avenue at a martial pace.

He understood he had won a victory.

Death had come close to him in the shape of two Gestapo men, stretching out their hands for his star, and then— nothing. Death had turned round, said something to itself and gone on. As if he had not even been there on the path at that terrible moment. As if the old woman had been walking along by herself talking about nicotine poisoning. As if the same thing had happened as that day in Havel Street. He was seen there although he wasn't there, and today it had been the other way round . . .

"When the master showed it to the doctor, the doctor said well, Mr. Kolb, you're a heavy smoker, aren't you?"

Kolb!

Heavens, it was Mrs. Emily Hobzek!

She had been talking about Kolb, who didn't know what to do with his twenty thousand!

He trembled a moment. Kolb's old housekeeper was a good woman, but everybody knew she never stopped talking, as though she was sitting in the kitchen telling tales all the time.

[23]

He knew he was in a bad way.

"I won't take all your cigarettes away at once," Mrs. Hobzek was talking about the doctor and what he said to Mr. Kolb, "I'll let you smoke ten a day, but not another one. Come back in a week's time. Next week the master went back to him and the doctor said, you've stuck it like a man, Mr. Kolb, just go on that way. And he let him have his ten cigarettes a day. Only the master thought he was all right again, and took a few more. Next morning when I went in to clean up there were six ashtrays on the table where he does his writing. That was three weeks ago, Mr. Mundstock. Well, he went back to the doctor again when the week was up, but when he got home he told me, Emily, he said, I didn't do so well today. I can see you haven't been obeying orders, Mr. Kolb, the doctor had said to him, and so there's nothing I can do for you. You've been trying to cheat me and so I can't treat you any longer. Can you imagine how awful I felt, I asked the master, I said, call him a doctor, I said, but the master just sighed and said there you are, Emily, a doctor like that's got an easy life of it . . ."

He had made up his mind. He would take all three tablets, even if he made himself ill. It was worth it for the moment's peace. He would be able to help Freda. And he'd have a look round to see what could be done about Simon. He'd take those tablets . . . His eyes were searching the passers-by. They looked at him shyly, encouragingly, frowningly, the last might have been whipping up those cats . . . The most diverse palette of glances of all shades and tones you realize only when they are fixed on you . . . It was strange he felt them so strongly just now, when his head was made of lead and the eyes that reflected them held no more than a flicker of life. Or was it just because of that . . . He noticed that though he could not see the end of the avenue he could see a crossroads in it. The ways parted under tall, slender trees.

He decided that when they got so far he would excuse himself and go off.

But it was woefully far away.

"And what do you think happened, Mr. Mundstock? Only a week ago the master came home so upset he could hardly get a word out. D'you know what's happened, Emily? he said the minute he got in at the door. That doctor of mine, you know the one, he didn't want to go on treating me for that nicotine poisoning, well he's gone too. Yesterday, with a transport of Jews to the concentration camp . . ."

"And then the master, dear man, said it's terrible, Emily, but I've got to hurry up and make that will . . . And from that dreadful day until this, whenever I pass his door in the night he's got the light on like he used to, only the dreadful thing is that he isn't up till two in the morning like he used to be, but even till four or till it's time for breakfast . . .

"And then when I go in to clean up it isn't ten ashtrays any more, it's twelve I have to empty now . . . Can you see how terrible it is?"

For heaven's sake, can't she stop, he thought to himself, this is no time to be telling long stories, we're not in the kitchen, we're in the park. The crossroads was coming nearer. If he turned to the right he'd come to the street along that path, and then he could be home in twenty minutes.

". . . it's all the same, Emily, whether I die of nicotine poisoning here or perish there, you can only die once . . ."

Home in fifteen minutes, it's safer there in spite of the letter box and the bell anybody can ring. That poor hen must be running about in a panic by now . . .

"And yesterday he told me he'd have the will made out in a week!"

Heavens above, if only she'd tell me how to make millet porridge there'd be more sense in it, but the crossroads was here and he felt instinctively that he ought to take notice of what the poor thing at his side was saying. He looked down at her and realized that all the time she'd been talking she had been looking up at him beseechingly and now she might be going to cry. Oh dear no, not that, he thought and hastily dropped his eyes. He looked at the toes of her shoes and trembled in case she hadn't said all she wanted to yet.

"Mr. Mundstock," she lamented on, "if only you would give me your advice. What ought I to do about it?"

Under his bag, his heart pitied her.

He said quickly that she'd better lock Mr. Kolb's cigarette ration card up in a drawer and he'd better go to another doctor. What about Dr. Propper? Then he remembered he'd had a stroke and said hastily he'd better go to somebody else. And would she remember him to her master and he wouldn't shake hands with her in case somebody noticed them in the park.

They had reached the crossroads.

At the last moment it occurred to him to warn her about something else. She should be careful and if anybody asked who the gentleman was she'd been with she should say she used to know him a long time ago but she'd forgotten his name. And if they asked what they'd been talking about she could say she'd only told him how to make millet porridge. Then, uneasy at his own words, he began to take his leave but the woman detained him. To thank him. Oh yes, of course, Mr. Kolb's old housekeeper. She was thanking him for his good advice—he was dumb for a moment—and promised she'd follow it since it was he who'd told her . . . and how happy she was to have recognized him, but she wouldn't have recognized him, he'd changed so much, and had he got anything to eat at all? Wasn't he ill? Her voice was kind and anxious, but there was no help for it. If he looked ill, he just did, he'd swallowed that soda, but they were standing at the crossroads! And out loud he said he'd had a bit of indigestion, taken some soda by mistake, and she nodded and said heartburn, of course, but he shouldn't really take soda . . . He was no longer listening.

She had probably turned left, he was hurrying along the path to the right that turned back in the direction from which he'd come. Dead leaves as yellow as the star on his coat were rustling under his feet and as he scurried along he felt his uneasiness growing even worse than when she was walking by his side, fear because he had been walking with her at all, fear of time past that cannot be thought out of existence, and then fear because he was hurrying, a hunted animal, alone, alone, alone . . . As he realized it he caught sight of the tower beyond the bushes at the edge of the park, the spot where the unknown man had been taken ill, and he saw the crowd was still there, the policeman's helmet gleamed through them. He realized he had come to the end of his tether. With his last breath he whispered the name he knew so well . . .

At that moment the crowd parted and someone came forward and he saw it was the one he had called out. Mon . . .

With Mrs. Hobzek . . .

When he reached the third street beyond the park he had to go a bit slower. He understood he had been going past the park when he was taken ill and sank to the ground. He realized his coat was covered in dust from the road but he couldn't stop to brush it clean because it would look like a provocation. He'd better get home.

Clutching his bag to his chest he dragged himself into the fourth street.

He tried to remember what had happened. He had fallen to the ground as he passed the park. Perhaps it was hunger did it, or perhaps because he'd eaten that soda the day before. People gathered round him and a policeman came up. A good thing Mrs. Hobzek had come along just then . . . He remembered her and the policeman helping him to his feet; she handed him his hat and took him through the park, and they met two men who took no notice of them . . . And Kolb, with his nicotine poisoning, thank heaven he didn't smoke, at least he wasn't making any will. This occurred to him as he reached the end of the fourth street.

He crept along the fifth street. As he passed the butcher's and delicatessen shop of Alois Klokocnik, which was just round the corner from where he lived, it occurred to him to wonder what he would do about a will, however much he smoked.

What would he have to leave anybody, poor Mr. Theodore Mundstock in his dusty coat with the six-pointed star, who had just got up from the ground, and Mrs. Hobzek took him through the park . . . Poor Kolb, what was the good of relying on that, when you couldn't leave anything to anyone these days! They could all be sent to the concentration camp and disappear from the face of the earth . . . With his bag clutched to his chest, stooping, his head peering upwards, he crept up to the house where he lived.

A bald, chilly looking man without a hat was standing in front of the house, and gave him a malicious, treacherous glance, and the name Mr. Korka flashed through his brain. One of the whippers-up of cats in the park! As if he hadn't had enough! He pretended not to see him, but he felt he was seen. His dusty coat noted. Well, what of it, my coat's a bit dusty, I fell on the road, what else do you want to know about me, for heaven's sake, and he scurried in at the house door but at that moment he remembered Mon. He had caught sight of him in the park, surely he wasn't still lying there? He had seen him get to his feet . . . He looked round, but there was not the tiniest shadow behind him. He knew none of the people behind him, except the chilly bald informer, Korka. Nor did any of them know him, except the chilly bald informer, Korka. A Mr. Theodore Mundstock, who lived in that house . . .

Then in his dusty coat and hat he started dragging himself up the stairs to the fourth floor.

Dragging himself up the stairs on his way back from that luckless errand he had had to make, because he was sent for to appear at the council office and be told which streets he was to sweep the dust and rubbish up in next . . .

CHAPTER 3

It was getting dark when he came out into the street. It gets dark early in November. He felt as though he was venturing on a journey into darkness, but beyond that imagined darkness he could see the lights burning in the Sterns' little dining room and this image, together with something he had found to smile at, gave him strength.

"It's a funny thing," he said to his shadow as he turned the corner, "but it really is a long time since I saw the Sterns. I suppose I don't like going since the war began. Well, anyway," he added as they passed Mr. Klokocnick's butcher's shop, "I'm not just going out of a sense of duty."

"Out of fear," Mon hissed, "in case anybody asks what he's going there for, out of fear."

"Oh no it's not," he waved that off; "fear wouldn't get me anywhere. There's something draws me to the Sterns's . . ."

He passed a woman dragging a little girl along, desperately anxious not to go home yet. Poor kid, he thought with a smile. It's getting dark, there's a mist gathering, it's nasty weather out . . .

Nasty indeed, he should never have stopped those regular visits. What was it really drew him to the Sterns's?

The idea of a cosy nook, a door always open to him. The idea of somebody to look after, somebody to watch over. He had had plans for their Simon. He had put great hopes in him. He had thought what a wonderful clear future lay before the boy; each time he thought of it he thought of delicate pink china, like a fairy spell, a fairy-tale pink; he was doing his bit for that future, he, who had neither wife nor children of his own . . . Three years ago the Germans with a single rough kick had broken it all up as though it was nothing but empty foolishness, china figurines, and he had dropped his regular visits to the Sterns'. And now he was remembering what it was that had created that atmosphere of beauty, clarity and rose-tinted happiness that he had last felt three years before.

"Thunder and lightning!" Mon exclaimed, "he's coming to life. We haven't even got there yet. Who knows whether we ever shall?"

"Nothing comes of fear of going anywhere," he shrugged it off.

He could feel it in his bones from the dark damp road that chilled him and irritated his throat.

As he crossed the road he almost got in the way of a truck. For a split second people on the pavement stiffened, but the driver went on and the dark damp road was empty again.

"There you are, you see, and he wondered whether we'd ever get there! No, the German boots would kick nothing to bits, life was too short, and what had he to show for it? Work and duty, duty and work, and life had slipped away between his fingers. He should never have stopped those regular visits. But now . . ." he wanted to go on dreaming a bit longer of the beautiful, clear pink image, but Mon spoke up:

"Suppose he's sick?"

"Of course," he whispered; he said he'd take the miracle tablets, but they made him feel sick, he turned pale, and the dreams vanished. He was back in the darkness and bitter woe and it was darker than ever. What a disgrace it would be! Hadn't he taken the miracle tablets so as to be able to stick it out?

He was drunk, he thought to himself. Three Swiss tablets and why should I be sick just when I got there? Didn't I take them so as to be able to stick it out?

"If he's as clever as all that, he might find out what that feeling of hope is that's been in his mind ever since the day before yesterday," Mon grinned.

"There you are, you see," he smiled, "even that's not impossible. Who knows whether it's really the valley of darkness and bitter woe? Grandma Stern may be quite wrong. She's hasn't got a single bit of proof, after all. She only says it because she's read it in one of those Hebrew books of hers . . ." He felt weightless as he walked along, imagining them in the Sterns's little dining room at that moment, waiting for him, as they used to do. Mrs. Stern would say, Mr. Mundstock will be here in a minute. Go and open the door to him, I must just run a comb through my hair . . . Maybe Simon was just saying something of the sort. Mr. Mundstock'll be here in a minute. I'm going to open the door. Or the grandmother. High time he was here, you go to the door, Freda, and bring him right in here, now where did you put my best cap . . . He was the only one, Otto, to sit and say nothing. Thinking to himself, he'll come, all right . . . That's the way they talk, but they're worried. About Freda and about the transports. Not about the cloth business, that's been taken away from them. He had worries of his own, too. Did anybody know what had happened to Ruth Kraus, for instance? He put that from him at once. Better ask about Mr. Vorjahren, only they wouldn't know about him. They had only known him by name . . . He passed a wall covered with ugly, damp posters he did not even stop to look at.

"*Herrgott, nehm'sie Brille, sie . . .*" a voice shouted as someone clutched at his forward-thrust body, pushed him off and swore as he went on his way. No need for glasses, the stupid fool, he was half turned to the posters and didn't see him coming. He recalled the evenings he had sometimes spent with them . . .

"Wine and dancing, I suppose?" came Mon's voice again. "A nice packet they made, didn't they?"

He started as though somebody had stuck a pin in him. Everybody thought the Sterns and their shop, a nice packet. A bit of slander the more sensible heads believed now and again. Nowadays they're spreading it for all they're worth, of course, like the posters that German was staring at. The poor Jew sitting on his sacks of gold. Here it is, take a good look, that's the way things used to be. What about Mon? He hadn't even known him before the war; it was only since the first day of the German occupation that they'd been together. He could point to the day of Mon's birth in the calendar, that's the sort of date you never forget as long as you live. Oh, well, you might say, what does it matter, even if they did drink and dance. Even if he himself had drunk and danced a bit. If only they'd had a single one of those sacks of gold they put on the posters. At least they'd have had some fun out of life, like other people. Like the people who had those posters printed, for instance.

They hadn't had anything out of it. Work, duty, duty, work, what would the neighbors say—that was what their life had been like, and now they were being tormented and hunted for it. Truly, though, it was not too late! There was still time to make up for it! No, no police boot was going to kick his happiness to pieces . . .

"Drunk, that's what he is, drunk," whispered Mon, "as though it was peacetime indeed and him going on a visit. It's those tablets have done it." He suddenly became aware of the trees.

If he cut across the park he would be there sooner. But there was the mist and it was dark, and if he met the cats they'd stop him. In the dark and misty park they might accuse him of sabotage . . . and he turned to go round the edge of the park.

As he went along he found that if he kept to the bushes he was walking on dry ground and didn't feel the damp in his bones nor in his throat, and he didn't need to avoid the people who passed like shadows in the dark although it was only twilight on a misty evening.

Laurel, lilac, laburnum.

If he hadn't felt so light-hearted he would have thought lucky things, the bushes are stuck in one place and nobody suspects them of anything, nobody threatens to deport them; in a week or two the snow will fall on them. People will pass them by and if they say anything it'll only be, look, it's been snowing. Then in spring when the sun started shining they'd put forth leaves and the flowers would bud and they'd watch the people and the trams and the birds in their branches and the children skipping about, and wars and persecution playing havoc with men were nothing to them. Of course, they were only bushes, they didn't need to prove their ancestry, he would have thought if he hadn't felt so light-hearted, people don't care whether it's laurel or lilac or laburnum standing here, they might not stand for fig trees or lemon trees, but these bushes are one hundred per cent native and nobody can take objection to them. How much better off they are than people who have to be watched and investigated, how much better to be a bush than to be a person called Mundstock who happened to be hurrying past.

"What about flowers?"

"Flowers are worse off," he answered his shadow as he hurried along by the bushes, "flowers have to wait where they are for someone to come and pick them. Somebody always comes along and picks them, and they must feel their end has come. You know," he said to his shadow and began to feel sorry for himself, "to feel your end has come is just as terrible as to lose hope."

"And anyway," he said after a little while, "if I was a bush I wouldn't be on my way to the Sterns's. And I couldn't even feel hope. It's better to be a man, after all. Unless I'm running after a mirage, some delusion of the mind . . ." He heard the sound of steps and thought, look out, one of the cats running out of the park. Then he realized it was Mon.

Where the park ended the bushes came to an end too. A new street stretched out in front of him, blue-black and damp, Rhine Street.

He hurried down Rhine Street looking neither to right nor left, and Mon muttered poor fellow, poor fellow. But he must not lose the game, whatever he said.

"No, I'm not a poor fellow," he hurried down Rhine Street, "I won't lose. I feel it in my bones. I'm not!"

"Oh, it's those tablets, but it doesn't matter. As long as he feels it in his bones. The only thing is," Mon looked at him suspiciously, "what is he going to tell them tonight? Has he decided?"

He felt in his pocket with a smile, feeling the packet wrapped in old newspaper.

"So he's got his cards with him. That's another story. What is he going to read from them?"

"Something will occur to me," he said, "there really are transports going off. To Poland, to Lodz. But I'll say there aren't any. Lodz? That's all nonsense, I'll say, pure imagination. You've thought it up yourselves, although I've heard it's really only the beginning, old Haus said so . . . And the war'll be over soon, I'll tell them, in spring at the latest, when the flowers come out again." And he remembered the idea of sabotage that came to him by the park.

"Sabotage!" cried Mon and pricked up his ears.

That's right, sabotage and strikes! And he felt pleasantly excited at the thought that sabotage and strikes would harm the Nazis all right. He went along with his eyes on the dark damp pavement in Rhine Street and thought about the meaning of the word "harm." It meant upsetting the life of the country. Upsetting the life of the country wasn't everything . . . and he had to smile.

[34]

"It's like this," he explained, "the Germans can only hold on a year if the life of the country's upset. I'll say a few months at most, till the flowers bloom in the spring. That means discontent. And *that* means people are fed up with the war and start making trouble . . ."

Mon was amazed.

"Trouble? Germans making trouble?" he sighed and his heart leaped, "where would that be? All over the country?"

"In Bavaria, of course," he laughed, "in Bavaria. Or in East Prussia and in the Rhine basin. So as to get both east and west in, you see."

"D'you think the Sterns are going to believe you?" Mon objected. "Doesn't it sound a bit unlikely to have the Germans making trouble while they're still advancing? Hadn't you better keep that in reserve until they started losing?"

There was something in that. But it was not so sure that he'd live to see the day. And so he'd say no. He could easily say there was trouble on the home front if he explained—his eyes fixed on the dark damp pavement he thought the matter over—if he said there were heavy losses during those big offensives. Yes, that was logical enough. Great loss of life, trouble on the home front because of that, and then trouble led to sabotage and strikes in the Rhine valley and in East Prussia. And he thought to himself a little sorrowfully that there was probably nothing on earth you couldn't explain away if you found the right reason.

"Fantastic," thought Mon, "thunder and lightning, the man's fantastic! The Sterns are going to be thunderstruck, they won't find a thing to say," and the thought of their amazement made him start jumping for joy.

He did not calm down until he came to the end of Rhine Street and there in the darkness ahead a familiar house stood out.

"Good Lord," he called out, "we're nearly there!"

"So we are. There you are," he said with a glance at the misty dark, "was it so bad going along the street, after all?"

"Well, I wouldn't want to get run over," he said, "but I've got eyes in my head. Run into a German? That's not the sort of thing that ever happens, don't be silly. Catch cold from wet feet? That's the sort of thing Mrs. Stern would say. What's there to be afraid of in the street, after all?"

"So that's what's worrying you? The police might ask to see my papers? They're all in order, that's right."

"A big J on the papers? That doesn't matter. They can't do me any harm for that. The Star of David on my coat?" he laughed it off. "They kill death and the star goes on shining."

"How can I have been so scared?" he sang. "It must have been nerves!"

"And now it's those tablets," replied Mon, and he sighed and plunged into the darkening mist towards the familiar house.

Mon began to get underfoot and willy-nilly he had to walk more slowly and look at the people round him and say to himself that it would really be better if he met nobody, so nobody would know he was going to pay them a visit . . .

"So he's afraid, after all," said Mon, "though he denies it."

"It's just a little calculation," he replied, dragging one foot after the other, "there are some people have gone wild and spend their time trying to find out who's been ringing at their neighbor's door. They think hard and then they make up a bit and taken together they've got the answer. And when they've got the answer it's gospel truth, especially after they've told somebody else about it." If he hadn't been feeling so light-hearted, he'd have thought to himself, is that what we're here for, to spy on each other? Is that the purpose of life? People going round spying on each other as if they were in prison . . .

"Who's talking about people in general," he replied, "it's the Sterns I'm thinking of, the ancient enemy, as the Nazis say. I'm thinking of Otto, and of Klara, and Freda, and Simon, and their eighty-year-old grandmother." And Mr. Mundstock, the enemy of the public weal as the posters maintain, who had just thought up that fantastic story of trouble in the country, sabotage and strikes, to comfort the poor unhappy Sterns, it really was sad irony, enough to make you cry. Is there anything on earth you can't explain away if you find the right reason? No, nothing. If he hadn't been feeling so light-hearted he might have thought about it, but not tonight. That was what the tablets had done for him.

"How stupid I've been," he said suddenly as he drew near to the house in the mist. "I've been a solitary sort of fellow all my life. I never used to go anywhere. Just an occasional movie, or a walk, and the place I used to go every day—that was all the life I knew except for the Sterns."

"The place he used to go every day, that doesn't sound like a solitary sort of fellow," Mon was skeptical; "he was very much at home in the Hlavovka Café, wasn't he?" but as he heard that he smiled sadly.

"There's not a word of truth in it, I wasn't thinking of the Hlavovka at all. The gentlemen used to ask me to join them, it's true, Fuchs the engineer and factor owner, Muneles the doctor, Fleissig . . . they invited me to sit there with them and read the papers and play a game of billiards . . . If I went there three times in my whole life that's a lot . . . Billiards? I don't even know the rules of the game . . ."

He saw that he had reached the Sterns' house. A chilly bald shadow flitted past.

"Gone wild," Mon whispered, "Korka . . ."

"He doesn't live here. And it's November, the man had a hat on, how could you see he was bald?"

He felt a twinge of anxiety as he entered the building.

"Up with courage, up with miracles," Mon whispered.

He set his lips and the anxiety fled.

A blue light flickered in the hall and a fat woman in a kerchief came round the corner on the ground floor. She passed him and noted his presence though she pretended not to.

"Bad luck," whispered Mon, "but never mind. He can pre-

[37]

tend he didn't meet her. Like the transports that don't go to Lodz, as he'll be saying in a little while . . ."

It might have been the janitress, and they're not usually a bad group, they're fed up with the Germans themselves. It depends on the house. He ought to ask the Sterns, at the right moment, who the fat woman in the kerchief might have been.

He went up the stairs as fast as he could, but met nobody else. On the third floor there was a card on one of the doors: Otto Stern.

"Let's hope," Mon shrieked, "let's hope the tablets last out!"

"Let's hope the effect doesn't wear off too soon!"

He shrugged and his brow was damp.

It dried off at once.

Before he had even stepped over the threshold they told him what he asked, for safety's sake, first thing:

The fat woman in the kerchief was Emily Taussig, a widow, who was leaving next morning for Lodz . . .

CHAPTER 4

"So there you are," he said somberly, sitting under the dim chandelier with the Stern family round him, "that's the way things are. By next spring." As he said it he thought to himself, that was a good piece of oratory, the best I've ever produced, may the Lord forgive me. And he added: "That's really the truth."

His fear had not got the better of him. His somber mood had come upon him when he saw them sitting in the dining room, touching in their close-knit affection, and felt no hint of sadness or distress. The fact that he did not dare to look them in the face arose from the unusual assurance with which he spoke, for the depth of this assurance had surprised even him. He waited with head bent, but calmly, for the first to speak and what their words would be.

The first to be heard was a voice framed in an old-fashioned white lace cap.

"Mr. Mundstock, sir," the voice began solemnly as though opening the speech from the Throne, and the glance which came from this voice soared above the heads of those present. "I am eighty-one years old. But for three years I have been telling them exactly what you have just said. What about them?" She gripped the arms of the plush armchair where she sat, and turning her head went on: "I would suggest you look round you. You will see four people. You should realize, however, who they are and into what company you have entered in crossing this threshold . . ."

They all looked at her in perplexity.

"As you see them sitting here, Mr. Mundstock," her hand described a broad circle, "they are not the four people you used to know, they are somebody quite different. And now you know whom you have to deal with you will understand why I fell ill. Wherever you look in this household you see fantasy at the helm. Truth stands in a corner weeping, and since you have brought her in with you, know that you will weep for it, and weep most terribly, and when you leave you will lament in sorrow that you ever came in here. These people have lost their reason and believe the exact opposite of whatever they are told.

"If you tell them this table is round," she went on without allowing any interruption, "they will believe it is square. If you tell them the light is on they will say they are sitting in darkness. And the worst of all, may the Lord forgive us, is that they believe the posters stuck up down there by the cinema . . ."

"Not those posters down by the cinema," Mrs. Stern burst out at last, tossing her head, "everybody knows that's only propaganda, but what about the news from the front? That's the trouble! Victories, victories," she cried, "one victory after another and not a single defeat. Have you heard of a defeat anywhere?" she was shouting now, her eyes circling his head, "Have you heard of one? Have you?" As he somberly kept silent she said more calmly: "There you are, you see. And now let me tell you something: we won't go anywhere."

They all looked at her in surprise.

"Didn't you hear me? Didn't I say it in Czech? We won't even pick up our suitcases. We won't go out in the street. It'll kill us here, in this very flat . . . Do you read the papers? They're full of lies, of course," she waved them away, "but you can't invent conquered cities. They are advancing and they're winning. Everybody is shaking in their shoes and surrendering. Armies collapse like matches as they advance. Just look at the map and tell me if there's anywhere they haven't hung out their flags yet. Go on, tell me, I'd like to hear it! People don't take it to heart, that's all. When they read it in the papers or hear it on the news they just shrug it off and go on believing what they want to. They're right, I wouldn't want to take their faith away from them. But our lives are at stake, our *lives.*" she was shouting again, and clutching her head in her hands. "If there's anybody surprised at us, surprised at our nerves giving way, if there's anybody bold enough to shake their heads over us if we dare to go mad, go on, tell me, it's no light matter, this isn't, for Christ's sake, I want to hear you say it!"

As nobody spoke she went on:

"It's all very well for Granny, she doesn't feel things the way I do." And she burst into tears.

"Listen to her shouting," the old lady retorted. "I don't feel things, eh? Lord God Almighty, turn Your ears from us. Do not punish our blasphemous words." She fell silent and turned her wrinkled face in its frame of white lace towards the ceiling.

In the fraction of dead silence that followed a voice spoke from the other end of the table.

"Mother's always on about it being all over with us. She sees herself in the concentration camp every day. They're going to lose the war by spring, and we won't be sent anywhere, will we?"

While Mrs. Stern was speaking he thought what a good thing it was that she didn't read the papers. When Grandmother called Heaven to witness he felt as though a warning finger was being shaken at him from the ceiling. But now, as Simon spoke, he felt terrible. The boy was gazing at him from the other side of the table with complete devotion in his great dark eyes, eyes in which there was not the shadow of a doubt that his words were true, and he felt the sedative tablets beginning to lose their power . . . And Otto, Otto just sat and sat with downcast eyes; he had not said a single word. And Freda? Her head was bent over the table as she stared at the tablecloth, her long black hair hanging about her face: she looked as though her soul had fled from her body. He involuntarily turned to the window, covered with blackout paper. The light of the dim chandelier above his head was engulfed in that black patch as if there was a candle there burning for the dead. Perhaps the feeling that the sedatives were losing their power, provoked by Simon's unlimited trust, had only been a momentary illusion. Something rose in him and this "something" pitilessly insisted that his sorry errand here was far from being over. That it was his duty to stick it out. And he said to himself it was for the love of God, and then, nodding his gray head, said:

"They'll lose all right."

This was the signal for an outburst of talking.

"You say they're going to lose," Mrs. Stern started off again, "but you don't say when. When? They're winning all along the line now."

Then she added: "Can't you see what things are like at home?"

He realized then there was nothing for it but to bring out the breaking down of morale he had thought up. That business about the Rhine and East Prussia.

"It's true," he said, "thank the Lord, the country's upset. Haven't you heard about the Rhine basin and East Prussia?"

He expected them to hurl questions at him from all sides, and was surprised to find a different reaction. Simon jumped up from his chair in excitement. Mrs. Stern shuddered in silence. Grandmother's face in its white cap grew cold.

"We know all about that, Mr. Mundstock," she said in a chilly tone, "we know that, I told them all about it the day before yesterday. I brought the news from the Backers. Trouble in the Rhine and Prussia. Now just look at them," she tossed a hand at those present and turned her eyes to the window.

He held his breath. The Backers, flashed through his mind, who would have thought it? A truthful orthodox family like the Backers! Fancy them getting the same idea! Trouble in the Rhine and Prussia . . . He began to wonder whether there wasn't something in the story after all, but before he could speak he heard Mrs. Stern's voice.

"Trouble in the Rhine and Prussia, I know all about that, but is there really anything behind the story?"

"That's right! Is there really anything behind the story?" Grandmother cut in, and turning her head towards him went on:

"You see why she said that. Because she hasn't read anything about it in the newspapers. Because she's got those posters down by the cinema to believe in. Because there's nothing about it on those posters of hers . . ."

Simon laughed and said: *"Sieg heil"* and looked at him to see how he would take it.

Before he could feel uneasy again at this simple trust Mrs. Stern answered:

"You know, Mr. Mundstock, when she brought the news from the Backers . . . I had to think whether there wasn't something wrong about it. I wondered whether it wasn't a lie. Honestly, now, trouble at home at a time like this—it just isn't possible."

He asked what, feeling in his bones . . .

"When they're winning everywhere."

He put a hand to his forehead. It was exactly what had occurred to him as he hurried here a little while back. He knew he would have to repeat his own words, exactly as he had thought it out by the park. He breathed a heavy sigh:

"It's like this, Mrs. Stern. They are winning all right, but you mustn't forget their losses in these offensives. The lives that are lost. That's what the trouble at home's about."

[43]

The words that now fell from Grandmother's lips almost threw him into a panic:

"Now you see for yourself, Mr. Mundstock. I told them the very same thing. The Backers said they've lost over a million. The civilians know about the losses and are fed up, fed up with the war. The Backers' news is reliable. They listen to the foreign broadcasts, only you mustn't tell anyone . . ." she added the last words to herself.

It was like a dream.

He realized that Mrs. Stern could not get a word out, she was swallowing with her mouth half open and her eyes were circling slowly round his head. He saw Grandmother in her chair with a cold smile of victory on her wrinkled face in its frame of white lace, her face yellow in the weak lamp-light, and it occurred to him that the poor old lady was smiling as though she lay in her coffin. Then he saw Simon's grateful look from across the table, his eyes sparkling as he said something about having known it was the truth the minute Granny brought the news. And he saw Freda in her long black hair hanging loose and smelling faintly of mignonette, and now she even lifted her eyes from the tablecloth a moment, to look at him under half-closed lids, but shyly: he thought she had been listening to him all the time, although she had never taken her thoughts off that one single person . . . And Otto . . . He could see Otto making up his mind to speak at last, and he felt that whatever Otto said would clinch matters. His words would settle whether he had succeeded or failed.

"Theo's right," he said glumly. "That's the way things are. We've only got to hang on a few months longer."

When the clock struck the hour Freda started tidying her hair and then stood up. She stood by the table with her hands at her sides and downcast eyes like a boarding-school girl. Mrs. Stern lifted her eyebrows and told her to go and get a bit of supper ready in the kitchen . . . She nodded and went out, and the moment the door shut behind her Mrs. Stern sighed.

[44]

"Poor Freda! She looks as though she's sleepwalking all the time."

"Bats in the belfry," said Simon from his end of the table, but his mother snapped at him and he hastily dropped his eyes.

"To tell you all about it, Mr. Mundstock," Grandmother began, and he knew he was now going to hear all about Freda's engineer. But he felt he knew more about it already. What it was all about. That he'd broken it off because of her non-Aryan ancestry, as they said . . . He suddenly felt extremely curious to know whether it was really the way he thought, putting his hand to his brow to make sure he was awake.

"To tell you all about it, Mr. Mundstock," Grandmother said, "This engineer gentleman told our Freda they'd better part company. You know, on account of her non-Aryan ancestry, as they say . . ."

He saw Simon as through a mist, nodding to tell him that was right and at the same time his eyes were asking what he had to say to it, what it all really meant. In a gray mist he saw Mrs. Stern staring silently at him. And Otto sitting there in a fog, as though he had nothing to say, his eyes turned sadly towards the blacked-out window.

"He made a long speech proving that marriage wouldn't save her while it would be the ruin of him," Grandmother went on. "Things would be different, he said, if he could save her by marrying her. He'd come and ask for her hand at once if that were the case. He would lead her to the altar. But with things the way they are now, it was out of the question. That's how things stand for our Freda."

So that's how things stand for Freda, he came to himself, exactly the way he had imagined it. And poor Freda looked as though she was sleepwalking, poor girl.

"And Freda looks as though she's sleepwalking," he said numbly.

"Bats in the belfry," said Simon.

[45]

Grandmother replied: "Unfortunately Mr. Mundstock has hit the nail on the head."

Grandmother's eyes blinked in their frame of lace and Mrs. Stern looked as though she was drowning and clutching at a straw, and then Otto turned his eyes away from the blacked-out window to look at him too, sadly and as if he were ashamed. But Simon's eyes were clear and trusting as he looked at him.

He nodded and gave a sigh.

"A sad business, a sad business, to drop her because of her race," he said.

"It's a sad business," he said again in a different voice, for he suddenly felt strength growing up inside him again, and looked round. "What's happened has happened," he said looking round again, "you can't expect everybody to have a heart of gold. Perhaps her engineer's afraid."

The thought flashed through his mind that he did not know the man and was perhaps wronging him, talking of fear.

"Perhaps I wrong him," he added quickly, "if so, may he forgive me. Perhaps it's the fault of his family."

Grandmother cried out:

"Mr. Mundstock, you might have read it in a book. That's exactly what he said to her. About his parents being against the marriage."

Mrs. Stern put in that that was what he said, anyway, and Otto turned his eyes back to the window again.

"There you are, you see," he went on in surprise, "so there's nothing to regret about it. You never know what sort of a family Freda would have found herself in. The break will have its good side, after all."

"It wouldn't worry me," said Simon, and propped his chin on his hand.

"You just hold your tongue," Mrs. Stern snapped at him, "I'd like to see what you'd say if it were you."

"It wouldn't happen to me," Simon smiled at him.

He had a remarkable thought.

"As far as I can see," he said with animation, "there are two things to be considered."

They all turned to him expectantly, even Otto, and it made him feel almost ashamed, but it did not shake his calm.

"In the first place, that engineer's making a big mistake if he thinks Freda can't be saved. Only of course it won't be him that saves her, it'll be the end of the war, and as I've said, that'll come before the spring. That's one thing. And then? The other thing is what to do about Freda till then. She has to get over this depression."

Four pairs of eyes were hanging on him and he felt he was bringing them under his spell. As if he had been transported back to the happy days when Mrs. Stern was frying cutlets in the kitchen and Simon was getting underfoot with his stamp album. As if the window were wide open and the Sunday-morning sun shining outside. He felt something green beginning to sprout inside him, as if he, the Mr. Theodore Mundstock that was, was rising from the dead. In that fraction of a second, as the feeling came to him, the image of the sedatives he'd taken flashed through his mind, and as he realized how wonderfully they'd helped him a mechanism started working within him, telling him the bright thoughts opening in front of him were not only due to those tablets. But there was no time to ponder over it. He reminded himself to ask what they were going to do about Simon, and then there'd be the fortunetelling, and all would be well. He turned to the people round the table again. He felt them coming under his spell.

"I would make one suggestion," he pretended to be thinking it over carefully. "What I would suggest is . . ."

And he began to explain his ideas.

"Everybody knows," he said, "that everything heals in time. Even the saddest things that can happen to a man lose the taste of mourning, as they say, in time, and then not a drop of sorrow falls into the soul . . ." He stopped short for a moment, remembering that on his way here he had wanted to ask if they knew anything about Ruth Kraus, and a drop of sorrow had fallen into his soul, nay, more than one single drop, but something within him wiped it away hastily and he went on. "Freda will forget her sadness in time," he continued, looking them in the eye calmly. "She'll just find somebody else and get married. Your Freda could have a dozen suitors if she wanted to."

He knew that was the truth, for he thought Freda very lovely. He had never had the slightest doubt about it. He felt they were all agreeing with him in their heart of hearts. Grandmother wanted to say something and so did Mrs. Stern, but Simon grimaced and rolled his eyes and Otto kept silent, and so he managed to go on without being interrupted.

"What we need," he said, "is to help Freda over the worst. Until she forgets. Then everything'll be all right."

"Just what I say," Mrs. Stern broke in. "You said next spring, didn't you?" He did not hear the ironic overtone in her voice.

"A couple of months, perhaps just a few weeks," he replied. "And we've got to help her get over it. She just has to make a painless change."

They all began to agree, even Mrs. Stern, but they looked at him rather uncomprehendingly, as though they were giving their agreement in advance . . . He went on:

"In front of Freda you must pretend the engineer was quite right and meant it for the best. If you can persuade her of that, it'll be a great help because it won't hurt so much. That's understandable. It won't hurt so much because she'll see he was really right and meant it for the best. And for her to see even better and for it to hurt even less, tell her he intends to wait for her. You can say you've talked to him alone, if you like, and he said so. That'll set her up completely. She'll see she hasn't been disappointed in him."

"But Mr. Mundstock, he . . ." Mrs. Stern started to interrupt, but Grandmother motioned for her to hold her tongue. She knew very well what he was going to say.

"You say he doesn't," he smiled at the lady of the house, "but it doesn't matter in the least whether he does or not . . .

That's the point of what I'm suggesting. What did I say? In a few months or even in a couple of weeks it won't worry Freda any more and she'll have got over it . . ."

"Suppose she doesn't, though, Mr. Mundstock, she's a very sensitive girl." Mrs. Stern spoke louder now.

"For goodness sake stop it, Klara," Grandmother snapped at her. "You're always raising objections. You see how it is, Mr. Mundstock. Always the other way around. If you say it's white she'll tell you it's black and if you say black she'll say white. It's no good talking in this house, Mr. Mundstock, it's all fantasy and imagination, nothing else . . ."

"Whether she's a sensitive girl or not has nothing to do with it. She'll have got over it and so it won't upset her. It won't upset her because you'll have told her what I suggest. And because she won't be upset, she'll forget all about it in a few months or a couple of weeks. That's all we need for the start. And then when things get normal again . . ."

"That's just what I'm worried about," Mrs. Stern was talking very loudly now, "what happens then. She'll go and see the engineer and then . . ."

"When things get normal again," he took her up with a smile, "she won't do anything of the sort because she'll have forgotten all about the engineer. How could she remember when you know she's forgotten all about him? Do you want me to go through it all again? There you are, you see. If she does remember, it'll all seem quite different. She won't be heartbroken about it any more. Everything will be all right. That's what time does in these painful things, I know all about it from myself," he said, remembering once again that he had thought of asking about Ruth Kraus, and more than a single drop of sorrow fell into his soul. "A painless change, that's all," he added convincingly.

Then suddenly, before anyone could say a word, he declared:

"That's a good *me-thod* . . ."

At that moment something stirred deep inside Mr. Theodore Mundstock. The moment he uttered that one ordinary everyday word. He did not see Grandmother nodding and smiling, he did not hear Mrs. Stern saying it all fitted in wonderfully, as though there was a magic piece of machinery, he did not see and he did not hear; something stirred. The sedatives couldn't have been responsible for that. There was something green sprouting in his consciousness. That mechanism in his mind, that must have been working inside him long before he got here. Something that had been there in the past and been forgotten these last few years, and now it had woken up and come to life in that one ordinary everyday word. He wondered whether it had anything to do with the strange feeling of hope that had come to him the day before yesterday as he went to bed, but now, just as a few minutes before, he had to be content with the vague feeling, the experience, and could not think it out clearly. He sat there under the gloomy light in the Sterns's little dining room, the center of attention for the whole family, who would not let him ponder over the strange workings and the strange things sprouting in his innermost soul.

"She ought to have her hair cut, too," Simon said suddenly, "before long it'll be touching the ground like Eve's in the picture where God's driving her out of the Garden of Eden. If I were her I'd go round to Luksch."

"The archangel," his grandmother corrected him, and Mrs. Stern made as if to box his ears, but her hand hung halfway. The door opened and Freda came in with the plates and they all stopped.

"Here's a bite of supper, Mr. Mundstock," said Mrs. Stern quickly and suspiciously brightly. And Grandmother added joyfully:

"Don't pay too much attention to what you're getting, Mr. Mundstock, you know how things are nowadays."

After supper it was time for fortunetelling. The little packet of cards wrapped in an old newspaper found its way to the table, cleared now, under the gloomy light of the chandelier.

He could see how impatient they were, he could see their grey, pale faces clearly. Otto was perhaps the only one who remained calm, and even smiled, a calm little smile. He smiled back at him. Why not? Fortunetelling from the cards was perhaps the most foolish of all the foolish things he had ever done, from the day he met that gipsy woman. He knew that he would not fail now, after the success he had just had. The cards were in his hands, entirely, after all . . .

They let Grandmother have first go, although it cost them all a great effort. Even Freda, for all her sadness and lifelessness. There was no help for it though, in her letter she'd said the cards were mainly for Grandmother. And anyway, the old lady was over eighty. When she cut for the second time they were all standing round him, the fortuneteller, the liar and the cheat. Otto was the only one sitting in his chair, silent. And Simon was kneeling on his chair on the other side of the table, his chin in his hand and his heels pressed against the back of his chair, watching with his great big shining eyes. He devoured every movement his grandmother made. She drew the Jack of clubs, the ten of spades and the ace of clubs.

"The ace," she gasped, "the ugly beast," and looked anxiously at him.

"The ace," he let his breath out, "that's not too bad. It means there's an honor awaiting you. It means dignity. And the ten of spades means an unexpected and happy event."

"What about the Jack of clubs?" she wondered.

"There's a man somewhere near you."

Simon squealed for joy. "Granny's going to get married, what a joke," and they all turned on him fiercely, but not really angry. The same thing had probably occurred to them all. For a split second there was merriment in the room, and only Freda grew suddenly sadder than ever. He felt it, and at the same moment they felt it too, and all fell silent.

"There's somebody here who's going to help you, he said, and added at once, "an Aryan," in case they thought he meant himself.

Mrs. Stern sang out:

"Mr. Kopyto!"

The others joined in: "Mr. Kopyto, of course, Mr. Kopyto, it couldn't be anybody else."

Actually only Grandmother and Simon joined in, Freda just whispered the name and Otto sat still and said nothing.

He thought it was a strange name and wondered who it was.

"You don't know Mr. Kopyto, he's a friend of the Backers," said Grandmother.

"He's a very learned man," Simon was laughing, "translates books in the German tongue."

"He's a scholarly man and a collector," said Grandmother.

"He wears big glasses and has a very deep voice," Mrs. Stern told him. "He had a throat operation, they say. The Backers are going to leave some of their things with him . . ."

"That is, if they have to go with a transport," Grandmother finished it for her.

"That's quite unnecessary."

"He said he'd hide things for us too, if we had to go," Simon volunteered. "He croaks when he talks."

"So you see how right you were," Grandmother stopped her grandson's flow of chatter. "Just as though you had guessed. Now what are things going to be like in general?"

"In general," he complied, "things are going to be like this: a man will bring you good news, you'll be pleased, and then there are these high honors you're going to receive. Now just cut again and take three cards . . ."

When she picked them out and turned them up, again there was nothing but clubs and spades.

"You will live to a great age . . ."

Then it was Freda's turn.

As she chose her cards he could see she was trembling.

From hers he foretold that she was worrying about something and that it was most likely an affair of the heart. He saw her stiffen, but the surprising thing was that he felt Mrs. Stern herself stiffen too. And even Grandmother. He wondered if they were all crazy and touched his forehead mechanically . . . The Jack of hearts she was thinking of, he went on with a gesture he remembered seeing by the River Vah, had the best of intentions. His plans were well laid. But for the moment she would have to make a small sacrifice, as they say. Something like a short separation. It wouldn't be for long and then everything would come out all right. He felt how relieved they all were, as though a burden had fallen from them. Mrs. Stern and Grandmother could be heard sighing with relief, and he shook his head in his own thoughts . . . When she wanted to know how long it was going to be, he made her take one more card, and even before he looked at it he said: "About four months. Till spring . . ."

Mrs. Stern cried out and the light of the chandelier flashed in his eyes: "Mr. Mundstock, you're absolutely right. That fits her case exactly," and she stared at him in amazement.

From her high-backed plush chair Grandmother exclaimed: "Mr. Mundstock, it fits absolutely to a T, how can you get everything exactly right like that?"

Simon flung his hands up to the ceiling and gave a loud whistle, and then fell off the chair and lay on his back on the floor.

"Look what you've done, you wild creature," his mother shouted at him. "I've a good mind to box your ears and leave you there on the floor," but he was rolling with laughter.

A shiver went down his back. These people have gone mad, every one of them, he thought, but he had to laugh at Simon too, and as he laughed he realized he hadn't had such a good laugh for a long time, perhaps not for the last three years, perhaps even longer than that. His laughter felt like a gentle shower, relaxing and liberating, and as though something colored a pale pink was flowing over his skin. He jumped from his seat to help Simon to his feet, and they both laughed. The thought flashed through his mind that Simon was supposed to have seen him in Havel Street, but to his surprise he went on laughing . . .

Even Mrs. Stern and Grandmother were laughing, too.

Otto was the only one to sit and say nothing, in silence.

Freda gave a little shake of her head and burst into tears.

When they calmed her down at last it was Mrs. Stern's turn.

He could tell she was burning with impatience, but at the last moment Simon bent over her and whispered something.

"Go on, then, and ask," and she looked at Mr. Mundstock.

"It's nothing, really," said Simon, "I only wanted to know whether you've still got that cockerel . . ."

"It's a hen," he answered with a smile, "and I still keep it . . ."

"Heavens, I thought it was a pigeon," Mrs. Stern exclaimed. "Don't I remember you telling us it fell off the roof one winter and you took it in so it wouldn't freeze? Heavens above," and she clutched her head in her hands.

What she said was soon forgotten, though, because she was simply dying of curiosity.

She was promised a three-room flat, that her children would make her very happy, and that she would be coming into a lot of money. A lot of money! He knew Otto wouldn't want his fortune told, and Mrs. Stern was the last, and so it had to be her who was going to come into the money. Before she got it though, there would be some worry and trouble. That was simple enough to explain.

"You can hardly be surprised, these troubled times," he sounded quite convincing. "It could hardly be otherwise, could it? The cards don't lie, after all."

As he left the dining room he suddenly thought of Ruth Kraus, he had the feeling he had not asked about her after all. . . . He thought, though, that he'd asked about Mr. Vorjahren and they didn't know anything. They only knew him by name . . . He knew very exactly, though, about his image of beauty, clarity, rose-pink, all his good and calm convictions had come back to him. What he had said had helped them, and Freda had been helped by that other business. but what about

Simon? He remembered it was no good leaving him anything in his will. He could not take him to the puppet show any more, it wasn't allowed and anyway the boy was too old for that now, and they weren't allowed in the Zoo, either. He had no chance to bring him stamps, now. He couldn't even watch over the boy's progress at school, the poor kid had been expelled. What could he do and what did the boy need most of all? His mind's eye caught a black jackboot hovering over dainty china figurines, but it was only a flash. No, no, nothing of that sort, he smiled. . . . As he took his coat down from the peg in the hall he tried to say to his hostess, in an aside, that next time they'd better talk more about Simon, and for these words Mrs. Stern looked at him so gratefully.

As he said goodbye he thought how contented they looked. He pitied them, but he didn't regret what he'd done. He knew they would sleep better that night, poor things, truth stands in a corner weeping. He pitied them. And yet even he felt better for the evening.

"You're such a calm strong man, Mr. Mundstock, you're just not afraid of anything," his hostess said as she wished him goodbye. "If I didn't know you I'd say you hadn't a care in the world. You can have a good laugh and you know so much more about things than other people do. But you really do need a rest. Haven't you forgotten man has a body as well as a soul? You're so pale," and she flapped her hands in front of her own equally pale face. "Don't you sleep well at night?"

Simon leaned over the banisters and waved as he went down the stairs in the half darkness.

"Mind you don't fall over," he heard Mrs. Stern's contented warning.

On the ground floor he quietly walked past the door where Mrs. Emily Taussig lived, the widow who was going to the concentration camp next morning.

As he came out into the street he heard footsteps by his side, and a voice.

Turning sharply, he saw Mon.

[55]

"The effect lasted," he whispered, "it really was a miracle. A pity they were the last I had. If I'd taken only one, there'd still have been two left."

He suddenly gasped for breath and began to shake and tremble all over.

"What's the matter, what's the matter," whispered Mon, but he was gasping for breath and trembling himself, too.

Oh dear, the effect was wearing off. But it didn't matter any more. . . . Full of fears he rushed through the blackout down the damp misty street, to get home as fast as he could. A thousand thoughts were running round in his head and not one of them could he get hold of properly. His fear began to be too strong for him to think of anything at all. There were a thousand thoughts in his head and yet it was empty. Only at the moment he hurried down the side of the park, past the bushes, the one clear sentence he had said at the Sterns' that evening came back to him whole: "It's a good method." But his fear made him forget it before he'd gone another step.

He got home safely.

He felt very distressed, but he had not been sick.

As he sat on the sofa, before turning it into a bed for the night, he began to wonder how things could have worked out so strangely, and how he had managed to foretell everything so successfully at the Sterns'.

The clock at the Cizeks' next door struck seven.

And it suddenly occurred to him to wonder if he wasn't a seer.

CHAPTER 5

That night the darkness round his bed seemed to take on an unusual shade of red. He had a feeling of heat, and so he attributed the redness of the dark to a raised temperature. I must have caught cold on the way to the Sterns', he thought, it's November and I caught cold. But he knew he hadn't caught cold. It's those tablets I took, of course it must be those tablets, he thought. But he knew it wasn't the tablets either. He had a faint glimmering of the real reason for his fever, and little hope that it would not break through into his waking mind.

A seer!

It was a terrifying thought.

He remembered having heard of cases, although they were very rare in the natural state. He could not remember where he had heard this, and he doubted very much whether it was by the River Vah that summer; an ordinary gipsy woman wouldn't be likely to know things like that. He tried to recall whether he'd suffered from anything of the sort before. He didn't think so. But people had obviously suspected him of this power. That explained why they were always stopping him and asking him all kinds of questions. If he had met Mr. Vorjahren, he would certainly have stopped to ask him something, too. That was not the real thing, though. The shocking thing was that this had appeared in him when least expected: at the time when the most terrible persecution of the Jews began, the transports to concentration camps, after months of indescribable suffering and exhaustion on his part. . . . There was still a terrible mystery hidden beyond this affair, and its name was "purpose." The purpose of being a seer. The word pushed its way into his thoughts, beating against his temples, demanding an explanation. He seemed to shout it out.

The purpose!

He felt Mon tear into the room.

He felt his panting breath and the heat of his body throughout his own limbs. He felt it in his thoughts and it beat at the temples of his mind. In his brain he could hear Mon's voice explaining and expounding, but he resisted his words as a horse resists the bit when his rider is plunging into an abyss. The darkness round him grew redder and redder and at the same time more sparse. It was a wild attack on his reason, with horror and physical pain wrought in with it until it became unbearable. When it overstepped the limits of reason and reached regions where there seemed to be nothing in human guise, his poor tormented reason surrendered.

A flood drowned his consciousness, carrying with it all that linked him to reality. All that floated on the surface were scraps of himself, transformed into the strangest creatures, and he realized what was hidden in all this.

The others were to be saved through him. In the hour that was to come he would be—the savior.

Mon's eyes flooded with tears.

The idea filled him with terror.

He, the savior of mankind, including those who wore the Star of David sewn on their coats!

The darkness in his room was unimaginably red and sparse.

The thoughts that flooded in on him then calmed him somewhat, and dried his tears. He recalled the feeling that had overcome him that Wednesday, the ray of strange presentiment that hope and salvation for him and for all of them were hidden deep within him. There must be some connection. The presentiment of hope and salvation! What could be more precious to the desperate in this valley of darkness and bitter woe, than the presentiment of hope and salvation? The worst thing that can happen to anybody is to lose hope and know the end is near. These thoughts did more than calm him down, they filled him with a sense of unexpected happiness. If, however, he was to be a savior, demands would be made on him. What would be the price of redemption? His eyes grew tearful again and his fever rose. Mon, poor Mon, what a fate is destined for you. To be the protector of mankind! It was a terrible thought. . . . And yet calm returned once more and Mon moved quietly away from his bed, though he could feel he was still in the room, wandering wide awake between the door and the writing desk; and it struck him that if he was a seer he ought to know how everything was going to turn out.

What was going to happen to him and to Mon, to the Sterns (oh, what did the future hold for Simon, for whom he had had such high hopes?), to Ruth Kraus (though he felt a strange reluctance to ask a plain straightforward question in this case), to Mr. Vorjahren (if he was still in the place), to the Radnitzers, to Kolb (was he being treated, and by whom), to the Backers, to Mrs. Heksch, had old Haus gone crazy communing with the spirits? Yes, he ought to be able to find all these things out. He tried thinking about it, but nothing occurred to him. The earth seemed to fall away from under him then, and the sun died away over head. With all his being he longed for what he had resisted and feared at first. He longed to be a seer, to fulfill his vocation, as the thirsty long for a drop of water and the blind for a ray of light, he longed to preserve and maintain his gift. Through these desperate prayers there rose to the surface one new aspect, and a hand seemed to tear the veil from something that had escaped his notice in the recent transformations.

He realized that he was a seer and a messiah, but the actual method, the way in which he was to put his vocation into practice was still hidden in his mind, just as it had been during these last days, with the only difference that now it seemed to be within reach; now he thought he might discover the road to salvation within himself; to find it became his first and greatest duty.

At intervals he tried to search his soul for it, but in vain. At intervals he realized, however, that some memory of his earlier life seemed to play an important part in this digging into his mind; this had occurred to him vaguely the previous day, when he was at the Sterns'. This was the point to which he finally came, lying there on his bed which was otherwise a sofa.

The darkness round him was still red and sparse, but he felt better and calmer.

All at once his head reeled.

This day he had discovered he was a seer!

A messiah!

With one bound Mon was at his bedside.

A wild roundabout began. The room whirled round Mon at a fantastic pace and the darkness grew redder and sparser as it spun round. A dreadful message forced its way through his head as the whirlpool of his thoughts raged and Mon lamented and cried and groaned.

Somebody had seized the door knob and opened the door.

There was a woman standing on the landing outside. He saw her through a red mist, but strangely enough he recognized her.

"Whatever's the matter, Mr. Mundstock? Are you feeling ill? I've been knocking hard these ten minutes."

"For God's sake, Mr. Mundstock, what's wrong, you look so queer?"

"For Heaven's sake, wait a minute, I'll get my husband . . ."

And then: "Evening, Mr. Mundstock, what's the matter, not feeling well, eh?"

"Come along inside, Mr. Mundstock, you can't stand here on the landing, you must be reasonable. You'd catch your death of cold out here on the landing, come along, now."

He suddenly saw quite clearly that he was sitting on the edge of his bed and that the lamp on his desk was lit. He felt the speckled creature with a yellow beak fluttering round his feet and looking at him curiously. Then he realized that Mr. Cizek and his wife were sitting on chairs by his desk, in green dressing gowns.

"Are you feeling better now, Mr. Mundstock?" he heard Mrs. Cizek ask him.

He felt himself nod and touched his forehead; there was something wrapped round it.

"You can take that off it. You're all right now."

And then: "Well, perhaps it won't be anything serious. I expect you're overtired. You didn't half give us a fright, though! It sounded as though you were pounding on the wall with your fists."

"I expect you had a nightmare and got out of bed still asleep . . ." Mr. Cizek said comfortingly. "Wouldn't you like a cigarette, Mr. Mundstock?"

"Thank you, no, Mr. Cizek, I don't smoke, you know," he found the strength to answer at last, and thought he must be looking terrible. He made a vague gesture towards his feet, as if to tell the speckled creature pattering about down there not to look at him.

"Of course, Mr. Mundstock doesn't smoke," Mrs. Cizek said.

"That's something to be thankful for, it's bad for you and the ration's so small . . ."

"What was it you wanted to ask, Mr. Mundstock, tell me,

[61]

and I'll do my best to answer if I can," Mr. Cizek interrupted his wife.

"Did I want to know something?" he asked . . .

Mr. Cizek looked at him soothingly.

"You just said something of the sort. Mr. Mundstock, is anything the matter?"

"When did I say so?" he asked uneasily.

"Just a little while ago. You said no thank you to a cigarette because you don't smoke, and you motioned with your hand, and said there was something you'd like to know . . ."

"Oh, yes, I remember now." And in a little while he went on:

"Are their losses really so big in these offensives . . .

And is there really trouble in the Rhine and in Prussia . . .

And will it really all be over by spring . . ."

Then he thought he was quite all right again. He looked at Mrs. Cizek and Mr. Cizek sitting there by his table in their green dressing gowns, their faces half lit by the lamp, watching in embarassment the creature strutting about in the middle of the room, and the thought flashed through his mind that he had completely forgotten, and what would the Cizeks be thinking? Was not salvation in his own hands? Was he not . . . And he tried to sit up a bit and hold his head erect.

"Just sit still, Mr. Mundstock, or lie down if you feel like it, you mustn't hurt yourself again," Mrs. Cizek calmed him.

And Mr. Cizek took his eyes off the creature and began to talk.

The foreign broadcasts had said that a hundred thousand Germans had been taken prisoner by the Russians . . .

It was going to be a hard and bitter winter for the Germans . . .

Sabotage was beginning in our occupied country . . .

The two Jews, Steiner and Knapp, flashed through his mind.

Then he heard about life as it was going to be.

All of us, black and white, will enjoy the same freedom.

A terrible thought struck him. Surely Mr. Cizek was not a seer, as well . . .

He rejected that at once. That was a blasphemous fantasy. Goodhearted Mr. Cizek with his comforting words . . .

He heard Mrs. Cizek telling him in a kind voice to go comfortably back to bed, they would put the light out and pull the front door to. If he felt ill again he should knock. He needn't be afraid. He wouldn't wake the children.

Then he felt his hand being shaken twice and heard footsteps.

And a voice in the hall.

Then the door closed to, the darkness was round him again, and all was quiet.

He suddenly realized that the darkness round him now was thick and black, soothing, as darkness ought to be at night, and at that moment he fell asleep.

CHAPTER 6

The future was a compact of horror. For all his skill as a seer he did not as yet know what it would be like.

From time to time he would meet the owner of the house he lived in, Mrs. Heksch, and the moment she saw him she would begin weeping softly. He assumed from this that she knew something about the horror ahead but he never asked. Sometimes a door would slam and she would hastily dry her eyes and hurry away. As a rule no door slammed and it was he who hurried away. Should he go and see Moyshe Haus? He thought about it but did not dare go a second time. Not because Moyshe Haus was an unfortunate creature whose mind was fixed on the spirits, but just because he had the latest news from the Community Office and he would not be able to hurry away. Before he ever reached his door there would be a thousand things to stumble over and he would find out all about that horror. And so he prayed he would not find it out from any other quarter, or, God forbid, discover it for himself. Yes, he was horrified at the thought of being a seer, horrified. It was wiser not to know what that horror was. It was enough to knock against the letter box and his nerves gave way a bit, and he could not bear it if they were to give way altogether. Man is a weak creature, and especially if he is called Mr. Theodore Mundstock and lives in the Nazi hell.

One day he was saved having to knock against his letter box. Mrs. Heksch found his mail in her letter box and gave it to him. She could not hurry away from him nor he from her. The mail was like the baton that had to be handed on in a relay race, two hands meeting; or like a common manacle. Because they were standing on the ground floor the janitress opened her door and joined them. She had a colored overall and wet hands.

"Just doing a bit of washing," she announced.

It was a picture postcard of a sea of roofs and spires, the sort they sell at the news dealers. As he turned it over he saw a neat hand and recognized at once the way Mr. Vorjahren used to write. All the years they had sat together in Havel Street. He scented catastrophe. But Mrs. Heksch was by his side, and Mrs. Civrna, and he had to bear up.

> *Dear Mr. Mundstock,*
>
> *I send you hearty greetings and wish you good health and all the best. I could not bring myself to pay you a visit, you must not bear me ill. You cannot imagine how I regret it. I am leaving tomorrow. Shall we ever meet again? If not, spare a thought sometimes for your old colleague in the string and rope business, and if you should meet Miss Ruth, which is hardly likely to happen now, remember me to her. May the Lord go with you.*
>
> *Samuel Vorjahren.*

He paled.

Seeing that, Mrs. Heksch began to tremble, but she had to bear up. Mrs. Civrna was standing there.

"A friend writes that he is leaving for the ghetto," he said with a sigh, and examined the postmark.

[65]

Thursday.

So he had left yesterday. For Lodz? Or Terezin? The card did not say.

"Perhaps they're not allowed to say, it's probably against the law . . ."

There was a flood of thundering words and a bright sleeve waved in the air. Looking up, he saw he was alone with the janitress. Mrs. Heksch had hurried away. The last thing he heard was that it might be written in secret lettering.

When he reached his room he lit the lamp and read the card held up against the light. When he had read it five times he knew it by heart but still had not found any invisible ink. Did he really want to know where Mr. Vorjahren had gone to? He opened the little box standing by the lamp and put the card away, as he did whenever he got one. There were six of them there, and a little pile of yellowing letters. It was a black ebony box and looked like a coffin where sad memories are laid.

Then horror flooded over him.

Lord in Heaven, Mr. Vorjahren!

A beak flashed yellow at his feet and tugged at his shoelaces.

Who was left?

The Sterns, Mrs. Heksch, the Radnitzers, the Backers, Kolb, Haus, Ruth Kraus . . . But the Radnitzers had already had their summons to muster in Pohorelec and the Backers were arranging to leave things in Mr. Kopyto's care. That left Mrs. Heksch, Kolb, and the Stern family. Haus didn't count, he would soon be mad. Ruth Kraus? . . . He dropped his eyes and gave his foot a shake. The winged creature had got the two ends of his shoelace in its beak . . . Poor thing, it wants me to go to bed, and here I am . . .

Mon was hiding behind the door, waiting.

"Here he is," he said, "waiting, because it could be his turn next, Mr. Theodore Mundstock."

Mr. Theodore Mundstock sitting there on the sofa with his shoes untied, counting up who had gone and who was left, a man with a graying face and scraggy neck, who could not sleep at night and had aged a hundred years in those three since the Nazis came and spread their brown darkness over everything.

What a cruel time that had done this to him!

He sat on the sofa with his head in his hands and felt the room fill with mist through which he saw the outlines of things and the creature dragging something along behind it . . .

Pitiless time, that had seized his unhappy life.

He sat on the sofa with his elbows on his knees and his head in his hands, and felt the room and the creature disappearing in the mist.

He saw a young man of twenty-three combing his dark hair before the mirror, straightening his green tie and arranging his pocket handkerchief. It was nearly eight but the young man seemed in no hurry. Then he left his hat lying on a chair and went out. Mr. Mundstock got up from the sofa and went out after him as though he were following his own shadow. Past the park, down Maisel Street and round past the Jewish Town Hall and the synagogue. Up the steps to the street, across, and there he was in Havel Street. In front of the well-known building, as green as the tie he was wearing. Through the passage and up the wooden stairs. On a door on the first floor was a poor-looking card: "Menache Löwy, String and Rope." He put his hand on the door knob and Mr. Mundstock slipped in behind him as though he was following his own shadow.

"Morning," said the young man, taking off his jacket and sitting down at his desk, "Morning," and Mr. Mundstock watching him like his own shadow thought it was a good thing for a young man to do his hair nicely and wear a decent tie, that was what people looked at first, when they didn't want to raise their eyes, that was what Haus said, who sold the things. But thinking so much about himself, as this young man did, and having mannerisms, no, nothing good would come of that, was it really him? But the young man began to speak.

He spoke to the man at the desk in front of his. He was

young, too, but not quite so young and not quite so careful about his appearance and he wasn't sitting in his shirtsleeves.

"Well, Mr. Vorjahren, what sort of a Sunday did you have?"

"Went to the football match. Sparta, of course. Quite a good game, but . . ."

"I went to the Botanical Gardens as usual," young Mr. Mundstock laughed, "and then on to the moving pictures to see Greta Garbo. We sat in a box in the balcony like princes . . ." and he stopped short, he had given himself away, but it was too late, and Mr. Mundstock watching him felt a pang . . .

"With the Kraus girl, I suppose," young Mr. Vorjahren at the first table supplied the missing words. "You know, that wouldn't be a bad match. She's a thoroughly nice girl and she was born on the seventh, that's your lucky number. You're a practical-minded young man . . ."

Oh, yes, he was practical minded all right, and Ruth Kraus really was born on the seventh of the month and a thoroughly nice girl, but the trouble was, she wasn't pretty. In fact she was downright ugly. You might say Ruth Kraus was even very ugly . . . Oh, dear me, no, that wouldn't do at all. Ruth Kraus was ugly, and twenty-three-year-old Mr. Mundstock was a good-looking young man who was careful about his appearance. Was he perhaps careful about his appearance to make up for what she lacked? God knows. But Mr. Vorjahren at the first desk knew that it was not the real point, and so he said nothing, not to embarrass his colleague Mr. Mundstock. . . .

Mr. Mundstock took Ruth to the Botanical Gardens where there were so many strange plants, trees and bushes and they walked along beneath the alders, ashes, and sycamores, beneath the beech and oak and chestnut trees, and a little farther beneath a pine tree and a fir tree, and then they went into the glass-house and spent at least a short time in the heavy, aromatic heat among the palms, figs and lemon trees, the tall aloes; they felt they were in some exotic part of the world, and then they went out and sat in the open-air restaurant. It was nothing more than a few tables and chairs among flowering rose bushes, and through the walls of the glass-house they could see their exotic world. He drank weak beer, because they had no other, while she sipped a raspberry soda through a straw. What did they talk about? Oh, nothing in particular; perhaps they talked about the book he had given her that day—but they felt happy enough. He mentioned the film they were going to see. And as they went to the cinema their exotic world and the flowering rose bushes went with them through the streets and then they saw it all over again on the deceitful screen with the pianist behind it playing the overture to the "Poet and Peasant" or the waltz "Southern Rose," and sometimes there was a violin too . . . Mr. Vorjahren at the first desk said nothing, not to embarrass Mr. Mundstock; he said nothing but he knew . . .

He knew that the visit to the moving pictures that Mr. Mundstock was happily talking about was the first for over six months, during which he and Ruth had not met, but only written to each other, letters which Mr. Mundstock put away in a little black box when he got home—over six months during which his life had stood still. For Ruth Kraus was a strange, queer girl. She had fits of anxiety, melancholy, despair, which attacked her ever since childhood, ever since the day she buried her father in a little country Jewish cemetery; she would tell no one about it, not even Mr. Mundstock her suitor, as though it would cost her her life, her all . . . When she was in that state some evil spell seemed to make her ugliness swelled to monstrous proportions in her mind. Perhaps some famous Jewish doctor could have helped her in these bitter, desperate states she got into, but she refused to go to a doctor about it, just as she refused to talk about it or about her father's burial in the village Jewish cemetery. When her trouble came upon her she would avoid everybody, except as far as she had to earn a living, and would not even meet her friend Mr. Mundstock, let alone go out with him . . . Ruth Kraus was a strange, queer girl. And Mr. Mundstock?

He was distressed and worn with worry over her, but as helpless as a thirteen-year-old. One day he dared to wait for her, in the belief that he would be able to help the poor girl. Was there anything better in anxiety than the encouragement of a trusted friend? Did it not work miracles to confide in a soul-mate? He waited for her late one afternoon, when the lights were going on in the street and she would be going home from the office. He waited for her in Plater Street, where she worked in the head offices of Bleckmann and Schoeller, heavy engineering, and he almost killed her. It was not long after he had given her a volume of stories by Gerhart Hauptmann, whom she enjoyed; she had told him one of the stories, "Lent Carnival." When she recognized him in the dim lamp-light in Plater Street that evening she stood stock still so that the people behind her had to swerve to avoid knocking into her; they looked at her in surprise and that made matters worse . . . Perhaps it was only the fact that she was attracting attention that got her moving again. She walked by his side as though she were in her death throes, as pale as death, and trembling. They went down Halek Street to the bridge. He told her at great length, full of youthful enthusiasm, that he wanted to help her; he asked her what was the matter, asked her to go with him to the doctor the next day or even that very day, and what had happened when her father was buried to make these attacks come back so . . . At great length, full of youthful enthusiasm, he tried to convince her it was nothing and would pass, everybody had some trouble to bear, nobody in the world was completely happy . . . When they came near the bridge and could hear the weir in the distance, he said he had two tickets for the pictures on Sunday and it was going to be a good film, they even said so in the papers; it was a film they had both been looking forward to. She simply must go and see it, have some fun, take her mind off things, and he shook his bare head . . . At this point she did speak. They had just reached the bridge. Did he want to be like the weaver Kielblock in "Lent Carnival?" she asked him in a hollow, empty voice, looking down at the thin covering of ice on the river, and terror seized him. He remembered the story of the weaver and his wife who perished with their child in the lake, after never-ending festivities, as the ice broke beneath the weight of their sodden sleigh . . . He had no idea how they had parted. He only knew it was at the tram stop on the bridge and that with her sunken eyes and half-open mouth she looked like a presentiment of death, the image of the drowned woman who after never-ending festivities. . . . No, the thing was such a shock that he never dared to try it again and offer to help her that way, with the encouragement of a trusted friend and confiding in a soul-mate, working miracles; it had been his fantasy, that was all. Perhaps famous Jewish doctors worked wonders that way, in other cases perhaps. And so he never again asked what had happened at her father's funeral, nor advised her to go to the doctor about it. He realized the only thing to do in those sad passages of her life was to leave her in solitary peace, as she had asked him in her letter, and wait until she came round enough to write to him. He would put the letter away with the others when it came, delighted to be able to meet her again, go to the pictures with her, go for walks, and do everything he could to make her happy. Until the next melancholy time, some months later . . . Mr. Mundstock liked pretty women, and it was Greta Garbo he admired most of all, but that was his fantasy, too, while this was his real life: Ruth Kraus.

Young Mr. Mundstock opened his ledger and began entering and adding up, adding up and entering, as if to smooth over the traces of his sorrow, so many months and weeks, so many meters, crowns and hellers, and he said never a word, never a word until he got to the entry for Excelsior, a ninety-millimeter rope; then he said "Excelsior, finest quality," and Mr. Vorjahren promptly turned round and said,

"Trash, but if you will have your own way of doing things, it's all right by me, it's all right by me," and Mr. Mundstock, watching it all like his own shadow, sighed a little and went out. . . .

The next day it all happened exactly the same.

Then the third, fourth, fifth day too, and the sixth was the Sabbath and the seventh Sunday, but after Sunday it all started again, up to Friday, and then again . . .

Mr. Mundstock saw one day that the man going downstairs was older. He went out of the house, past the park, down Maisel Street, respectfully he passed the Jewish Town Hall, came up on to the pavement by the synagogue, and crossed over to Havel Street. Now he was in front of a gray building. Through the passage and up the stairs. On a door on the first floor was a glass name-plate: "Löwy and Rezmovitch, String and Rope." He put his hand on the door knob and Mr. Mundstock slipped in behind this older man, following his own shadow.

"Good morning, gentlemen," said the older man and hung up his coat and hat. Then he sat down at his desk. Mr. Mundstock, watching like his own shadow, nodded. It was all as it should be, his hair was not nearly so neat, and anyway it wasn't as black any longer, either; and the tie was just an ordinary one, gray like the building, which was no longer green, as it used to be, what did it matter, anyway, if that was what people looked at first when they didn't want to raise their eyes, as Haus said in the days when he sold the things, before he changed over to a second-hand store? No, no, thought Mr. Mundstock, this wasn't the young man who used to sit here, it's beginning to look more like me. . . . And the older man began to speak.

"Well, Mr. Vorjahren, how did you spend your Sunday?" An older man sitting in front of him turned round.

"I was out at Chuchle at the races. Horses, you know. Quite a good race, but . . ."

"It was a pleasant Sunday," said the older Mr. Mundstock,

"I went to the Botanical Gardens and then to the cinema, to the Alfa, to see Great Garbo in 'Countess Waleska.' We sat downstairs in the fifteenth row . . ." and he stopped short, he had given himself away, but it was too late, and Mr. Mundstock watching him felt a pang. Even now . . .

"With Miss Kraus," said Mr. Vorjahren, "you know, that wouldn't be a bad match. She's a thoroughly nice woman and she was born on the seventh. And you're such a practical-minded man, not so young . . ."

Oh, yes, he was practical minded all right, and not so young, not that it was surprising, Ruth Kraus was not so young either, and couldn't be what she had been at twenty . . . Anyway, everything was all right now, the older Mr. Mundstock no longer took so much care about his appearance, either. Was that so he wouldn't be so different from Miss Kraus? God knows. But Mr. Vorjahren knew it was not the real point, and so he said nothing, not to embarrass his colleague Mr. Mundstock . . .

He knew that this visit to the cinema was the first for six months, during which he and Ruth had not met but only written to each other, letters that Mr. Mundstock put away and kept; Ruth had been having her attacks of melancholy again, and he knew that Mr. Mundstock was as helpless about them as he had been twenty years before, and that he would never have dared to try and help her with the encouragement of a trusted friend and confiding in a soul-mate, and questions about what had happened at her father's funeral, and advising her to go to the doctor; he knew there was nothing to do but wait until she wrote to him; he would put the letter away with the others when it came, and they would meet, go to the cinema, go for walks, the older Mr. Mundstock and the older Miss Kraus, until the melancholy fit came on her again. Mr. Mundstock used to like pretty women, and the great actress he admired most of all, but that was his fantasy, while this was his real life . . .

And the older Mr. Mundstock bent over his ledger, writing

and calculating, so many months, meters, crowns, and said never a word, never a word, until he got to Excelsior, and then he said "Finest quality," and Mr. Vorjahren sitting in front of him said, "Trash, but if you will do things by your own special method, excuse my saying so, don't take it ill," and Mr. Theodore Mundstock, watching it all like his own shadow, sighed a little and went out . . .

Yes, that was really what it used to be like.

All those years he had been going to Havel Street, day after day except Saturday, when they kept the Sabbath, and Sundays, highdays and holidays, on and on, year in, year out, not bothering to count any more, until one fine day . . .

The sky was a dirty gray and snow mixed with sleet was falling. An elderly man was hurrying past the Town Hall, past the synagogue, into Havel Street, into the gray building, up to the door with the name-plate on it. He hurried in, but did not say "Good morning" this time, did not even hang up his wet coat and hat, for hell was let loose.

Desks lying open, drawers upset, chairs knocked about, a pile of papers where Mr. Vorjahren used to sit. Good Heavens, hadn't he made a mistake and come in on the wrong floor? And someone yelled *"Ausweis"* at him . . .

He saw in front of him a man in a gray-green uniform, astride and arms akimbo, staring at his worn gray tie . . .

He thought the color of the uniform was like that of the building over two generations.

"Also was denn, sie Hure, worauf sie noch warten," shouted the striding figure, *"sie sind doch Theodor Mundstück oder Mundstock,* aren't you? A clerk in this shit-ass rope business? *Also, sie sind entlassen, sie unverheiratete jüdische Sau . . ."*

He realized he was an unmarried Jewish sow and sacked.

He realized—it was the end.

He took his papers and went out.

Down the wooden stairs.

Out through the passage.

Out of Havel Street.

Across the muddy street and round the synagogue and the Jewish Town Hall.

After thirty years.

He crawled up to his flat.

He unlocked the front door and went through the hall into the little room. He did not take off his wet hat nor hang his coat up. He sat on the sofa and went on sitting and sitting and the sleet dripped off him and went on dripping and dripping and something inside him *split in two*.

His head sank into his hands and a mist came over him.

He was weeping like a boy, like a thirteen-year-old boy at his parents' funeral, like the dirty gray sky outside, his tears mingled with raindrops running off the brim of his hat, an unmarried Jewish sow weeping, he thought, and at the moment he thought that, something inside him *split in two*.

From the rain and tears at his feet there rose a *shadow*.

Its name was Mon. He could not call it anything else.

Sitting on the sofa with his head in his hands Mr. Mundstock remembered everything and burst into tears. Finished, tormented, afflicted, round him a mist through which he saw the outlines of things and a creature running wildly about with his shoelaces in its beak, and he knew it was the end.

The mist round him was dispelled and everything became sharp and clear; he stepped over the creature pecking wildly at his shoes, stepped over the shoelaces it had dropped, and staggered out into the hall on feet that were sliding out of unlaced shoes. The door slammed behind him and the catch slipped. The only thought he was conscious of was that Mr. Vorjahren had been wrong. All those years with Excelsior rope. What about the Sterns was not a thought, it was only a flash. What about Ruth a fraction of a flash. He was in the hall, tearing down the curtain, reaching into the cupboard and pulling out a piece of rope, a souvenir . . .

Wild chaos had broken out in the room. Something was banging on the door as though despair itself had wings and was beating them against it. The door shook and trembled and quivered but the catch had slipped. From the other side blows were falling on the outer door and there was a human voice on the landing . . .

He lay motionless on the floor by the cupboard with the rope round his neck, while Mrs. Cizek trembled on the landing outside as her husband slowly but surely forced the lock with a skeleton key and calmed her fears.

Then, when they had got the door into the room open again as well, they saw something lying on the threshold. Mr. Cizek picked it up and took it over to the window. It was a pigeon with ash-gray feathers, brick-red legs and a dark beak. Its wings were broken and drops of blood had clotted on its breast feathers.

CHAPTER 7

An unhappy man with a rough reddened mark on his neck was bound to find that house terrifying. There were stone pinnacles jutting from the first and second floors, with Gothic windows and gargoyle-like heads with long undulating necks. The third floor was ornamented with a simple cornice. Perhaps he lives on that floor, he thought to himself desperately, perhaps. . . . But as he stood on the opposite pavement gazing up at the big Old Town apartment house, he lost the courage to go in. All at once he did not even dare to cross the road . . . At last it occurred to him that there must be a back door, leading from the yard, and he made up his mind to find it and not to go in the front way. The idea calmed him a bit, and even seemed to make his neck less sore; it delayed the moment when he would have to put his intention into effect.

He walked a little way along the other pavement, past windows draped in heavy curtains. In the dark windowpanes he saw his own moving figure mirrored. At the end of the street he plucked up courage to turn round and make sure he was not being followed, then he crossed over, turned one corner and then another, until he had got right round the block; then he went into an unknown house and through the hall into the yard at the back. He scurried through two more yards, a maze of garbage cans and carpet-beating stands, until he came to a small door. If only it isn't locked, he thought. Anxiously he put his hand on the knob, and the door yielded.

The house breathed a stone sepulchral chill, suffused with a gray half-light. In front of the list of names he struck a match. The tiny yellowish flame showed him that the card with the name he was seeking was marked Third Floor, thank Heaven. He told himself not to be so scared. He knew the man he was going to see, even if he had never been inside his home before; he had known him for years, he was a man of flesh and blood like anyone else. The doors around him were more dangerous, for many of them could open at any moment; behind him was the street door, the one he had not come through, and that, too, could open and let someone in at any moment. That forced him not to dally. He climbed the staircase in the gloomy half-light, and the bannister on which he leaned bent six times at a sharp angle before he reached the third floor. Striking a match he found himself face to face with the door he sought. Cold sweat burst out all over his brow. He had reached his goal and it was cruel.

An elderly woman he did not know opened the door to him.

He whispered his name and the person he would make so bold as to speak to.

She whispered to him to enter. In the dark hall she asked him to leave his hat and coat . . .

Then she led him into a room without announcing him.

It was a large, dark study. He felt by instinct rather than saw that there were bookcases all over one wall, while on the others hung large and small pictures in red and gilt frames; in one corner hung a tapestry. He thought there was a small table there with a candlestick on it. And two closed doors beyond, the one he had come in through from the hall, and the other obviously leading into the next room. The gray light of the street entered through two windows, but he did not notice what shape they were.

There was an erect shadow sitting at the desk facing him, but it could not be him. It was no human being sitting there, but a phantom evoked by too vivid an imagination and the pain in his neck. He was in the next room beyond one of the doors. He could hear the woman speaking next door, probably saying that he had come and was waiting in that room. Then the woman's voice fell silent and a dead quiet spread over the place. Nobody came into the study.

He stood there in front of the desk for five minutes and watched for one of the doors to open, but nothing happened. Then another five minutes and still nothing happened. Then he stood there fifteen minutes and nothing happened and then nearly half an hour and still he did not come. He began to feel it was odd. He stood there an hour and his legs began to ache. He would have liked to sit down. A step away from the desk, just facing the erect shadow, was a piece of furniture that seemed to be an armchair. For a moment he considered the propriety of sitting down when nobody had invited him to. Suppose he came in and found him seated? He decided to go on standing a bit longer. Another hour passed and no sign of him. The flat seemed dead. It began to seem suspicious. Had he forgotten him? Forgotten he was here waiting? If he had forgotten, suppose he happened to come in and find him there? The very idea made him feel upset. He put his hand to his neck and felt his throat dry and burning; he would have liked something to drink. If only he could disappear, he thought. Unobtrusively slip out into the hall, take his hat and coat and go out through the door on to the landing. But it would be dangerous to leave suddenly; he realized he would not have the courage. Suppose he heard him just as he was leaving, and suddenly opened the door? What would he say? That he was just going? That he had suddenly felt thirsty? It would look as though he had stolen something and was furtively trying to get away with it. Whatever he did was embarrassing: standing there, or going out. He did not know what to do.

At last there was something of a change in the darkness of the study. The erect shadow behind the desk seemed to move a fraction.

It raised a hand as if to touch the dark air in front of its face and make sure whether there was anyone standing there . . . A dreadful thought occurred to him. The shadow behind the desk might be him after all. That would mean that all the time he had been standing there he had been watched. As he looked doubtfully at the armchair, turned round to look at the door, felt his neck, thought of going away . . . He trembled in terror. Then it seemed too fantastic. It would be impossible. Unless . . .

Unless, the thought struck him, it was *him* after all, but he could not see his visitor. Could not see he was standing there. He realized in horror what that would mean . . . Seeing that shadow feeling the air in front of it, the dark shadow and the empty air, and looking towards the windows through which the half-light of the street filtered into the room, he thought they rose in Gothic arches and he must be not on the third, but on the first or second floor, and then he thought it must be a blind man there in front of him . . .

His legs began to give way beneath him, his nerves quivered, in wordless horror he felt his neck swelling up again, but before his strength deserted him and let him fall on the carpet in front of that desk the shadow spoke, just in time:

"*Shalom*," said the shadow. And then: "Take a seat, Mr. Mundstock, and pour yourself a drop to drink. There is a little wine mixed with water in that decanter," and he pointed to the decanter in front of him on the desk. . . .

"At the beginning of the twelfth century there lived among the people of Israel Rabbi Yehuda Halevi. You may have heard me speak the name."

He remembered, yes, yes, he had heard the name. Once

[80]

during Adar Sheni before Purim, in the Old-New Synagogue. Many years ago.

"And this Rabbi Yehuda Halevi said to the King of the Khazars:

" 'Israel among the nations is like the heart amid the organs of the body. It is the richest in sickness and the richest in health.'

"And when the King of the Khazars begged him to expound his meaning, the Master said:

" 'The heart is always being pursued by sickness. It is a prey to anxiety, fear, sorrow and terror. Its temperament is constant flux between too much and too little. Food and drink work on it, movement, hard labor, sleeping and waking—all this wreaks its havoc with the heart while the other organs are left alone.'

"The king then said:

" 'It is now quite clear to me that the heart is richer in sickness than the rest of the body. But tell me, Master, how it comes about that the heart is richest in health also?'

"And the Master replied:

" 'Is it possible for the heart to gather poisonous sap within it? For the heart to suffer from swellings, cancers, ulcers, wounds, loss of sense or even paralysis? Is it possible for the other organs of the body to suffer in this way?'

"And the king replied to this:

" 'It is not possible for the heart to gather poisonous sap within it, for even the smallest drop would mean death. The heart resists the sap that would destroy it, fighting against it to the utmost, and driving it out. The other organs are not so susceptible, and that is why poisonous sap can collect there and cause sickness.'

"And the Rabbi spoke and said:

" 'You have spoken truly. The sicknesses of the other organs cause the heart in its tenderness many painful moments, but this is the very reason why these sicknesses are driven off before they can enter the heart and settle there.'

[81]

"Thus it is not only with Israel and the nations of the earth, but with the heart and organs of Mr. Theodore Mundstock also."

The calm smile behind the desk came to him through the twilight of the room.

He experienced a feeling of relief. As though shadows had withdrawn from him, shadows that were metamorphosed thoughts of being a seer and the salvation of his people.

"There have not been many true prophets and messiahs, but many false prophets," he heard the voice behind the desk say, "many false prophets who were deceived in their own hearts. That was two or three hundred years ago. But they died the moment their deceit reached their hearts. They were indeed unhappy creatures who were the playthings of the Devil, may the Lord have mercy on them. You may have heard me speak of this, too."

He remembered he had heard of it, in the Old-New Synagogue at Rosh Hodesh, the new moon. Many years ago.

"We are apt to receive prophetic and messianic visions, but it is essential to distinguish between the true and the false. There was a rabbi who recounted the following story:

"The only son of the Emperor fell ill. One doctor ordered them to spread a stinging ointment on a piece of linen and wrap it round the naked boy. Another opposed his view, saying that the child was too weak to endure the pain the ointment would cause. A third suggested a sleeping potion, but a fourth feared it might damage the child's heart. The fifth doctor suggested that the sleeping potion be given in very small doses every hour whenever the pain woke the prince up. And his advice was followed.

"When the Lord sees that the soul of Israel is sick, He wraps it in linen and sends down as much sleep as it can endure; not to endanger the soul He wakes it every hour with a vision of some false prophet or messiah, and then sends it back to sleep until such time as the true prophet or the Messiah shall come.

[82]

"Mr. Theodore Mundstock should sleep on in peace . . ."

He observed a smile on the face beyond the desk. He felt a pleasant emptiness within him. The shadows that were metamorphosed thoughts of being a seer and the salvation of his people had receded from his mind.

"Our life cannot pass without suffering. Suffering is our vocation. In our suffering we are eternal.

"Two and a half millenniums have passed since the Babylonians conquered us and destroyed our first Temple, the symbol of our civilization and the shrine of our people's freedom. They carried us off into their own land. Yet we have survived them. Two thousand years have passed since the Romans conquered us and destroyed our last Temple, and carried us off into their own land. Yet we have survived them. Today the enemy that has sworn to kill us all is murdering us and burning our synagogues, but we shall survive him. What makes this possible? The fact that we steadfastly declare principles which are themselves eternal. *Ahavot hateryot!* That we are the apostles of charity, truth and peace.

"Mr. Theodore Mundstock will go quietly home and cast out from his heart sick thoughts he will not give in to again.

"Mr. Mundstock thought he could be a seer and a messiah, and take his own life, when he used to be a sensible, practical, logical man with a method of dealing with everything?"

He fell silent for a while and the room was quiet.

The half-light seeping in through the windows grew paler, as though a gray cloud outside had parted.

Then he went on:

"Although we are the Chosen People and are eternal, each one of us must do his share. The worse off we are, the more essential it is for every one of us to contribute the best that is in him. We must set an example for those around us, for our city, our country, the whole world.

"*Olam khesed yibaneh.* The world must be built on charity. We must know how to make people see our affection for them, and how to bestow on them our love and charity. Not only when we ourselves are happy and contented, for we would not bestow much that way; but when we ourselves are living in misery and suffering. . . .

"Mr. Mundstock must remember that he is a Jew, and not try to flee suffering and avoid his grave responsibility.

"Mr. Mundstock must take his place in the great history of the Jewish people. . . ."

He rose to his feet behind the desk, and holding his aging hand high in the air, said:

"May the Lord God of Israel bless and protect thee in this day and hour. May the light of His countenance shine upon thee and be merciful unto thee. May the Lord turn His countenance upon thee and grant thee peace."

"Amen," he replied as in a dream.

Then he heard the voice telling him to think over all he had heard, sensibly.

And as he reached the door:

"You need have no fear, and go out by the front way."

Standing outside the house that looked like a nightmare castle, and coming to his senses somewhat in the chill air of the evening, he discovered that far less time had passed than had seemed to him when he entered that darkened study and stood in front of that desk.

He could not have been there over an hour.

CHAPTER 8

The damp chill of the evening before had turned to bitter frost.

The bitter frost was running wild in the streets and people were fleeing from it, wrapped in furs and scarves, as they would have fled from a runaway horse. They kept popping in and out of the half-empty shops looking for something to buy, watched from the edge of the pavement by a pair of half-dead piteous eyes. Clutched to his breast was his bag—what was hidden in it was worth its weight in gold—and he considered: Christmas shopping was beginning, it was December the sixteenth, the beginning of Hanukkah.

"That's right," he said to the shadow at his feet, "the beginning of Hanukkah. Last year Hanukkah came late, but not this year. It's a moveable feast. Or isn't it? I could find out if I had a Jewish calendar, but I haven't. I haven't even got a perpetual calendar with which—with the help of the Lord—the holy days can be calculated right to the end of the world. I never thought that one day the perpetual calendar would be the only way of finding my way about in time. I've had to decide for myself when Hanukkah begins this year."

"True, I could have asked yesterday, when I was out visiting, but it just didn't occur to me. I'll ask somebody in the street, shall I?"

A fattish woman was approaching, with a pleasant, good-natured smile on her face. She was carrying a parcel done up in pretty paper.

"Excuse me, madam," he made bold to ask, "do you happen to know when Hanukkah begins?"

She looked at him, puzzled, once or twice, and then with a sudden shiver she left him standing . . .

"That's nothing, that's nothing," his shadow cried, "she felt cold and then she was a bit ashamed of not knowing the answer, poor thing. Perhaps she was even scared of his tormented eyes. This gentleman looks as though he would know, though, and he isn't likely to be scared, I shouldn't think . . ."

A gentleman in a beaver coat with gold pince-nez came along, his parcels decorated with sprigs of fir.

"Excuse me, sir," he asked sadly, "do you happen to know when Hanukkah begins?"

He took one look at the coat behind the bag, staring over his gold pince-nez and his beaver fur, and pulled a face. He passed by. . . .

"That's nothing, that's nothing," the shadow at his feet squirmed, "the frost has deafened him and he couldn't hear properly. He probably thought it was a beggar asking for money. Look at these two fellows, now, they're sure to know, hurry up and ask them, hurry up, do . . ."

Two youths were coming up, hands in pockets, shoulders hunched in worn coats, collars about their ears. A cigarette hanging from one corner of the mouth.

He clutched his bag to his thumping heart and opened and shut his mouth helplessly.

"I ought to have asked yesterday, on that visit," he said sorrowfully, "I'm never going to find out in the street like this. And I'm so cold . . ."

"What on earth is he standing here for if he's cold?" his

[86]

shadow exclaimed so sharply that the pavement vibrated. "Why doesn't he go home to the warm like other people, he's got a little flat, hasn't he? He's got a stove and a bit of coal to burn in it. Why doesn't he go home?"

He looked down and said nothing.

"Why!" his shadow screamed at him.

He stared miserably at the pavement, trying to silence and soothe the dreadful voice.

"I've got a little flat to go home to, and a stove and a bit of coal to burn in it, I'll go back in an hour or so, before it gets dark. Not yet, though, I don't want to go back yet. I'm standing here because I've got to! I'm standing here to get a bit of warmth.

"Of course, that's it, to get a bit of warmth, a different kind of warmth that coal can't give, don't you understand?" his teeth were chattering.

On the first day of Hanukkah he simply had to be with people. He had to get out of his flat, that had been made into a cemetery two days before, a cemetery with a polished floor and a rug, a cemetery without a handful of earth that he could gather in his palm, kiss and sprinkle over the body . . . He hoped to find a cemetery outside somewhere, have a funeral and then get warm in human company. Christmas was drawing near, and people's hearts would be growing warmer. . . . He wasn't asking for much. Not for ardent affection or heartfelt embraces, not that; he would never even have thought of expecting such a thing from people he did not know. All he hoped for was a tiny little flame.

Trams and cars were speeding along the street and pedestrians thronged the pavements. He was standing a pace away from them, holding his bag, and nobody took any notice of him. He was probably too far away from them, that was it; he ought to move away from the edge of the pavement and come nearer.

He took a step forward and found himself in a whirl of humanity.

[87]

He was carried away and rushed forward, he knew not in what direction but it did not matter, he was among people and there were people where he was going. He found himself moving against the stream and it carried him away again in the other direction, backwards, he knew not where, but he was among people and there were people where he was going. He was carried back and forth, people knocked up against him, pushed him about, those coming out of the shops and those going in. The shadow dodging round his feet flapped about like a gasping fish and the bag clutched to his chest, swelling with something worth its weight in gold, bobbed about.

At the corner of the street the whirlpool flung him up between two low houses, where there was a patch of frozen gray grass in the corner.

He opened his bag and took out the dead little feathered body.

As he was taking it out a pair of bloodshot eyes peered over his shoulder and stared at his hand. The pair of bloodshot eyes had a collar turned up and hands in pockets. There was a cigarette hanging from the corner of his mouth.

He recognized one of the youths he had spoken to a little while back.

The upturned collar came round in front of him and pulled a face.

"Nice bit of grub," he spoke through one corner of his mouth. "Black market? What did they charge you for it?"

The world reeled round him.

He ought to call for help.

How could he? He! And anyway, they were alone here.

The other was watching round the corner and came to join them. His collar turned up and hands in pockets. He spat out the end of a cigarette and took his place by his side. He was caught between them in a pincer movement.

"Just ready for the pot—pigeon pie," the first youth hissed through clenched teeth.

[88]

"In God's name, I was going to bury it, to lay it to eternal rest, you couldn't do a thing like that, you couldn't," he managed to whisper, clutching the handful of feathers with helpless dangling head close to his chest.

They laughed, a loud, icy laugh.

"He's going to throw it away," the first youth said, taking his hands slowly out of his pockets. He retreated before them into the corner between the two low houses.

There were some people coming past.

He stood there squeezed into the corner and they pretended to be talking to an old friend.

"So he isn't selling," the first youth said when the people had passed by, "he wants to give it to the worms. What's he trying to pass off if he doesn't want to sell the pigeon?"

The other was kicking at the frozen grass.

"Cats'd scratch it up, here," he said.

The first youth looked him up and down with his reddened eyes and then said:

"If he found it dead it'll be tainted."

"It wasn't found dead, it died," he lamented, "it met its death, it passed away, and I'm going to bury it."

"Lay it to eternal rest, we've heard that before," the first youth retorted. "Our janitor had the same idea about a cat." He jerked his head in the direction of the door of one of the low houses. "That's the hospital garden through there, just the spot for a funeral. Come on!"

"Come along, come along, we're off to a funeral," he repeated, and between them they pushed him towards the door of one of the houses.

More people came past.

"Get a move on," they said, and pushed him through the door.

They marched him down an unknown corridor as though they had him in chains. He was afraid to twist free and try to run for it, and it was out of the question to call for help. At the end of the corridor they kicked a door open and he found himself in a little yard with two bare trees, a scrap of frozen grass, and a garbage can. A few feet away was a wall.

"Drop it in here," said the bloodshot one, and lifted the lid of the garbage can.

"No, oh no," he protested as he saw the ashes and the horrible rubbish inside, "for God's sake don't make me do that, have a heart . . ."

"All right, then, in here," and the other scuffed at the ground. Then he bent down and scraped at the soil.

He made a little hollow in the ground.

"Thought better of it?" snapped the first youth, and took his hands out of his pocket for a moment.

"Are we supposed to sing hymns?" they asked.

He covered it over with handfuls of earth, pressing them in with his hands, kneading and pressing so that nobody could disturb it afterwards. He knew it was no good. He had guessed what the two were thinking of doing. As soon as his back was turned they would come back here and dig the poor little creature up. He could have wept.

"Funeral over?" asked the bloodshot one.

He got up from the ground stiffly, thinking to himself that if only he had known what was going to happen to it after death . . . As he got to his feet his eyes were wet.

They went back the way they had come.

Through that corridor.

He went along between them as though they had him in chains.

"So you ain't got nothing to sell?" the second of the two said menacingly.

The first youth suddenly barred his way.

"Waiting to be sent to the concentration camp?"

They were back in the corner between the two low houses, by the scrap of frozen grass.

He did not reply.

Then he whispered: "None shall come to save us."

They looked at each other. Then the second youth took his hands out of his pocket and lit a cigarette.

"What d'you mean, none shall come to save us, who're you talking about?" he didn't take his eyes off him.

Then they looked at each other again.

"What d'you want to do about it?" the bloodshot one said.

As he stood there and said nothing he went on:

"Get a move on! You go in front and we'll be a step or two behind . . ."

He was carried away by the throng again, swept forward and pulled back, and the two youths behind him. They hadn't gone back yet, they hadn't dug the creature up yet; he could have wept. He got out of the stream and caught at the wall like a weak man drowning. Turning to look back he saw they were no longer behind him. They had disappeared.

Blue-gray clouds poured down the street and from them came a rattling, thundering, rolling noise. Like a storm raging down the street.

He saw wheels, smelt rubber and gasoline. He saw steel helmets wearing coats with ammunition belts over them. They were on their way to murder. On December the sixteenth, the first day of Hanukkah.

He heard a voice behind him.

"This man standing here, madam, was a seer yesterday."

"This man, madam, was a messiah yesterday."

"Ladies, ladies, didn't you know this man had come out to get warm today?"

He heard laughter drowning in the crowd.

A freezing shudder seized him and the thought flashed through his mind that he could throw himself under those wheels. But he knew, since the previous day, that he must not . . .

Suddenly he saw the familiar face with bloodshot eyes in front of him.

"Look here, this isn't doing you any good, you know."

"If you're waiting for the Zebra you're wasting your time. And there's somebody watching you over there."

"They'll have the Zebra in cop tomorrow and you'll be in trouble," he hissed and drew a finger across his throat. "We're warning you!"

The trucks had gone and there was a wood on the other side of the road. A little forest of Christmas trees on sale. A mother in a shabby coat was dragging her equally shabby little girl away from them for all she was worth, and the child was putting up desperate resistance.

He took side streets to get home.

His head was hanging and his eyes fixed on the pavement.

He observed that the people passing him were walking in just the same manner. Heads hanging and eyes on the pavement.

Those two youths thought he was selling black-market stuff, he thought.

He had no idea they were following him right up to the house he lived in, and the one with the bloodshot eyes went inside to look at the name-plates and to listen for the sound of a door banging and see which floor it was . . .

Had he found a little warmth, as he had hoped? He could not have said. But perhaps he had, a little.

Snow began to fall.

The sky above the blacked-out city seemed sprinkled with stars. It was the first day of Hanukkah.

In the cupboard in the hall he found the menorah candlestick he had inherited from his grandmother, who had it from her mother, and from her parents before that. He carried it into the room and stood it on the little table, which he carried over to the blacked-out window; it was not hard to find the right direction, he had been placing it this way for at least thirty years. What about candles? Whatever else he might lack, in the depths of this wartime misery, he had candles for the Feast of Lights. They were still those he had bought off Moyshe

Haus, heaven only knew where he had got hold of them, but he didn't ask more than thirty hellers a piece. Moyshe Haus would not try to make on Hanukkah candles. They were so thin that he had to wrap paper round the ends to keep them upright in the cups of the menorah. He put one of them into the first cup on the right, and another, the *shammash,* into the detachable cup. He lit this one and the flickering flame threw a shadow.

Holding the *shammash* in his hand, he softly sang the *brokhe.*

"Blessed be the Lord our God, who has sanctified us by Thy commandments and enjoined us to kindle the Hanukkah lamp, and in its light to remember Thee, who hast done wondrous things to our fathers in days of yore at this season."

Then taking the *shammash* he lit the candle in the menorah from it and sang the *Moauz tsuryeshuosi.*

> *Moauz tsur yeshuosi*
> *Lekho noe leshabeakh*
> *tykain beis tefilosi*
> *veshom taudo nezabeakh*

The shadow began leaping round the candlestick.
He gazed at the flame and his heart ached.

> *oz egmaur beshir mizmaur*
> *hanukkahs hamizbeakh.*

He gazed at the little flames and thought of Hanukkah, the feast of peace and goodwill. The Jews were sitting round their candlesticks, remembering and rejoicing. He wondered what. . . . He thought of Ruth Kraus. Perhaps at this moment she too was holding the *shammash* candle in her hand, lighting the menorah and softly singing the *brokhe,* poor Ruth, perhaps she was . . . He thought of the Sterns. Mrs. Stern and Otto, dear sweet Freda, Grandmother, Simon. Simon! The boy's great dark eyes were staring at the flame of the first

Hanukkah candle, full of wonder. The flame flickered and was reflected back from his magnificent eyes . . . He bent his head to the candlestick and the shadow at his feet trembled again.

"There's something pink flying about," he whispered, "something pink fluttering."

Outside the snow was falling and the sky above the city was full of stars.

Then he went on putting another candle into the menorah every day for eight days, at this evening hour; he sang the *brokhe* and the hymn *Moauz tsur yeshuosi*, and thought of the Sterns, of Simon, of Ruth . . . And on the last evening the whole of the Hanukkah candlestick was alight and by the end of the feast thirty-six candles and eight *shammash* candles had been consumed.

On the last day of Hanukkah, though, the Christmas trees were lit up, carols were being sung, bells were ringing and incense burning, for the last day of Hanukkah was Christmas Eve. Christmas Eve, peace and goodwill in the middle of a war.

It was quiet in his little room.

He was alone with his shadow.

But there were many lights in his room.

A menorah full of flickering lights.

And it was not quiet in his little room.

The radio could be heard from the Cizeks' next door, and the voices of Charlie and Molly mingling with it.

Nor was he alone there.

A piece of yellowed paper lay on his knee. . . .

He unfolded the yellowed paper, Ruth's last letter to him, two years ago; it was dated December 24, 1939.

> *My dear Theo,*
>
> *I send you warm greetings. Things are going ill with us, I can feel it. I cannot talk to you about our future, and even if I had the opportunity, I do not think I would be able to. It is sad and grim. Yet I think you should know*

something of what is going on, and not live in the belief that ignorance is strength.

There is a rumor that we are all to be evacuated to the east, to build villages there where we shall live isolated from the rest of the world. There is no knowing whether it will really come to pass. The war may end before we expect it, and if they had had time to move us out there perhaps we could endure it for a while. But I have heard far more serious rumors—that they are setting up concentration camps like they have in the Reich for their political enemies, but these will be only for us, and there in some way as yet unknown we shall all perish. There are many among us who do not believe this; I talked to the Streckers, who just laughed at me. But I no longer fool myself with dreams. We have been flung into a terrible hell.

I look worse and worse these days, Theo, you would be shocked to see me. Yesterday in the street I heard someone say "ghastly sight," and I felt a stabbing pain in my head. I thought they meant me, and I remembered father's funeral.

I have never told anyone what happened that day in our village cemetery, but today I will tell you, after you've known me for thirty unhappy years. You will probably expect to hear of some extraordinary event, but it was something very small, that did not even last a minute.

We had just finished the Yisgadal and were throwing soil into father's grave when somebody climbed up on the wall and shouted: "Go and bury yourself with him, you Jew-monkey," and that was all.

I have told you about the concentration camps. But, Theo, I have no strength any more to fight against fate. I shall not suffer their torments. You can save yourself from them, you can, Theo, even if you're quite alone; however weak you are, it's so simple and easy. If I have to go, Theo, I shall never get there. I really shall go and bury myself with poor father, in the only place in the world where there *is peace and quiet. It will be the best thing for me, and if you wish me well as you have always done in the past, you will admit that I am right and you will not sorrow over me. There's only one thing I beg of you: don't try to talk me out of it. Consider what you would be talking me out of and that there would be no sense in it. Your last attempt would fail as completely as your first, that evening thirty years ago in Plater Street. We should only spoil our long years of understanding, weave a web of sorrow round our friendship, and that would not be the right way to end our lives.*

I want to thank you, now, for all the kindness you have shown me, for thirty years of true understanding. I know I have spoiled your life for you.

May the Lord God reward you a thousand times over.

I am going to stay shut up at home now, as far as I can, and not go out anywhere; it's the only thing I can do, to wait underground like a gopher. Perhaps I shall not be sent away anywhere, and then I won't have to do that. I am sure you will survive. Then when it's all over we shall meet again as we used to do, and we shall know we have come through hell-fire with our dignity intact. We shall go to the Botanical Gardens—perhaps it will just be the time the trees are in flower. We shall go to the pictures, and start our lives again.

Meanwhile, keep as well and strong as you can, and keep your courage up.

I wish you a joyful Hanukkah 1939/5720.

From next door came the sound of the radio, mingled with children's voices.

Yes, they had asked him to come in and join them, not to sit there all on his own; he could spend the evening with them. He excused himself with a thousand thanks. He would only spoil their pleasure and upset the children.

He was a Jew and he would stay by his menorah.

[96]

The Jews were sitting round their candlesticks, remembering and rejoicing. . .

He sat by his menorah remembering and whispering *"yevonim nikbetsu olay, azay bimey khashmanim,"* in a quiet little room whose walls rang like those of the seven cities with the carols all around; he whispered *"beney vino yemey shmono, kovu shir urenonim,"* alone, deserted, saddened.

There was a fluttering sound. Something was flying round, he whispered by the candlestick. Something pink was fluttering about.

At that moment the bell rang.

He got up and went to open the door as if in a dream.

The two on the landing had their hands in their pockets and their worn collars up above their ears.

He wanted to cry out but his throat was suddenly constricted.

They pushed their way into the hall and into the little room. For a moment they were taken aback; they saw the lighted menorah. Then they saw the letter.

"Nice little place you've got here," said the one with the bloodshot eyes and took out of his pocket a black, shiny thing he weighed as he held it in his palm.

"Nice little place and you got a letter for Christmas," said the other looking round, "only the paper looks old and yellow."

"Surprised to see we found our way here, aren't you?" the first said with a loud, icy laugh and went on weighing the black metallic thing in his hand.

Then he put it down on the table.

"Only a bit of cheese," he said, "the old man works in a dairy."

On the table lay a white paper packet tied up with a bit of old ribbon.

"We're off to the Reich tomorrow. Forced labor."

"For Heaven's sake," he cried in a state near to fainting, "you must have made a mistake, gentlemen!" They burst out laughing.

"The gentlemen," the bloodshot one answered, "did make a mistake. We thought you were the guy what was supposed to wait for the Zebra on account of some stuff, we were supposed to warn you and take it off you. It was all this fool's fault, here," and he jerked his head towards his companion.

"He hadn't got a star on, had he? So I didn't notice and what the . . ." said the other and went on examining the menorah.

He did not understand what was happening but he was beginning to come to his senses. He suddenly realized they had come to pay him a visit on Christmas Eve and brought him something, and here was he never even offering them a seat. He thought they might at least like a cup of tea.

"Don't bother, we can't stay anyway, it's Christmas Eve."

He opened the packet and saw pieces of cheese wrapped in silver paper.

"No money, it's a Christmas present," and before he could say anything they had gone out of the room.

"You must stay a minute, gentlemen, please," he tried to detain them, but they had opened the door and were out on the landing.

"Who was that woman in the colored dress downstairs," asked the one with the bloodshot eyes, "she looked a bit sharpish."

"Oh, that's only the janitress, Mrs. Civrna," he smiled.

"What the devil brought her out on the landing on Christmas Eve?" said the other.

"That's all right, you needn't worry," he smiled again. "She's a good woman. But I'll go down with you if you like."

"Merry Christmas and make the best of it . . . that was some funeral, wasn't it? That pigeon's still lying there, and if you don't believe me you can go and look. Take care, though, if you do. . ."

He believed them all right, except for its being a pigeon, but he didn't say it aloud. He was smiling as he wished them a merry Christmas and safe return from Germany. Would they come and look him up if he was still there? . . . Of course they would, and the bloodshot one said they'd sure come and see him after the war, because they were going to do a skip and a jump and made the motions of running away. They laughed and turned their collars up about their ears, waved and disappeared down the stairs.

He went back into his little room with his head in a whirl. It was like a dream.

Ruth, the Sterns, Simon, these two fellows, the white packet on the table. He could hardly believe it.

The menorah was flickering and from next door he could hear the radio; he suddenly felt himself as light of heart and content as if he had been taking some tablets.

CHAPTER 9

The Feast of Hanukkah passed, and a new civil year began. Mr. Theodore Mundstock was sweeping the street. . .

There were plenty of people in Saltpetre Street, even in winter. In the morning they went from the church near the tram stop towards the cinema and the sports shop. In the afternoon from the cinema and the shop towards the church and the tram stop. In the early morning and at midday there were children going both ways, for there were two schools in the street. Some days he swept Saltpetre Street in the early morning and before noon; other days it was midday and the afternoon. In his old black coat with the yellow star that showed up so well that he could be recognized far off. Perhaps because there were always people about when he was sweeping Saltpetre Street he began thinking about people and getting ideas about people.

It is true that we have survived all kinds of suffering, he thought to himself as he tipped his dirt into the handcart they had given him for the day in the city dump, we have survived . . . And as the men and women in fashionably cut winter coats passed by on the pavement carefully looking in the other direction, or furtively catching his sad glance, the thought came to him that his was the most ancient people in the world that had survived to the present day.

With broom in hand he encouraged himself then, telling himself that they had been alive under their forefather Abraham and even long before that, when the empires of Egypt and Babylon were flourishing, in the days of the Assyrians and Sumerians, the Amalekites, the Philistines and the Phoenicians, and what all the peoples were called; and there was no trace of Saltpetre Street then, the road he was just sweeping. What had become of all these ancient peoples? They had melted in the stream of humanity like mist. Or could it be said that the gentleman over there waiting for the tram was an Assyrian, or the elementary school teacher just crossing over, could be a Sumerian? Was that a Phoenician woman standing in front of the church? Was the young man looking down from the film poster the latest Philistine actor? The dust of the earth had buried them all thousands of years ago and nothing remained but bits of stones and broken fragments of tiles in museums, dug up out of the ground; yet their empires had been great and powerful, and one had even built a tower to touch the stars. Yes, it had all passed away; but they were still as they had been at the dawn of history, whatever their names; it was a drop of the same ancient and yet eternally young blood, however much it had mingled long ago with others, so that finding a fragment inscribed with Hebrew letters today was to find a scrap of a living language, a bit of official and vernacular speech. Was suffering the price of their ransom? At this point he recalled the old man's words that suffering was their vocation, and then he told himself that their persecution was perhaps the price of their survival.

When the children with their schoolbags came rushing out yelling, a storm seemed to tear down the street. As the boys reached the spot where he was sweeping he blushed with shame as he stood among them with his yellow star, holding the broom, and thought of Simon. For Simon was not dashing out of school yelling, he was not permitted to, and it always came to him to ask why Simon? What had Simon done to deserve that? Had he done an evil or a great thing when he was born in the cradle with the Star of David? Had he lived before he was born?

What would have become of Simon if his birth had worked out otherwise, the thought always came back to him in this street, if his parents had never met. If Otto had married somebody else and not Mrs. Stern, or if Mrs. Stern had taken another husband than Otto. Such things could happen. The fact that two strangers met depended on quite insignificant trifles. If their paths had never crossed would it have been Simon here, or somebody only half like him? And what would have happened if both Otto and Klara had stayed single? Would there have been a Simon or not? Was it thinkable that there would have been no Simon when Simon existed today? Yes, it was chance that Simon had been born in the cradle with the star, of a royal line, and on account of that he was not permitted to go to school now; just as it was chance in his case that he was born in the same royal cradle and was now engaged in sweeping the street . . . Whenever he noticed a young married couple or a pair of lovers coming along with happy smiles he wondered what poor Freda was doing now that her Aryan engineer had jilted her and she wasn't likely to get over it. He did not even dare to think of Ruth Kraus.

When the school children had disappeared and the street was quiet again, and he pushed his cart as far as the church wall and had a moment's rest, pretending to tidy his little heap of dirt, he recalled the old man's words that he must do his share, set an example, and take his place in the history of the Jewish people.

The advantage of Saltpetre Street was that it was fairly clean. Considering that plenty of people came that way and there was a school at each end. He rarely had more to sweep up than scraps of paper, tram tickets, burned matches. Occasionally apple cores. But never banana skins or orange peel. At first he used to be surprised, because children like oranges and bananas, after all; but when he caught sight of the uniforms and jackboots, the columns of military vehicles, and when he smelled the gasoline and rubber, he woke up to reality. There was a war on, and the country was occupied. In wartime and in occupied country there was no room for oranges and bananas, only for hand-grenades and rifles. And one thing became clear to him: as long as he, the Jew Mr. Theodore Mundstock, was forced to sweep Saltpetre Street, there would never be a banana skin or a piece of orange peel for him to sweep up. And he swept up the tram tickets and burned matches.

Soap Street, which he swept on Saturday mornings, was quieter, but far dustier. He only had to raise his broom and a cloud of dust rose from the pavement with it, and as he went on sweeping the cloud grew until he and his handcart were lost in it. His face and mouth and lungs were full of it and his black coat turned gray and so did his yellow six-pointed star. Hidden in his cloud of dust he turned his thoughts in a different direction.

He remembered the days when he still used to go to the Old-New Synagogue on holy days to hear the old man preach; from his lips he had heard of the dust and the stars. . .

I will multiply the seed as the stars of the heaven, and as the sand which is upon the sea shore.

Rabbi Yehuda bar Elai explained these words thus:

This people is likened to the dust and likened to the stars.

Falling, it falls to the dust.

Rising, it rises to the stars. . .

As he went home along Soap Street he could feel the dust, feel it in his face, his mouth, his lungs. Not until he had got home and dusted off his old black coat and washed behind the curtain in his little hall did he begin to feel better. For a while he had got rid of the dust of Soap Street; but fear and torment at the thought of the day to come accompanied him everywhere like his own shadow.

[103]

One day an incredible thing happened.

One day in this time of fear and torment, when he did not know himself how he managed to keep going and to keep sane, in his place in the Jewish history of suffering, the moment came when all this changed.

Mr. Theodore Mundstock discovered something he had only dimly felt so far, something vaguely guessed. He discovered what it was that seemed to be sprouting and budding green in his mind.

The way out of the Jewish history of suffering.

The secret of salvation.

It was the happiest day of his life.

It was a Friday and he was just sweeping Armorers Lane.

He felt himself begin to rise to the stars.

CHAPTER 10

It was just an ordinary Friday, not too much sun, not too many clouds, neither too hot nor too cold, just an ordinary natural Friday. The only remarkable thing about that Friday was that Armorers Lane seemed to have gone mad that day. As though everybody who lived in Armorers Lane had got together and said they were going to do their spring cleaning all at once. There was no other explanation. Armorers Lane looked as though it was being cleaned out. On that memorable day there were piles of rubbish in front of every house. The edges of the pavement were adorned with old tin cans, battered buckets, cracked basins, and all stuffed with the wildest assortment of rubbish—ashes, rags, old bottles and jars, saucepans, pokers, hobs, stovepipes, sofa springs, all kinds of scrap iron, a bit of an old mattress, rusty dustpans, and a mangy broom. In front of the biggest house there was even a pile of bricks and ornamental tiles, looking as though someone had taken a tiled stove to pieces. It was a fantastic collection of the entrails of the homes and houses, the homes and houses turned inside out, as it were, and spilt on to the street. The entrails ended at the corner of the street where the chemists' shop was, in the shape of a piece of old hose-pipe. And all this Mr. Theodore Mundstock was supposed to pile on to the little handcart they had given him for the day in the city dump.

When he reached this street about midday and saw what it looked like, he felt certain he could never get it all in. After the weeks he had spent sweeping the streets he had some idea of what he could get into his cart. For a while he stood gazing at the uneven cobblestones, trying to remember what holiday was on the doorstep. Christmas had come and gone but it was still a long time to Easter and the spring. As he wasted his time wondering about possible holidays he seemed to notice queer people in the street, people he had never seen there before; they seemed to be watching him furtively as if they wanted to see how he was going to set about his job, and it occurred to him that this was a trap that had been set for him, this street. So that he wouldn't be able to sweep it clean and they could accuse him of disobedience, of refusal to obey orders, and even of sabotage. In his mind's eye he saw his letter box and in it a white paper with the official heading on it. If that's the way things are, he thought, I'm done for.

As he stood there hanging on to his cart with one hand to prevent himself collapsing on the ground, trembling with despair and bathed in sweat, he looked sadly and helplessly at the handcart; it seemed smaller than usual, and he thought perhaps they had purposely given him a smaller one that day. As he stood there men and women of all ages and sizes passed by on the pavement, wearing all kinds of coats and hats, carrying dispatch cases, handbags, shopping bags, or just empty-handed; from little shopping expeditions, from errands, going home to dinner; some of them carefully looked in the other direction as they passed him, others furtively caught his glance, and some looked into his eyes for a moment, with pity or as if they wanted to encourage him; it was sure, though, that not one of the people passing by had any idea what was going on in his mind, what a terrible thing he had to deal with, this man in his worn black coat with the yellow star, pushing his cart along with its broom; they could not guess his very existence was at stake.

Only those strange people who slipped furtively across the street and watched him from a distance, fingering his death-warrant in the pockets of their overcoats, smiled menacingly.

Thus began the memorable day, the happiest day in the life of Mr. Theodore Mundstock.

Then his destiny began to be fulfilled.

From the very moment when, with trembling hands and bathed in sweat, he began emptying the first tin of rubbish into his cart and sweeping up what was left on the pavement in front of the corner house. . .

He remembered how he had once come down this street on his way to the Backers, so as to avoid nearby Havel Street. He remembered the years in Havel Street and he felt like weeping.

By the time he had trundled the cart along to the second house the bottom was already covered with a nasty little pile. And he had only just begun! He saw that he could never cart it all away, at least not in one trip.

In front of the third house he resignedly swept up the dirt and threw the old bottles and rags into the cart. Then he noticed a bit of old rope lying there. Poor papery stuff, he thought, and it brought his memory back to Havel Street again. Excelsior, now, that was quality for you! Finest quality! And Mr. Vorjahren said: Trash! Yes, that was what poor old Mr. Vorjahren used to say, and by now he had been taken away somewhere. And it occurred to him that soon he was *not* going to meet him there after all, because he'd be facing a charge of sabotage and the penalty for that was death. Sabotage was a surer death than all the nooses in the world, of whatever first-rate quality. He took out a handkerchief and quietly wiped his face as though he was sweating. But they were tears he was wiping away. He realized he would be finished sooner than he thought. That he would never even get to the end of the street.

In front of the fourth house the heap of rubble, bricks and

tiles was waiting for him, for the fourth house was the biggest of them all. It was impossible; unless he made three trips. If it were possible to come back a third time, anyway.

"If you will have your own way of doing things . . ." the words of Mr. Vorjahren suddenly formed in his mind. "Such a practical-minded man, doing things your own way, *prac-tic-al* . . ."

He was resignedly throwing old hobs and stovepipes into his cart when the Sterns came to his mind with an ache. The way she used to be frying veal cutlets. And Freda. Don't worry, Mrs. Stern, she'll get over it. You do as I advise you. Thus and thus . . . It's a good method, you see, a *me-thod!*

At that moment a man in a black hat and gold eyeglasses passed by and seemed to nod approvingly. He looked like a university professor. He remembered the chief rabbi. Mr. Mundstock thought he could be a seer and a messiah, and take his own life, when he used to be a sensible, practical, logical man with a *method* of dealing with everything.

He remembered and for a split second his hands hung in mid-air.

A method and a way of doing things, a method and a way of doing things. Mr. Vorjahren, the Sterns, the old man, not to mention many others. Sensible, practical, logical. Such a *practical*-minded man . . . The same thing, over and over again.

After all, he thought, in heaven's name, it's true. He had always been like that. All the years he had been going to the Sterns', and there, just round the corner from here, to the place in Havel Street. Why had the string and rope business made a profit although the customer had never lost on it? Why did the string and rope business make no profit but still the customers were not robbed? Why did the string and rope business occasionally lose money but the customers never, although it did not happen often? Because he had always known what ought to be done. Because he was practical minded and sensible. Why were they glad to see him at the Sterns'? For the very same reason. And he told himself to cast his mind back to those old days, here in Armorers Lane as he stood in front of that terrible pile of rubbish he could never cart away. The piles that had been put there on purpose to trap him so that they would have an excuse to punish him. He ought to remain calm and think things over properly, he told himself, and his hands trembled in the air, but not with pure fear and horror now. This was the beginning of a queer excited feeling . . .

He looked at the pavement on both sides of the street and back at his cart, seeing them both through mingled tears and sweat; then suddenly through his tears and sweat he saw something he had forgotten till then. The hooks along the side of the handcart, the hooks to rest the broom on when he had finished work and was wheeling the cart home, and on the other side were two more hooks for the broom he didn't have with him. And he realized he'd not been doing it sensibly. He could carry away all the rubbish and even the houses themselves if he went about it the right way. If for instance instead of tipping the contents of the tins and buckets into the cart he left it in the tins and buckets and hung the tins and buckets themselves on the hooks. He would save space in his cart and only put in the rubbish from the basins that couldn't be hung on the outside of the cart, and the heaps on the ground. The tiles and bricks could be piled up to take the least room possible. And then he could pile the basins upside down on top when he had finished, to stop the rest slipping down. In fact, he could set about arranging it methodically. The rubbish from Armorers Lane.

His eyes dried in a moment and the sweat stopped pouring off him, and he set to work. He filled the tins and buckets with rubbish again and hung them on the hooks, arranged the tiles and bricks in piles up against each other. The ashes and dirt he pressed down carefully . . . Men and women of all ages were passing by, watching furtively to see what the old man in the worn coat with the star was playing at. They pretended not to notice, though, looking in another direction and hurrying. He struggled along the uneven cobbled street, hanging tins on his cart, packing the dirt in, piling things up neatly, and then when he reached the end of the street he saw that the cart was full, covered on top with upturned basins and hung all round with tins and buckets full of rubbish, but Armorers Lane was swept clean. He had cleaned the entrails up. He felt that the strange people who had furtively been walking about and watching him behind his back had disappeared too. Of course they had. He had stood up to the test, hadn't he?

It was two o'clock in the afternoon as he left the street.

His handcart was so overloaded it creaked, hung round with dreadful tins and buckets of incredible filthy rubbish; threaded through the spokes of the wheels were pieces of black hose-pipe and over the top of the cart was an armor of upturned broken basins, with the broom crowning the lot. Not even an Italian ice cream man could have had a more decorative handcart on whatever festive occasion. In all the streets he passed through people stopped on the pavements and looked after him with amazement, and the policemen on point duty stared embarrassedly at the streams of traffic, blindly motioning him to pass on quickly. He had the feeling that were it not for their embarrassment they would have held up the entire traffic for him to pass.

And Mr. Mundstock trudged on and on, the sweat streaming off him, his eyes filling with tears, yet he was not frightened and terrified now, but filled with a strange excitement.

He wanted to get to the city dump with his cart as soon as he could.

He wanted to get home to his little flat, into his little room, as soon as he could.

For something had begun to dawn on Mr. Theodore Mundstock.

On that memorable Friday in the month of January, 1942,
Mr. Theodore Mundstock
could be seen
hurrying along
hands in pockets and head bent forward

in an old worn coat covered in dust
with the yellow six-pointed star
leaving the City Ash and Rubbish Dump
passing along Gate Street Straight Street Anthony Street
Heinrich von Kleist Avenue
Gluck Road and Stuck Road
round Zavis of Falkenstein Park
under the railway bridge by the Main Station
along General von Schwerin Avenue and Rome Street
across Thirty-first of January Street
and down London Street
home.

Houses, streets, avenues, viaducts, parks, cars, trams, shops and people had all ceased to exist for him. If any of the passers-by had had sharp enough eyes they might have seen his shadow Mon running in and out between his feet like a performing dog in the circus ring. If any of the passers-by had had sharp enough ears they might have heard him whispering like tiny rustling leaves, murmuring like young wine, whistling like a dancing clarinet, chiming like a bell or like a boy in the circle of his companions. But there was nobody like that about. There were only people who saw an elderly man hurrying along in a worn and dusty old coat with the six-pointed yellow star, hands in his pockets and head bent forward.

And not one of these passers-by had the slightest idea what had become quite clear to this elderly man hurrying along with the star on his coat covered in dust:

That he must constantly think the same way as he had done that afternoon in Armorers Lane. That if he thought the same way as he had done that afternoon in Armorers Lane, method and a practical approach could save him. He would be *saved!*

The first methodical question which occurred to him as he hurried home full of hope and salvation, did not occur to him but was methodically thought out by his mind; it was as follows:

Who could survive the concentration camp?

[111]

And the first methodical answer which came to his mind did not just come to his mind but was methodically thought out; it was as follows:

The man who went about things sensibly, with a logical method.

The man who was thoroughly, properly prepared for everything in a logically planned manner.

Mon was running about under his feet and he was strung up to a high pitch of excitement. He would have liked to shout for joy. Houses, streets, cars, trams, pavements, shops, people, had ceased to exist for him. It all slipped past him as though a conveyor belt was carrying it in the opposite direction. The passers-by saw an elderly man in a worn and dusty coat with the yellow six-pointed star hurrying along. Those who had a kind, sensitive heart pitied him. But senses sharp enough to know what it was all about there were none. Mr. Theodore Mundstock stopped in front of the house where he lived.

Near the front door he caught sight of the gaunt bald head of the informer Korka. He was talking to somebody. Mr. Hetzel from the second floor. He nodded at Mr. Hetzel and turned away to the door so that Mr. Hetzel could not return his greeting. He was talking to an informer.

Who could survive?

He who was thoroughly prepared for every eventuality.

As he hurried up the stairs to his fourth floor he thought of the letter box. If only the official summons had not come yet! Not today! Not yet! He took two steps at a time.

He reached the fourth floor, opened the door, and his shadow Mon flung itself on the letter box. It was dark in the hall but Mon felt for what he wanted. There was nothing there. He switched on the light on the wall, but the letter box was empty, graying with nothingness. At that moment Mr. Mundstock had won his race with time.

His first move was to go behind the curtain to the calendar of Alois Klokocnik hanging over the burner. Reaching for a pencil he put a ring round that memorable Friday. He knew for certain now that he would remember this day as long as he lived. The mists had cleared and the road to hope and salvation had been revealed.

Cheerfully he took off his old coat, shook the dust out of it, and washed himself in cold water. Feeling fresher he went into the room; it was growing dark, for it was a quarter past four. He lit the lamp and wanted to say to Mon: "There you are, you see, dear old friend. I've found my old self, the way I used to be before you'd ever heard of me," but he could not see his shadow anywhere. He turned round, but there was no shadow behind him. His shadow had disappeared. Only on the lampshade Columbus's ship came sailing towards him . . .

CHAPTER 11

In his little flat Mr. Theodore Mundstock was making his preparations. Sensibly, methodically, with a practical plan.

Im Namen des deutschen Volkes, Reiches und Reichkanzlers the family of Mr. Richard Backer packed their bags, each of fifty kilograms, and were sent off to the concentration camp. Before they left they gave Mr. Kopyto some things to keep for them. A few pictures, some jewelry and a fur coat. The coat belonged to Mrs. Backer, it had been a wedding present and she said she was fond of it. Mr. Kopyto said it was no wonder, we were only human and everybody had something he was fond of, and that made him the hero of the hour. He carried it all away from their flat in good time, although they were valuables and to be caught carrying them off meant the death penalty. It was stealing official Reich property. Mr. Kopyto did not seem to mind taking the risk and had the Backers' valuables out of the place in no time. He was the hero of the hour. And they were sent off.

Im Namen des deutschen Volkes and all the rest Mrs. Heksch the property owner who had long since ceased to have any property to own was sent off too. With a little travelling basket which could not have weighed ten kilograms. Mrs. Heksch was elderly and could not have carried any more. Mr. Kopyto was at hand to help. All unobserved he carried off in good time several of the most valuable things in her flat, including the picture in a gilt frame that she had inherited from her mother. She had been very fond of that. No wonder, said Mr. Kopyto, we were only human and everybody had something he got attached to. He carried it off and that was risking his neck. He was the hero of the hour. And Mrs. Heksch was sent off.

In Namen des deutschen Volkes the earth swallowed up the Radnitzers too. Their flat had been taken over a long time before by the family of a Reich official, with all that it contained. Except for the valuables that Mr. Kopyto managed to carry off. And the thousand crowns he had borrowed from them in time, saying his family was dying of hunger. He was really an excellent saboteur. Robbing a Reich citizen of his rightful property and risking his life to do it. But who wouldn't do what he could for his neighbors? The Radnitzers disappeared from view.

The Grünwalds hanged themselves, the Streckers gassed themselves, Albina Schick jumped out of the window, Kohn got himself run over by an express train near Chuchle. *Im Namen des deutschen Volkes, Reiches und des Führers und Reichskanzlers.*

Before all that happened Mr. Kopyto had carried something off from their respective homes.

The Sterns were the only ones still hanging on.

Only old Moyshe Haus in Benedict Street went doddering on.

Nobody knew anything about Kolb.

What about Ruth Kraus . . . ?

Mr. Theodore Mundstock had worked out his practical method. He was making his preparations night and day. Step by step, sensibly, methodically, with a practical plan.

What did Mr. Theodore Mundstock's method consist of?

In the colossal investigation of every possible situation, the working out of a method of action in each of these situations, down to the last minute detail, including all possible eventualities, and fantastic perseverance in practical training for them all. In the understanding and thorough comprehension of reality, at the same time stripping it of all fantasy, illusion and invention.

That was the method.

He felt as though he had been born again.

CHAPTER 12

Mr. Theodore Mundstock was watching. Watching attentively. But what he saw was not his room. Not his round table and the chairs, his desk with its lamp, the mirror by the window, the sofa that was turned into a bed at night. Mr. Theodore Mundstock was watching attentively and saw—a railway station.

How could he fail to see it since he was standing there and watching attentively?

He was standing on the platform. An enormously long train, ready to leave, was standing near by. Fifty paces, perhaps a mere forty paces away from him, but he knew very well that those forty paces to the train which was ready to leave could be a terrible distance. He pricked up his ears. A voice echoed down the platform; a loudspeaker was probably announcing the departure time, he thought, at least I shall know what time the train leaves. It was not a loudspeaker. There was someone shouting on the platform, "You filthy swine there, *sie eine Sau!* Get a move on or I'll break your legs for you." The voice roared through the station and made the lamp on the desk flicker with horror and the mirror slipped on its nail. What was to be done if the voice yelled like that? He caught sight of a figure in a uniform of the color of two generations. Great heavens, he thought, I've seen that fellow somewhere before. It's our old friend. Get a move on. . .

What about Mr. Vorjahren?

Mr. Vorjahren could see him too, but unlike Mr. Mundstock who was only watching the scene, Mr. Vorjahren was the one who had to get a move on. With a suitcase weighing fifty kilograms he had to get a move on towards the train which was ready to leave. He had another forty paces to go, a terrible distance. His legs were bending under him like a pony's and his face was drawn in weakness and fear. The engine was panting to be off, getting up steam and hissing, it was a heartless machine that could not feel pity for the struggling Mr. Vorjahren. Then suddenly the man in uniform leaped towards Mr. Vorjahren and Mr. Mundstock thought to himself it had taken him long enough to cotton onto the idea that he could help the fellow! But the soldier ran at Mr. Vorjahren and landed a kick at his suitcase. Mr. Vorjahren, forty paces away from the train, grew pale and staggered, and the case dropped from his hand. When Mr. Mundstock saw that, he paled too. That sort of thing never used to happen, people being shouted at and called swine, and having their luggage kicked about. Whoever had seen such a thing? He remembered once, when he was on his way to spend a holiday in the Vah valley, and went to buy a glass of lemonade on the station, that an unknown man had bumped into him, but he had apologized immediately, I beg your pardon, sir, and that had been an insignificant accidental nudge. Of course, that was in the old days, the days of normal people, when he was buying a glass of lemonade on the station and was going on holiday. This was nowadays, the days of madmen, and Mr. Vorjahren was neither going on holiday nor buying lemonade. Mr. Vorjahren was going to the concentration camp. And that was a very big difference.

Mr. Vorjahren, pale, pulled himself together, picked up his suitcase and dragged it on, like a pony whose knees were giving way, ready to fall at any moment. And no wonder, said Mr. Mundstock sadly to himself, with a case that size. It would be all my butcher Mr. Klokocnik could do to carry that. He watched attentively and observed a strange thing: to carry a case of that weight along a station platform what you need are not legs but—arms!

Hands!

In his own mind, as he watched Mr. Vorjahren, he asked: Exactly how is he trying to carry that suitcase? Does he change hands at all? Of course he must, he answered himself; Mr. Vorjahren is changing hands, nobody would claim to be able to carry fifty kilos in the same hand all the time, not even Mr. Klokocnik. What does it mean, then, if in spite of that he keeps dropping it? Mr. Mundstock drew significant conclusions from his observations.

The important thing was how often the fifty-kilo suitcase was shifted from one hand to the other.

He decided that it was best to change over every ten paces. That happened to be double the figure of the weight, but it was immaterial. Later the weight could be shifted at every fifth pace and that would be the same figure. Later on, of course, when there were only those last forty paces left. The moment he reached this conclusion he wanted to shout after Mr. Vorjahren to change hands every fifth step, but he couldn't. Then he noticed something else.

Mr. Vorjahren's free hand.

Heaven forbid it lie idle! It was no good just letting it flap uselessly at his side, as poor Mr. Vorjahren was doing. The free hand must carry out relaxing exercises! The fingers must move to and fro briskly. Moving the fingers and flapping the hand from the wrist were the best way to get the blood flowing properly and the hand rested. Unfortunately Mr. Vorjahren had never heard of anything like that. He wanted to shout after him, for heaven's sake, Mr. Vorjahren, flap your other hand from the wrist and move the fingers about, you'll get nowhere the way you're going on. You're digging your grave right there on that platform. But he could not shout. There was knowledge rushing in on him from all sides.

Mr. Mundstock realized, too, that it was necessary to know how to hold the suitcase.

It was a strange thing, he thought, but it was true, that people did not even know how to hold their luggage. A suitcase must be held properly with the handle in the palm of the hand, not hanging from the fingers. At that distance he could not see how Mr. Vorjahren was carrying his, but it was probably by the fingers. No wonder he could not manage it. Fingers get cramped and weak. And so—he saw—you had to have a handkerchief.

Hold the handle in a handkerchief!

But not in a fine silk one like Mr. Vorjahren used to wear in the pocket of his black suit when he went to Purim dances. You needed a good thick one, that stands to reason. Even better than a handkerchief would be a piece of flannel.

Flannel!

Of course, flannel is not only thick, it's soft as well. Of course Mr. Vorjahren had no piece of flannel with him, and so the man in uniform could swear at him and kick his suitcase about, that was only logical.

As Mr. Mundstock stood there on the platform watching Mr. Vorjahren struggling to get to the train he suddenly moved off and disappeared.

He disappeared into the little hall, behind the curtain, and opened the cupboard. Down on the bottom shelf where he kept his shoes, rope and bits of string, he would find a bit of flannel. Red flannel. Just big enough to cover the palm of his hand. When he put the scrap of flannel in his hand it reminded him of blood. As though his hand were bleeding. He felt that a man with a bleeding hand would look suspicious. That fellow in the uniform might even take his bit of flannel off him, he might dislike such things. He hurriedly returned the red flannel and looked for another piece. Among the tangle of string he found a gray piece. It was the color of his worn tie, of the building in Havel Street, of the uniform of that shouting soldier if you subtracted the green tinge. That was not at all noticeable, but it was too big. It would be enough to cover his head, not his hand, it was the remains of a pair of pyjama trousers. And so he had to go and cut a piece of the gray stuff off. Six centimeters wide and five long. Or the other way around? After careful thought he cut a piece twice that size, so that it could be folded in two. Then holding it in the palm of his hand he went over to the mirror hanging by the window in his room. There he found that the gray flannel could not be seen in his gray-white hand, as though he had nothing there. It faded into the gray-white of his hand as though it was one and the same thing. It was enough to make you cry, the way the two faded into each other, but he felt happy about it. For heaven's sake, though, what was going on down on the platform?

Excited, he rushed to the platform again and saw that Mr. Vorjahren had almost reached the train with that suitcase of his. The poor fellow still had about ten paces to go. If only he could make it before that mad soldier got at him again, thought Mr. Mundstock anxiously. The engine was steaming impatiently, it had no thoughts to spare for that poor man with his case. A soulless machine without feelings, interested only in its own levers and wheels. The poor fellow was at the end of his strength, jerking the case along, pale, stumbling, desperately staring at the endless row of coaches ten paces away; the engine whistled and quivered with impatience. Callous, as though it was a living thing.

And Mr. Mundstock, watching Mr. Vorjahren and his desperate struggle, realized suddenly that for the business to have any sense at all he would have to see how it would work with a suitcase, one like the unfortunate Mr. Vorjahren was just dragging along.

A really big suitcase.

A warm feeling flooded over him, as if he had found what he was looking for.

Mr. Mundstock moved away from the platform again and ran into the hall, where he had just such a large suitcase. He used to say he would take it with him if, God forbid, he had to go. It was a good quality case, he had taken it with him on his holidays in Slovakia. He took it into the room, up to the mirrow by the window. Then the bit of gray flannel in his hand, and he held the case firmly by the handle. He looked into the mirror. . .

Just at that moment the engine hooted and with a quick movement Mr. Mundstock managed to catch sight of Mr. Vorjahren disappearing inside one of the coaches with that terrible suitcase.

He breathed a sigh of relief, thank heaven he had managed it, but he realized that his task was not yet over. There was still something missing. And he realized the most important thing: the way Mr. Vorjahren had exhausted himself carrying that dreadful case! That was it. The case he was holding in his hand was empty, and it was supposed to be heavy. There was no point playing about with an empty suitcase like that. That wouldn't be preparing himself for anything at all.

And Mr. Mundstock standing there on the station platform began looking for heavy things to put in his suitcase.

The engine was puffing and blowing and letting off steam. As he searched for something to put in it he found himself enveloped in a cloud of steam, as if he was up in the clouds. He searched, up in the clouds. Then he found something. There was a paperweight on his desk, shoes under the table, an iron in the hall, and an iron off the stove. He found them, up in the clouds. Then he felt in the bookcase for books to make up the weight. The case was full to bursting. He could hardly close it and it was a wonder the locks held. Suppose anyone were to kick it, he thought, such an unthinkable thing! He took his bit of flannel and ran out of the clouds and over to the mirror.

The engine gave a last whistle and the wheels thundered

over the rails. Burning with a fever the machine began to move.

Mr. Mundstock put the case down by his side and held his hand to his eyes to peer at the windows of the coach Mr. Vorjahren had got into. He was not to be seen. Unknown faces were leaning out of the windows, pale ones, gray ones, yellow ones, terrified, gaunt, sad, some seemed to be fainting as they waved and called and wept. Poor creatures! And Mr. Mundstock decided that the compartments were so full that Mr. Vorjahren had not managed to get near the window. He could not even wave goodbye to his unfortunate friend. He resignedly lifted his case and moved away.

Then began the training in lifting his suitcase.

Here Mr. Mundstock made his last discovery.

As he lifted the case, up, down, up, down, ten times over, the sweat pouring off him, and then with the case in the other hand, up, down, up, down, another ten times, the sweat running down his face, he discovered that his left arm was not as strong as the right.

His left arm was weaker!

Of course, it's the same with everybody; most people are right-handed, he thought. The only thing is to realize it in time. Mr. Vorjahren hadn't realized it in time.

The last coach of the long, long train was disappearing in the tunnel with its red light, and Mr. Mundstock knew he would have to practice lifting his case with the left hand, every day. It was hard work and made him sweat. But here was no help for it, the times we were living in. He took out a notebook and jotted down: lifting, left hand, one hour.

The red light on the last coach disappeared in the tunnel.

The station platform was empty and quiet.

Mr. Mundstock realized he was alone on the station with his suitcase; he looked at his watch and saw it was time to be moving off. Why not? he thought, he'd done what he set out to do. That would be manageable. He'd get to the train all right. If that was the worst. . .

He wiped the sweat from his brow, picked up his case with

his bit of flannel, and set off. His steps rang through the empty station so that's that, he thought, but poor Mr. Vorjahren had a bad time of it, that's what happens if you don't make proper preparations in time. Now he was in that tunnel. . .

The table with its chairs, the desk with its lamp, the sofa. The sofa that he would soon be making over into a bed.

Mr. Mundstock's blood was up.

Ignoring the fact that his arms were aching, he had to go on; he knew there would be no meaning in it otherwise. It was just waste of time to be playing about.

He got up from the sofa in great excitement and took a step towards the window, where his mirror hung. Suddenly he stopped stock still, his legs would not take him further. He was in a terrible crush, standing there, unable to move; he felt very hot. He wanted to look round but it was dark all round him, so dark that he could not even see Columbus's ship on the lampshade. The darkness would pass, it was already thinning, pale light shot through the gloom and the daylight made his eyes ache. The ship sailed into view.

They were out of the tunnel.

He looked round the packed compartment and towards the corridor, and saw that things were worse than he had thought.

A yard ahead of him poor Mr. Vorjahren was squeezed in.

Was he gasping for breath, or was it hunger made him do that? He was probably hungry, because he had just tried to move. He was trying to bend down and get at his awful suitcase on the floor. Only hunger could make him do such a thing, he must have got bread in the case. As he bent down he pushed into his neighbor, no wonder, in that crush, the other man pushed against the next, and so on, and oh, dear! the soldier was just coming along the corridor.

"What's going on in here? Filthy red swine, I'll pitch you out on the line."

That was addressed to poor Mr. Vorjahren. He paled and began to tremble, left his suitcase alone and tried to straighten up again. Mr. Mundstock paled, too. Whoever heard of such a thing, shouting filthy swine and threatening to throw people out of the window. The soldier must be mad! When he last went on holiday . . . but that was in the old days. The compartment wasn't packed. They were all sitting down and could open their suitcases and even take out a napkin. And there were no soldiers marching about there at all, let alone mad ones; there was only the ticket collector with his clippers and then the man in a white coat who brought beer round. Mr. Vorjahren ought to have realized he wasn't going for a holiday. Mr. Vorjahren was on his way to a concentration camp! Mr. Mundstock looked at the desperate Mr. Vorjahren a yard away from him and thought how stupid it was to put your bread into a big suitcase like that. How could the poor fellow have thought of that? And he realized a very important thing.

How very important it was not to try to move about too much in a packed compartment.

From this he drew another significant conclusion: he must have a piece of bread in his pocket.

Filled with pleasurable excitement, like a man who has discovered a new corner of the world, he pushed his way through the crowded compartment to the hall and behind his curtain he cut himself a slice of stale bread, put it in his pocket, and calmly squeezed back into the compartment.

As he stood there, squeezed on all sides, he could not reach for his suitcase and so he did not push into his companion. In that cramped compartment he did not even take the bread out of his pocket. All he needed to do was to crumble it in his pocket. He would satisfy his hunger better that way, too, breaking it off bit by bit. Like drinking beer by the spoonful. And it wasn't so noticeable, either, as if he were to take the whole slice and bite it.

The uniform-clad madman came along the corridor and stopped to look in.

Mr. Mundstock was merrily breaking off bits of bread in his pocket and carrying them to his mouth with the minimum of motion. He pricked up his ears but could not hear a word. The mad soldier was as dumb as a fish. He could not even accuse him of eating, let alone call him a swine. Mr. Mundstock did not push against anybody. He did not push against a single one of his companions. . .

In his delight he would have liked to shout at Mr. Vorjahren and tell him for heaven's sake to behave sensibly in that crowded compartment, look, that was how he ought to be doing it. In his pocket. Breaking it off bit by bit. But he couldn't shout. And anyway, the heat was getting too much for him.

He pushed his way out of the compartment again, into the corridor the soldier had passed along a few minutes earlier, and took a deep breath. He wiped the sweat off his face and said to himself that it was going fine, thank heaven, and so far so good. It wasn't much, yet, though. Looking back into the compartment he thought, poor old Vorjahren, still trying to push about in there.

Poor old Vorjahren, who hadn't known that in a crowded compartment you have to have your bread in your pocket.

Mr. Mundstock knew well enough that he was not through yet. It was going to be far worse when they got to their destination.

Their destination!

Was there anything to be done about that?

You have to take things as they are, complete, and not just a bit here and there. Playing about like that would be no preparation at all.

Excited and worked up as he was, Mr. Mundstock had to take himself in hand, sigh, and start on another sorry stage of his preparations.

The train slowed down beneath his feet and came to a stop. It was standing by the sort of raised siding they use for freight trains. Crowds of uniforms were rushing about under the windows in jackboots and yelling. Probably: All out, please, *bitte aussteigen*. Mr. Mundstock strained his ears.

"*Heraus, Schweine, heraus!* Get out, you swine, get out!"

The thought crossed his mind that perhaps there was a

wagon of pork attached to their train, and of course it would have to be unloaded quickly; he had never eaten the stuff himself. Then he saw that the people were tumbling out of the train. Pale, grayish, yellowish faces, all the faces that had been waving and weeping at the windows as the train left the station, and among them Mr. Vorjahren with his terrified face, dragging that dreadful heavy suitcase after him. The men in uniform were yelling like madmen. Mr. Mundstock could not catch the words, but he had the feeling they were not yelling, "This way, please." He went out and on to the siding last, putting his case down by his side and looking round calmly. Almost as though he were looking for a porter. What he saw, though, was something terrible.

The men in uniform started hitting about them. They struck at everyone within reach, as though they were working at a conveyor belt.

What had become of Mr. Vorjahren?

He did not have to look long. He saw Mr. Vorjahren reeling, pale in the face, as he dropped his case. The poor man had caught one of the blows. Mr. Mundstock paled as he thought of it. That sort of thing never used to happen. When he got out of the train that day, going on holiday . . . but he had better not think about it. The men in uniform were obviously quite mad, you couldn't shout and call people swine and beat them up like that, the moment they get out of the train. Normal people don't do things like that. And as he watched the chaotic scene, Mr. Mundstock noticed an interesting fact.

The people at the edge were getting the worst of it.

Mr. Vorjahren, for instance, was standing on the edge of the crowd when he was hit.

Mr. Mundstock was glad he had noticed that.

But Mr. Mundstock went on watching and so he noticed much more: far more blows were aimed, for instance, at those who were remarkable in any way.

Mr. Vorjahren had made a big mistake to stand on the edge

[127]

of the crowd as they stood on the siding, but Mr. Vorjahren was also terribly noticeable, for heaven's sake. He had only just realized that. He was dressed as though for a Purim dance! He even had a silk handkerchief in his breast pocket! For God's sake, Mr. Vorjahren, you're not on your way to a Purim dance, you're going to the concentration camp, what an idea to dress like that! No wonder you keep getting hit when you're all dressed up like that. The madmen might think, look, there's one of those rich Jews. You're not rich at all! Mr. Mundstock would have liked to shout after him, but Mr. Vorjahren couldn't undress there on that siding, anyway. And he couldn't even shout. He thought tempestuously that he would be careful not to look like that. Oh, dear, no! The only coat he could think of wearing when he went to the concentration camp would be the one he swept the streets in. Or perhaps he'd better not. It was old and black, and they might think he'd done it on purpose. Pretending he was going to a funeral. He'd take his other, the dark blue one he hadn't had on the last ten years.

Mr. Mundstock standing there on the siding behind the thousands crowded there with Mr. Vorjahren moved quickly and went into the hall behind the curtain. With a warm feeling flooding him he opened his cupboard and took out the dark blue coat. Back in the little room he put it on and went up to the mirror. He looked at himself carefully. The coat was too big for him, of course, he had lost seventy or eighty pounds during those three years, everything he had got was too big for him, now, he couldn't find anything to fit.

But as he looked at himself in the mirror he felt there was something about that dark blue coat that stuck out a mile. Much worse than the old black one he wore to sweep the street in. It was funny, unreal, somehow, not like a coat at all; it was like something out of another world. If the engine had been standing there letting off steam he would have thought he was still in the clouds. What on earth was wrong with it? Just that he hadn't had it on for ten years and wasn't used to it? That might be it. Then all at once it dawned on him.

There was no Star of David on it!

Yes, that was it, the star was missing. Of course, it was bound to be missing when it was a coat he hadn't worn for ten years. You didn't wear stars in those days. The fashions were very different, indeed! And Mr. Mundstock made a note to sew a star on the dark blue coat. He knew he would feel courageous enough in it then.

And so he did.

Back on the siding, in his dark blue coat without the star—if anybody noticed it, it would be there when the time came—he picked up his case and mingled with the crowd like one of themselves. He caught sight of Mr. Vorjahren, on the edge again, of course. Then the soldiers started lining them up and that was something new again.

Mr. Mundstock was counting the people.

He wanted to be in the middle, to be as far as possible from those flailing fists. If they were in ranks of seven, he wanted to be the fourth. Then he'd have three on either side. It would be worse if they were drawn up by sixes. He'd have three on one side and only two on the other. In pairs would be a catastrophe, but that was the way children walked, and how long would their procession have to be? It would stretch to the end of the world. But it wouldn't be rows of seven or of six, because seven was their number and their star was six-pointed, and the soldiers wouldn't want that. More likely to be rows of five, and that wouldn't be too bad. He would have two on each side. But that wouldn't be it, either. He remembered the Cizeks telling him one day about the five-pointed red star. That would be the Communist star, and the soldiers wouldn't want that, either. That left only rows of four, and that would be awkward. Two on one side and on the other only one. Rows of three would be better than that . . .

While he was thinking it over at such fatiguing length the

men in uniform were beating people with the butts of their rifles and yelling at them. The column of no particular shape or size set off. Mr. Mundstock counted three on either side of him. So it was the Jewish seven after all. Might they not have to weep for it! But Mr. Vorjahren got no good out of it. He was far away in front, dressed up as though it was Purim, dragging that case along with him; he was second from the edge and even worse, he kept turning round. Just you keep turning round and looking about you, he thought, but he knew very well, himself, what ought to be done.

As he went off from the station in the middle of a row, in his insignificant coat, he would not turn round to look at anything. The more you look round the more you see, and the more you see the more you are likely to be seen. And so if you don't see anything yourself . . . It's best to look at the heels of the man in front, and count your steps. Count up to ten. Later on count up to five. Change hands, shake and move your fingers. He would walk like that, trying not to be noticed, until they got there . . .

In his dark blue coat and a piece of flannel in the hand holding his tightly packed case, Mr. Mundstock marched, not turning his head, attentively watching the heels of the man in front, counting one, two, one, two, up to ten, shifting his case to the other hand and shaking and wriggling his fingers, from the window to the desk, from the desk to the sofa, from the sofa to the door, and round and round like a lion in a cage, until his legs ached and he had to laugh. It suddenly seemed so funny. It took no doing, after all! It was only a sort of merry-go-round, that was all. You only needed to be properly prepared for it. Mr. Vorjahren had obviously not prepared for it at all. But *he* had. He had gone through that part of his preparations thoroughly. And so he thought to himself that he had earned a bit of a rest, and sat down.

He was on his feet again at once.

How could he be allowed to rest? Fine sort of preparation that would be. The reality contained far more than one march from the station somewhere. They had got to go on until they arrived somewhere! They would have to be quartered somewhere! Full of expectations, Mr. Mundstock went in—to their quarters.

Quarters!

It was evening and they were getting ready for bed. The unhappy Mr. Vorjahren was getting ready too. His bed was in the corner.

The door suddenly burst wide open and a soldier with an automatic rushed in.

He's come to say good night, thought Mr. Mundstock, leaning calmly against the wall near the door, a good sleep is just what they need after a hike like that from the station, with fifty kilograms to lug about. But he knew very well the soldier hadn't come to say good night.

Down! ordered the soldier, waving his gun, Down! Trash like you.

Mr. Vorjahren lay down on his corner bed, trying to make himself comfortable.

What are you wriggling about for, that swine in the corner, son-of-a-bitch! the soldier raised his gun and aimed.

Mr. Vorjahren turned pale and lay as still as the dead. Mr. Mundstock raised his eyebrows a little. Why should Mr. Vorjahren have been so uncomfortable when he lay down? Was it the way the soldier swore at him? No need to annoy him unnecessarily, though. Mr. Vorjahren would just have to get used to being called the son-of-a-bitch, these days. Mr. Mundstock felt he was beginning to get annoyed. The way the soldier banged the door when he went out angered him. Of course he was mad, in normal times he wouldn't get a job even in the poorest hotel. Swearing and banging doors, only a psychopath would behave like that. But although he was angry at the man, he noticed nevertheless that a splinter flew off the door as it banged, a tiny little splinter. He nearly cried out loud in his surprise, why, everything's made of wood here, the walls, the floor, the ceiling, and—of course—the plank beds!

Plank beds!

What a good thing he had noticed them!

It dawned on Mr. Mundstock.

That was why Mr. Vorjahren had wriggled about so when he lay down. He wasn't used to a plank bed. It felt hard. Of course it would. Mr. Mundstock flushed with pleasure. He had made another discovery.

He was not used to a plank bed, either.

For more than thirty years he had been sleeping on the soft bed he made up every night on the sofa. For over thirty years it had been a sofa by day and a bed by night. Now there would be a radical change, he was aware of that. A bed? It was the end of all that nonsense. In a little while he would be going to bed, and he'd get his ironing board and put it on the sofa. For the moment he waited, leaning against the wall. How could he go to bed, when it hadn't come to an end yet. They were all lying down. Night had begun.

Night.

Mr. Mundstock went out into the middle of the room and looked round at them.

It was as dark as in that tunnel. He could not even see Columbus's ship on the lampshade. People were laid out all along the bunks, some of them—the most fortunate—asleep. Others were only dozing, delirious in their despair. But most of them were wide awake, gazing into the darkness. Mr. Mundstock could not see their faces but he could guess how pale they were, how gray, how yellow; a storm of protest rose in him, but he subdued it. He must not stir, or he would frighten them.

All at once it began to grow light.

The ship of Columbus's day sailed out of the darkness and began to move through the gloom alongside the dreadful bunks, where the pale, grayish and yellowish faces were coming into view too, thinner and more tired than they had been the night before when the soldier came in to say good night. It was nearly morning.

Mr. Mundstock guessed that they would be getting up in an hour or two, and his disgust at this ghastly place grew even stronger. At that moment the door flew open and uniformed men rushed in.

Good morning, gentlemen, did you have a good night, the first you spent here? Get up nice and slowly, now. That was not what they said. They were waving their guns about and barking *rasch, rausch, rasch, rausch,* like mad dogs, until the walls of the hut shook, the walls of his little room shook, and the ship on the lampshade rocked. *Rasch rausch, rasch rausch.* Mr. Mundstock felt like spitting as he stood in the middle of this wild barking. He felt he had had enough, and he had to keep a firm hand on himself to keep his attention lively. He saw that people were finding it hard to get up, in fact someone over in the corner was finding it very hard indeed. He couldn't get himself up off that bunk.

Oh, Mr. Vorjahren!

That's what comes of having slept in a bed. Let's hope it won't make too much trouble for him. Before he had formed the words in his mind he saw one of the soldiers spring across to Mr. Vorjahren and start pulling him off the bunk.

"*Sie, faule Sau,*" he was swearing at him until the walls shook, "lazy swine, how much longer d'you want?"

Mr. Vorjahren almost collapsed. That's what comes of not having had any training in lying on a plank bed. Let's hope the beast doesn't start kicking him. They're all quite mad. Suppressing his indignation Mr. Mundstock watched every movement Mr. Vorjahren made, and realized that knowing how to sleep on a plank bed was not everything.

You need to know how to get up from that plank bed, and like a flash, the moment they come and wake you.

It was certainly earlier than eight o'clock, which was the time he was used to getting up on the days when he was not sweeping on the early shift. He would just have to get used to that, too, the thought flashed through his angry mind. Who knew when they were supposed to get up in that awful concentration camp? He looked at his watch; that was something he had not yet found out. Perhaps old Haus would know, in the news he got from the Community Office. He ought to go and ask him. Perhaps seven would do?

The people were getting up off their bunks, the soldiers were barking, and it was not yet light. Day was only beginning to dawn.

Was it six? But that was their star. Still, seven was their number. That didn't mean anything. He would get up from his ironing board at six. Angrily, he finally decided on five. Even if that was the Communist red star. This seemed to be an idle coincidence that made no difference. Five it would be!

"The extra hour won't hurt me, here," he said as he looked at his watch, "but there I might have to pay dear for it. Like Samuel Vorjahren." He would learn to lie on a plank bed, to get up from a plank bed, to get up at five, and then nobody would be able to bark at him to stop wriggling about in the corner, there! And to be on the safe side he would not lie in the corner, anyway; it was logical enough. Why hadn't Vorjahren thought of that? Why make things worse?

Mr. Mundstock took a last look round the hut and said, well, that's the night over, it wasn't too bad . . . And he went and sat down in his armchair to calm himself.

Then he thought that after all, that couldn't be everything. There must be worse things, the real thing that you had to go to the concentration camp for; but never mind. Those things would come to him in time.

Another five minutes passed and Mr. Mundstock sat there and thought, but nothing came to him. Perhaps he ought to go and see Haus, after all; Mr. Haus, he would say, you get news direct from the Community Office, tell me what else goes on in those places. Of course, as long as old Haus wasn't mad by now. He couldn't go and see him at that time of the evening, anyway; he'd have to leave it until the next day, and he would have liked to carry on his preparations there and now.

There was no point in stopping yet, he thought, his head in

his hands. Just a bit of the brutality that really went on, for heaven's sake, it wouldn't do for all his preparations to be useless.

He had already progressed so far that although he was uneasy on the point, he no longer fell a prey to his uneasiness.

He felt that he looked well in spite of what he had been through.

He wondered, then, whether it was not a mistake to look too well. They might send him to hard labor. In matters of health it would be wise to stick to the middle way, too. Then it struck him that they might do it all the same . . . what then? It was like a flash of lightning. Mr. Mundstock leaped from his chair.

At the last moment he had discovered the quarries . . .

He hurried into the hall, behind the curtain, where the poker was propped against the wall. It had probably belonged to his grandmother, the Lord bless her. In a few moments Mr. Mundstock was off to work in the quarries with his pick over his shoulder.

It was a large quarry, with dwarf trees growing at the top, and dust and clatter everywhere. Wherever he looked he could see unfortunate creatures stripped to the waist, and among them the uniforms in their jack-boots. He threw off his jacket and shirt and found himself faced with a really enormous block of stone. At first he couldn't do a thing with it. He struck again and again, until the lamp nearly fell from the table, but nothing but splinters of stone flew off. He strained himself to the utmost and struck again and again, until the pick was red-hot and the wall was shaking, there were sparks behind his eyes, and then he felt he was beginning to get into his stride, and he realized why. It was all thanks to his unstinting training with that heavy case. In the quarries it was arms that counted, too. In the end he said, well, it's pretty much the same thing, the quarries wouldn't be too bad. Where had Vorjahren got to? He wasn't there, most likely, how could he be, weak and sickly as he was; that was heavy work, and they'd only take the strongest men for it. No place for a poor creature like Vorjahren of String and Rope . . . Then the whistle blew and work was over.

He wiped the sweat from his brow contentedly.

Now let those monsters in uniform say something to him!

He wanted to dress and go off, the others round him were dressing too, when all of a sudden one of the monsters sprang up in front of him and yelled at him frightfully. Mr. Mundstock turned and stood stock still. Before he could open his mouth to speak he remembered the blow on the face . . .

It was getting near midnight.

For the first time in thirty years Mr. Mundstock did not turn his sofa into a bed. He brought his ironing board in from the hall, and for the first time in thirty years Mr. Theodore Mundstock turned his sofa into a bunk.

As he lay down in the darkness on his concentration camp bunk, his whole body quivered from that blow on the face. It is true, he had first thought of it out there on the railway siding. But only here in the quarry had he realized that it was going to be a serious matter. Out there on the siding he had easily avoided the blow, because he was not standing on the outside of the column, but in the quarry he was face to face with the beast. Would he stand up to a blow like that? It never used to be done, hitting people in the face, and he'd had no experience of that sort of thing. The man in uniform yelled at him fit to split his throat, then he lifted his hand and he felt the monstrous mad hand stinging his gaunt cheek, and he saw sparks behind his eyes. Keep calm, keep calm, he said to himself lying on his plank bed in the dark; that would never do. He could taste blood on his lower lip, and tried to think back, whether he had clenched his teeth too hard and bitten himself. That might look as though he was furious. It might annoy the mad creature in uniform even worse. It was no good clenching your teeth and biting your lips. More thoughts began to assail Mr. Mundstock as he lay in his bunk in the dark. After it had happened he would not look the mad creature in the eye. That would seem like an invitation to repeat the performance. He would have to fix his eyes somewhere lower down. On his tie, like Haus used to say in the days when he sold the things, on his brown tie. He himself used to wear green and now he wore gray. Did Haus keep brown in those days? He hadn't got a single one, but he'd have to get used to them. He could dye one of his own. Buy the dye at the druggists'. What would happen if the fellow in uniform knocked one of his teeth out for him? As he lay on his plank bed Mr. Mundstock's legs sank with the thought. He realized that the lout might knock several teeth out at one blow. Then what? It would be best to spit them out at once, the mad creature would see he had not missed, and stop at that. He would turn round and go away. Perhaps it would be as well to have a tooth ready in his mouth, in case. He suddenly thought of Dr. Schleim, the dentist whose wife was an actress in the German Theatre; he had been dead six years, the Lord rest his soul, and he thought, heavens above, I've got those false teeth I've had for six years. That plate. That was settled, then, he thought, he could pry it loose with his tongue and spit it out, may the Holy One bless Schleim. Then he could pick it up and put it back in his mouth when the monster had turned away. Or in front of him, if he realized it was false and told him to pick it up. Things were going very well, he thought, very well indeed; yet as he lay on his bunk in the dark he could not help thinking of one serious drawback: he had had no practice in this extremely difficult business.

It was no easy matter to receive a crashing blow and immediately think of how to loosen your teeth and not clench them and not bite your lip and not look the beast in the eye but at his tie, and the Lord only knew what else. That would be no trifle at such a moment.

How could he prepare for this possibility?

Mr. Mundstock felt that this was going to be more difficult than training with a heavy suitcase or hammering at stone. That he could arrange on his own, but for this . . .

Mr. Mundstock turned over on his bunk and stared at the

[137]

darkness. He explained it, worked it out, thought it over, and began to feel unhappy. Nothing came to his mind, no approach he could use, no practical method, nothing at all. His eyes were beginning to close with fatigue and he was dropping off to sleep when the idea came to him at last.

How could I forget that? he thought, and his heart leaped for joy.

His plank bed was hard, the darkness was all around him, and with his eyebrows slightly raised he was smiling to himself; he felt as though he was in the most wonderful bed in the world.

CHAPTER 13

The next day Mr. Mundstock could hardly wait for evening to come. For five o'clock to come round, the time (as the experience of those miserable war years had taught him) when there were fewest people in the shops. At half past four he put on his old black coat and looked through his pockets. His key, a handkerchief, of course. His purse with a couple of crowns in it, he needed that. And most important, the meat coupon the Cizeks had given him, for fifty grams of their ration. He picked up his bag, the shield of his star, but he did not pick up his hat; today it would have got disastrously in his way. He went out of the flat.

With a coupon for fifty grams of meat, his bag, no hat, but a carefully laid plan.

How could he have forgotten about that practical-minded man who always had his own way of going about things? Why, he had brought the misery of the last three years on himself! Just by forgetting that one thing. And he had even invented a sort of shadow for himself—Mon.

"Get away," he said, seeing a shadow in the gloom of the ground-floor passage.

"It's only me, Mr. Mundstock. Good evening to you . . ."

"Oh, it's Mrs. Civrna. Good evening. Where am I going? Only round to the butcher's."

"That old thief? My respects to him."

He knew that for the first time he would not be giving her message to the butcher. He could not give him Mrs. Civrna's respects today. It would not fit in with his plan.

His plan, in which every sentence was carefully arranged and every word accounted for.

He went out of the house.

He reached the corner of the street.

And his heart thumped a little, after all.

This plan he had decided on was rather bold, he thought it over; it was really very dangerous. It was the most carefully thought-out plan he had ever laid, but suppose it did not work out in the end? What if Klokocnik called the police? He rejected the idea almost before it had formed. Klokocnik and the police, that didn't go together. Nowadays, and because of him. Hadn't he known him for years as a peppery, hot-tempered and thoroughly decent man? Wasn't Mrs. Civrna of the same opinion? Ever since the Germans had come he'd been wilder and more irascible. No, he would not let him down. He clutched his bag to his chest and the other hand clutched the purse in his pocket, the purse with a few crowns in it and a coupon for fifty grams of meat. He was prepared for all eventualities except the police, and they were out of the question, so what could go wrong? He began to notice the people passing by, and smiled indulgently.

The clock in the tower beyond the park chimed five.

The signboard, painted red and white.

Alois Klokocnik, Butcher and Delicatessen. Prime Fresh Meat. Home Killed.

Underneath was a decorated card:

> *Buy my prime meat*
> *And save your purse.*

I guarantee
Your money's worth.

The man who had the bar in the next street had composed that for him; he fancied himself as a poet.

The blackout on the shop door was not properly fixed, one of the corners was curling up and there was a light inside. But it was only five o'clock.

He opened the door with a thumping heart, and went in.

There was only one customer in the shop, a woman without a star, buying a hundred grams of black pudding. For her own and her husband's supper. They're going to have a feast, he thought, and smiled commiseratingly, pressing his bag to his chest. The woman looked at him and gave a commiserating smile too, nodded rapidly and said good evening. He was alone in the shop. Alone with the man behind the counter . . .

There he stood behind the counter, legs astride, in his white apron with his great paws on the glass top covering the sausages, a great hefty muscular giant with his shirt open at the neck and fearsome mustaches, a real butcher. He stood there looking at him and waiting for orders like an enormous dog. Mr. Mundstock felt a momentary pang, but gave no sign of his misgivings. I've been through worse things, he told himself, didn't I stand up to work in that quarry? And with an energetic gesture he silenced his own thoughts.

"A hundred grams of salami, this one at four crowns," he said, slapping his hand down on the glass counter top.

The large silent dog on the other side of the counter twitched his mustaches (perhaps he thought Mr. Mundstock sounded funny today, the way he spoke), felt under the glass with his big paw, and started cutting the salami. He slapped it on the scales without a second glance, and at the same moment Mr. Mundstock looked the other way. He knew the scales pointed to over a hundred grams. If he let his heart soften it would be the end of his carefully laid plan. Then the scales clicked back and the meat was weighed.

He felt in his pocket for his purse, opened it and handed the butcher the coupon for fifty grams. Alois Klokocnik, Butcher, barely glanced at the coupon, lost in his vast paw, quite prepared to say nothing and drop it into the drawer. That was the first hurdle. Mr. Mundstock had foreseen it and was prepared.

"What do you think you're doing, looking at the coupon as though there was something wrong with it. Accusing me of swindling, eh?" he burst out according to plan. "Didn't I give you a hundred? What d'you mean, looking at it as though it was fifty?" And he scowled ferociously.

The butcher gave him a glance and twitched his mustaches. He was embarrassed to have to bring it out and show that it was really only fifty. Mr. Mundstock had expected precisely this development. It was the second hurdle, and he was ready for it. He declared according to plan:

"I know very well I gave you a hundred. You must have mixed it up in that paw of yours."

The butcher's eyes nearly dropped out of his head.

Mr. Mundstock knew he must not give the hot-tempered butcher time to get his breath after that serious accusation. Before he found words to reply, Mr. Mundstock flung his coins down on the counter and said:

"Take your money. Four crowns is plenty to pay for that rotten salami. All the stuff you've got here is bad. D'you always sell tainted meat? Fit for the zoo, that's what it is."

The butcher had got his wits together:

"For heaven's sake, Mr. Mundstock, there's a war on, you know what I'd like to do with the whole lot, but you can't say it's tainted meat, Mr. Mundstock, sir, it's not and you can believe me, I wouldn't have it in the place . . ."

He felt it was not going quite as he had intended. He had expected the butcher to start working up into a fury, and here he was apologizing. Never mind, he would have to ignore it and carry on with his plan. That is to say, act as if the butcher had turned purple and shouted menacingly: Now then, Mr. Mundstock, what d'you mean by saying my meat's tainted.

And so he shouted back:

"What did I mean by it? You're no butcher, that's what I meant. A decent butcher would be ashamed to have the stuff in the place. You ought to be doing some other job."

"There's a war on, Mr. Mundstock," the thief was fidgeting his big paws about on the glass top, apologetically, "you can't get poultry. They've gobbled it all up themselves. You know what I'd like to do with . . ."

Once more he felt it was not going as he had intended. He had expected the butcher to be yelling by now, and here he was apologizing all the time. What had happened to his famous temper? What was the matter with him? He was angry, it was true, but at *them*. At *them!* There was nothing left but to do some quick thinking and turn his anger in the right direction.

"That's everybody's excuse, these days, blaming it all on to them," he tossed his head skeptically. "Everybody throws it back at them, as if they were responsible for everything. Everybody's innocent and they're the only ones to blame. It's the easiest thing in the world to sell bad meat and then wash your hands of it like that . . ."

He noticed the butcher getting uneasy. He was looking at him very queerly. It must have been what he'd just said. He mustn't think I'm going mad, the thought occurred to him, that would never do. And he determined not to waste any more time.

"Throwing it back at them, when they can't help it," he shouted, so loud that the glass counter rattled, and seizing his hundred grams of meat (it flashed through his mind that it was decidedly more than a hundred, he had a feeling for weight) he was ready for the culminating moment.

As the butcher stood there behind his counter, leaning on his huge paws, he threw the meat back at him, hitting him in the neck with a dull slap.

The butcher was dumbfounded.

Keep calm, keep calm, and stick it out, he whispered to himself, his whiskers are bristling, that's a good sign . . .

"What on earth do you mean, Mr. Mundstock, such a thing's never happened to me all the years I've been here," Mr. Alois Klokocnik said at last, after a long pause; he spoke in a strange dull voice as though he had to make an effort.

"What do I mean? What I said! You can eat your own dirty meat, if you want to know. Call yourself a butcher! Haven't even got the strength of a butcher in those fat paws of yours. You don't even know how to cut a piece of real meat, that you don't . . ."

Klokocnik the butcher looked as though something had just stung him. He turned purple, leaned over the counter and put a heavy paw on one of Mr. Mundstock's shoulders. "Mr. Mundstock!" he started shaking him, "Mr. Mundstock, sir!"

Two of his front teeth fell out on the counter in front of the enraged purple face. His mouth half open, he fixed his eyes on the thief's throat, at the spot where a brown tie would be . . .

"Christ Almighty!" the butcher shouted, and the purple faded from his face in a flash. "Mr. Mundstock, what have you done? Oh, dear, what a terrible thing, have your hurt yourself, are you bleeding? What on earth has happened to you?"

Then he saw across the counter a man with the happiest smile in the world, a man in an old worn coat with the yellow Star of David, the calm, kindly, mild elderly gentleman he had known for the last thirty years, and heard him say: "That's all right, Mr. Klokocnik, that's all right, there's nothing wrong. You can't imagine what it's all about, and what a service you've done me. Don't worry about those teeth, they were only false ones. I've got five more like that at home."

It was quite a bit later when Mr. Mundstock left the shop of Alois Klokocnik, Butcher and Delicatessen, with two hundred grams of salami in his pocket and a coupon for another two hundred grams in his purse; the butcher had only accepted the eight crowns. Good, kind Alois Klokocnik, he reproached himself and the tears almost came to his eyes, poor fellow, he was upset, but what else could I have done?

Evening was falling and tiny flakes of snow were drifting down, here and there one settled in his hair. The blackout lamps in the street were still off, though. He went home thinking that was another thing done. The worst, and it was over. Thanks to the Lord and Alois Klokocnik the butcher. How well things work out when plans are properly laid! The hurdles he had had to get over! And even a few deviations. But it had worked out all right. Thanks to the Lord and a carefully thought-out plan.

He went into the hall, pulled down the blackout blind, switched on the light on the wall and hurried behind the curtain. Without a second glance he slapped the two hundred grams of salami on the blue frying pan with a scrap of margarine, and lit the gas. There would be a real feast that evening. That evening he could set the table properly and read a bit out of Shulhan Aruk. Or he could go across to the Cizeks' after supper. To those kind neighbors, the Cizeks, who helped him all they could and were not afraid. Then he remembered he had a lot to do after supper. Shulhan Aruk and the Cizeks would have to wait till the next day. He looked to see how the salami was getting on, shook the pan, stirred a bit, added a pinch of salt and a drop of water. Then he took off his shirt and put on a clean one, to enjoy his meal properly and to be ready for the troubles of the evening. More troubles that were waiting for him that evening. With a happy smile on his face Mr. Mundstock sighed helplessly.

And added in his thoughts: Let's hope it's not pork salami.

CHAPTER **14**

It was morning and Mr. Mundstock was hurrying to the baker's. To Jacob Pazourek the baker, because he had run out of bread, to the man with the well-kept hands and the fine face. But it was not bread that mattered for the moment. Mr. Mundstock was hurrying to the baker's for a much more peculiar reason.

The baker in his white coat was standing by the shelves at the back of the shop, counting something, and said, "One moment, please," glancing back at him from time to time, and going on counting. He's a baker, thought Mr. Mundstock, and so he has to count his loaves, but what is he looking at me like that for? It must be because I haven't been in here for so long. Never mind, I must be patient if he's to fall in with my plan and do what I'm going to ask him to.

The baker suddenly exclaimed and dashed to the counter.

"Well, I never, sir," he cried. "I kept thinking to myself was it you or wasn't it, sir, you've changed so. I'm so sorry, Mr. Mundstock, to keep you waiting like that, I hope you don't mind."

"That's all right, Mr. Pazourek," Mr. Mundstock smiled at

him, "just carry on. You were counting the loaves and now I've got you all muddled up."

"Not at all, Mr. Mundstock, what should I be bothering about counting loaves for. I was calculating how much they've put the price of the French Chanel up, I like Chanel perfume best of all. You must have been using egg yolk, Mr. Mundstock, now don't say, or ultra-violet rays. You couldn't possibly have such a good color without. A better color you can't see even at Madame Lavecka's . . ." Behind his counter the baker clasped his well-kept hands and gazed adoringly at his customer, forgetting all around him.

Mr. Mundstock kept silent, thinking that if the baker knew why he had come he'd be surprised, indeed, and only smiled.

Just then someone called from the back for the baker to come and fetch the bread, and he said, "What a nuisance," and disappeared behind the shop with an elegant gait. In a moment he was back again, hot and bothered, bearing in his arms a great basket of loaves of bread. He dropped it on the floor and gasped:

"What a weight! Ruins your hands in no time."

Mr. Mundstock saw that his luck was in, and hastily added his bit:

"I'll say it does, a laundry basket like that. You haven't got any flannel, either."

"What did you say I hadn't got?" the baker inquired.

"Flannel."

Mr. Pazourek's delicate features stiffened in the effort to comprehend, and so he explained:

"Flannel, Mr. Pazourek, it's the most important thing, and that's just what you haven't got."

All at once it seemed to Mr. Mundstock that the baker was uneasy and did not know what to reply. How could he, when he did not know what the flannel was for. In a little while he would tell him what he had come for, and explain the whole business, and then the baker would open his eyes. He must prepare him for it a bit more, first.

"So you think I'm looking well, do you?" he asked.

The baker pulled himself together and sighed, yes, indeed. As if he had just come from Madame Lavecka's beauty parlor, perhaps Mr. Mundstock knew it? But Mrs. Schleim, now, he added sadly, she looked bad. You would hardly recognize her. She used to take such care of her appearance.

"That's the actress from the German Theatre," Mr. Mundstock nodded, "Dr. Schleim's widow."

"It must be because she's expecting her summons any day," the baker said and looked at Mr. Mundstock with renewed admiration. "I thought they didn't take real ladies like that."

Mr. Mundstock said nothing but purposely looked at his hands, and the baker took the hint:

"Is it a French cream, the Flannel you're talking about?"

Mr. Mundstock shook his head with a smile.

"Where would I get hold of French cream these days, Mr. Pazourek? Just ordinary flannel."

The baker let out a sigh of excitement and said:

"Yesterday Madam was telling me about a Mr. Haus. She said he used to have a *Trödlerei,* but I don't know him, I'm afraid, . . . Well, he's doing all kinds of queer things in his rooms and last week he tried to drown himself in a washtub, she said. *In einem Waschtrog . . .*"

Mr. Mundstock was rather shocked at this, and thought, I hope he hasn't started calling up spirits, and the baker asked:

"Is it something of your own invention?"

As Mr. Mundstock nodded secretively and said nothing, he sighed again:

"Madam's afraid they'll take this Mr. Haus off to the mad-house. Mr. Haus, *der alte Trödler,* the secondhand dealer, she said, will be finding himself in the madhouse if he isn't care-ful. *In einem Trottelhaus . . .* You're obviously not expecting a summons, looking as well as you do . . ." the baker added in a low voice and looked at him inquiringly.

Mr. Mundstock shook his head.

"What an idea, Mr. Pazourek, I'm expecting it just the same

as everybody else. Waiting for it and waiting for it. There are transports going off every day, you know . . ."

"I know," the baker replied sadly. "I know they leave every day. Madam is expecting her summons too. *Schrecklich, aber wahr,* she said. *Arme Teufel,* no difference any more. *Und der Arme muss überall in den Sack,* she said."

"That's what the theatre does for you," Mr. Mundstock shrugged it aside huffily," *der Schrecken ist oft grösser als die Gefahr,* if Mrs. von Schleim is interested, poor thing. What is going on today, Mr. Pazourek, is not a stage play as Mrs. Schleim seems to think, but the real thing. You have to be prepared for it. Method, method, that's the important thing! It's no good making up fantasies. I'll take half a loaf, if you don't mind . . ."

Mr. Mundstock handed the baker his bread coupons and the money and took his half-loaf. He turned as if to make sure there was nobody else in the shop and went on:

"As a matter of fact, Mr. Pazourek, that wasn't really what I came for today. You say I'm looking well, but of course I don't go to beauty parlors, especially not nowadays, they wouldn't even let me in. I've got quite a different way of going about things. What would you say, Mr. Pazourek, if I were to help you in the shop, now? Carrying those heavy baskets for you, for instance, but that's really nothing, that's not what I was thinking of—I might watch the oven for you when the bread's baking, and take the loaves out, that's the sort of thing I was thinking of . . ."

The baker looked to Mr. Mundstock as though he did not know what to say in his embarrassment.

"Of course I shouldn't expect to be paid for it," he said hastily. "I'd like to do it just for fun, so to speak, I don't need money. It'd just be something to fill in the time with . . ."

"That's out of the question, Mr. Mundstock," the baker pulled himself together, "the oven would kill you, it's terribly hot work, the heat simply roars out at you. I couldn't ask you to do anything like that, and you looking so well now . . ."

[149]

The bell tinkled as a customer came into the shop.

"Well, we'll discuss it again another day," said Mr. Mund-stock with a smile, "and I'll tell you all about the flannel and what it does for you if you use it . . ." and he went out.

He was cheerful on his way home, although he had not actually come to any agreement with the baker over the matter behind his visit, but it did not matter, for he felt sure the baker would fall in with his plan. He was thinking of him and the enthusiastic way he held the door open for him, but he was thinking, too, of Mrs. Schleim who was constantly expecting her summons, and of old Haus, who might even have started calling up spirits and was said to have tried to drown himself.

Poor things, he thought, they would never survive it.

Then he suddenly quickened his pace.

He hurried home with his bread.

Unlocking his door he dashed into the hall and opened his letter box. Hadn't it come while he was out at the baker's? The letter box was empty. There was not even a postcard in it.

CHAPTER 15

Just before five he sat down at the table with the Sterns.
Mrs. Stern and Grandmother could not get over their aston-
ishment.

Simon was surprised.

Freda just looked at him.

Otto said nothing.

He sat there smiling modestly and saying that wasn't what
he had come for . . .

It was Grandmother, in the end, Grandmother in her plush
chair and dignified lace cap who brought the subject up . . .

"Thank the Lord you've come, these people are at their
wits' end again. It's bitten them badly this time."

"Just imagine, they've started doubting again that it'll be
over by spring."

"You wouldn't be looking so well if you lived in this house!
You'd age in a night, like I did."

Simon had knelt on a chair on the other side of the table
and with his chin in his hand was gazing at him with those
great trusting eyes of his.

[151]

Freda was staring at the tablecloth, her hair hanging loose round her face.

Mrs. Stern said:

"I just can't believe it any longer. She talks about spring. Hasn't spring come? Isn't it April? Hasn't Pesach come and gone?" And then she said: "Have you heard that Mrs. Schleim has gone too? Did you know her?"

He said he had false teeth made by her husband. She had been expecting it.

"What you expect always comes," said Grandmother. "Mrs. Schleim expected it." And she added: "May the Lord not punish you!"

This was the signal for an outburst from Mrs. Stern.

"Why should the Lord want to punish me?" she cried. "I suppose I'm lying and she hasn't gone? Or perhaps I hoped she'd go, did I? I hoped Mrs. Schleim would go, I said so, didn't I? . . ."

"Drop the subject, do," Otto spoke up before anyone expected him to, but to no purpose.

"I should drop Kolb, too, I suppose? He hasn't gone either, has he?" she turned on him sharply. "I suppose he's still sitting at home with Emmy to look after him, not long ago I heard she'd done roast turkey, and he's getting ready for a trip to Italy. To the seaside, you know," she turned to Mr. Mundstock; "they say everything's in bloom down there now that spring has come . . . And the Neufelds aren't going, I suppose," she cried. "They haven't been fixing anything with Kopyto, have they? That's the collector," her voice took on a calmer tone all at once. "I must tell you all about him. The Nettles have been gone about a month, did you know?" She was getting upset again. "That is, if they're still there—Freda had a dream the other night," her voice began to rise again.

"A dream needn't mean anything," Freda whispered and lifted her eyes to his.

"She dreamed we'd all been shot," Simon blurted out, and looked at him inquiringly, head in hand. "There was a man in uniform there, on a sort of shooting range place, and he'd got a machine gun and we were all standing in front of him and he started firing the gun at us. He couldn't see us standing there, I s'pose, he wouldn't have fired if he had . . ."

"Yes, of course, it's an overwrought imagination," he nodded, "people are imagining an awful lot these days. You have to take things as they are and not believe whatever you happen to hear. That is the way to salvation!"

"But Mr. Mundstock," Mrs. Stern exclaimed and pretended to be surprised, "that's exactly what I am doing! Taking things as they are and not believing what I hear. And that's just what doesn't go down in this family. That's what they nag me all the time about. And why? Because they don't like the look of things as they are. They try to get out of it. They'd like to think it was still peacetime. You ought to have seen the way they went for me when I said Otto's stores had been given to a German. Where did I get such ideas? they said. Just imagine it! As if I'd invented it myself. It's his, of course," she jerked her hand in the direction of her husband, who just sat there in silence, "he's standing there behind the counter measuring lengths of corduroy. You ought to see how well the business is doing, too! Raking in the money, he is . . ." Simon giggled rudely. "There's no need for you to laugh," she turned on him, and then went on: "Is it any wonder my nerves are going to pieces? Where can you turn for strength? I don't blame people for escaping into dreams, I certainly don't. You've got to find a refuge somewhere. How can we just go on holding out? I'm only waiting for them to start reproaching me for saying my prayers. Reproach me—that isn't the word. In this family we don't reproach each other, Mr. Mundstock, we abuse each other! You fool praying! As bad as a concentration camp, it is," Mrs. Stern was practically in tears. "Just let them start," she began to rally, "I remember when we were children there wasn't a feast we didn't go to the synagogue. Pesach, Shevuoth, Hanukkah, the New Year, the Day of Atonement, but now they'll say I'm turned foolish, I suppose?"

[153]

"Nobody has reproached you with anything of the sort, Klara," Grandmother said sharply.

"Oh, no?" she cried. "You're just afraid, that's all. You see," she explained, "they heard that people don't blame others for it in the concentration camp. One rabbi sings *Mole el rakhamim* there . . ."

"It's time you learned to speak properly," said Grandmother, but Mrs. Stern burst into tears and they all fell silent.

Then, as she wiped her eyes, she asked him:

"Have you been to see Mr. Haus?"

He sensed danger and hurriedly said, no.

"So you don't know about him trying to drown himself?"

Relieved, he said, yes, he'd heard.

"Otto went to see him the day before yesterday," Mrs. Stern went on. "He's going from bad to worse. He's out of his senses by now."

"For goodness sake," Otto spoke up for the second time, and Grandmother said sharply:

"I'm not surprised at him, an old man like that."

"There's a ginger-haired girl there reading fairy stories to him," Simon called out from the other side of the table, and gave him a mysterious smile.

"The Community Office have sent a girl to look after him and cook him a bit to eat," Grandmother said sternly, "she's an orphan and sometimes she reads to him from a book of fairy tales."

"Not sometimes, all the time," Mrs. Stern interrupted her. "She sits by the window in the corner and he sits on a chair listening to her. That wouldn't matter, though," she turned to Mr. Mundstock; "but he lights candles and calls up the seventy-two angels of the Shem ha-Meforash. Have you ever heard of such a thing? Do you know what they are? I don't. Maybe I haven't got it right. Go on, you tell Mr. Mundstock what he told you, instead of just sitting there," she turned on Otto.

"Drop it, can't you?" Otto shrugged her away and went on sitting in silence.

"Just listen to me, then," Mrs. Stern went on and he had the feeling that the others were listening silently. Grandmother even turned one lace-covered ear in the direction of her daughter's voice. Only Simon went on kneeling on his chair at the other side of the table and smiling at him.

"He said that there wasn't really any war on at all, and we were all living on a star, I've forgotten the name of it, now, it's just billions of miles away . . . the war and living here on the earth is all something we've dreamed. Up there on the star there's plenty of everything, nobody wants for anything, but when we go to sleep at night, up there on the star, dreams come to us, and that's what we are doing down here. The best thing is to take sleeping pills and then we don't have these awful dreams. To take sleeping pills at night, up there on the star, of course. Do you make sense of that?"

"It's his fantasy," he declared.

"He said he'd sold the king a white statue and built himself a house with the proceeds, and that's where he's living now. On the star, I mean. Only the nightmares are troublesome, and that's why he dreams he's living in a dirty hole in Benedict Street where he hasn't even got a bath."

"Can't you leave him alone, poor fellow?" Otto growled.

"And just think, he says he can hear with his eyes and see with his teeth! So when he doesn't want to hear anything he shuts his eyes, and that's the trouble, because then he goes to sleep and starts dreaming he's down here on the earth and there's the war on. And if he doesn't want to look at things he shuts his mouth, and so he's stopped talking altogether now. That's what he told Otto, anyway."

"He was talking then, all right," said Simon, his hand over his mouth and devotion in his eyes.

"What about the orphan, the girl he's got there?" his glance passed to Simon.

"She never leaves him," Mrs. Stern replied, "just sits there in the corner by the window and reads him fairy tales. He says that's the only good thing about his dreams of the earth, the fairy tales. Every evening when he goes to sleep he takes the girl to his house on the star with him. He takes the sleeping pills in Benedict Street, though, he keeps those down here . . . If you work it all out he thinks the evening is the morning and the day's the night and the earth's a star. Only the pills are right . . . Does it make any sense at all to you?"

Otto was frowning as he sat in his corner, and the others held their breath for him to speak.

"Does he get news from the Community Office?" he asked.

"He does," Mrs. Stern nodded. "It's only just round the corner from Maisel Street to Benedict Street, and the orphan brings him the news. That's another trouble, though, he thinks the news is all part of the nightmare. Just imagine that, the Jewish Community Office and he thinks it's a nightmare! Because it's down here on the earth, you see, close to Benedict Street, it's all a dream . . ."

Poor old Haus, he thought, he thinks the news from the Community Office is all a dream. He really ought to go and see him and find out more details about the concentration camps, he really ought.

"But I didn't finish telling you about the Neufelds," Mrs. Stern went on excitedly, and Otto just shrugged and turned away to the window again. "They're preparing to go, too, and they've given stuff to Mr. Kopyto to keep for them. Bed linen."

"And a fur coat," Simon added.

"Yes, a fur coat as well. So did the Backers before they left," his mother went on.

"It's premature," Otto spoke with his back to them at the window.

Mrs. Stern raised her eyebrows and turned round.

"It's not premature," she cried, "it's too late once you have to leave. He'd like to wait until he'd locked the flat up behind him," she waved a hand disgustedly in his direction, "and is on his way downstairs. How can he know who's spying on him? They're terribly strict about it," she stressed her words, "if you give things to people to keep they call it embezzlement of

Reich property! One informer in the house is enough and there's trouble. We're lucky, as it happens, only decent people live here, but even so we have to be careful not to talk too loud. Simon's got the bad habit of talking at the top of his voice and you can hear him right down on the first floor. You've got an informer in your place, haven't you?"

"That's right, Korka," he answered, "but I'm not afraid of him."

"It doesn't seem sensible to me," said Otto.

"It doesn't seem sensible to him," his wife repeated sarcastically.

"Your Mr. Kopyto may be a crook, you know, Mrs. Stern," he said, and turned to Otto.

"Now that's too much," she interrupted. "He's not as bad as that. And even if he were, what does it matter? At least there's a grain of hope . . . anyway, I'm sure he's on the level. Mr. Kopyto is a decent honest man and not a cranky creature, not at all. He's only started getting on Granny's nerves lately."

"He comes to see you?" he was surprised.

"He drops in sometimes."

"Can't you stop talking about it?" Otto begged.

"Because he talks too much," Grandmother said. "He's always promising things and making plans and giving advice and explaining things and I simply don't trust him. You know, Mr. Mundstock, the more I listen to him the surer I am that he's putting it all on and that he's just a common rascal who could do us a lot of harm."

"He's a learned man, a collector!"

"A learned man and a collector!" Grandmother snorted. "He came and borrowed a hundred crowns off us."

"I wouldn't hold that against him," said Mrs. Stern, "he hasn't got much to spare these days . . ."

"We have, I suppose?" Grandmother retorted. "We're rolling in money, Mr. Mundstock, you must know that. They don't know what to do with the stuff. They're just talking of buying a car and going to Italy, to the seaside. It's said to be lovely there in the spring. And a house, of course they're going to buy a house, almost as nice as the one poor old Haus has up on his star . . ."

Simon laughed and gazed at him with devotion.

"Don't let's talk about that man Kopyto," Grandmother waved the subject aside with disgust. "If he is a *schlammasel schmusser* the Lord God will find him out and hold him to account. I won't worry about it. Good heavens, it's half past six already," she said suddenly and turned to Freda. "Freda dear, run along and make that miserable oatmeal in the kitchen . . . It's the food you eat on the fast of Zom Gedalyah, Mr. Mundstock, but perhaps you won't find it too bad."

Freda leaned against the edge of the table, shook her hair back on her shoulders, and went out.

"Before I forget," he felt in his pocket, "I've brought a couple of flour and margarine coupons along, and something for Simon's sweet tooth. He's the baby of the family."

He put the coupons down on the table with a slab of chocolate.

"Good heavens, it's chocolate!" they were all amazed.

"My neighbors gave it to me, the Cizeks," he explained. "They've got children themselves, but they gave me this packet. They got hold of it somewhere. Simon can enjoy himself—the baby of the family," he repeated softly.

Simon jumped up and down on his chair and smiled. He could not take his eyes off him.

There was a sudden silence which seemed embarrassing, all at once.

"Aren't those the Bolsheviks?" Grandmother asked in a muffled voice.

He nodded silently.

"They must be kind people," she spoke more calmly.

"I've never been in favor of communism, that I have not," Mrs. Stern burst out suddenly and tossed her head angrily.

"D'you think anybody's going to ask you?" Otto said.

"I suppose you hold with them, don't you? You've been one

of them as long as you can remember, haven't you? Did you know we were a Communist family, Mr. Mundstock, and he's the Commissar?"

Simon laughed outrageously and rocked on his chair.

"Just you sit properly on that chair before you fall off like you did last time," his mother shouted and wagged an admonishing finger at him.

"For heaven's sake stop talking so wildly, Klara," said Grandmother, straightening her lace cap. "Freda's out there in the kitchen and you're wasting our time with that nonsense."

"Well, Simon saw her walking up and down Rose Street, you see," Mrs. Stern told him while Freda was outside in the kitchen making the porridge. "Wandering about like a sleepwalker."

"You've forgotten to say that that's where he lives, if you must talk so much. It doesn't make sense otherwise," Grandmother put her word in.

"Mr. Mundstock has known that long enough," she snapped.

"She wasn't wandering about," Simon broke in hurriedly. "She was only walking along next to the wall and looking up."

"So she hasn't forgotten him yet?" he asked.

They shrugged their shoulders helplessly and Simon looked questioningly at him.

"Well, it isn't six months yet since I was last here," he said almost apologetically. "Still, I hope she doesn't cry over him any more?"

"No, she doesn't cry, but she's very thoughtful all the time," her mother answered.

"I wouldn't let women spoil things for me," said Simon. "She's not as bad as she was, either."

"You hold your tongue," Mrs. Stern shouted at him. "You're a silly boy . . ."

"What's silly about that? He's right," Grandmother interrupted. "He's got a lot of sense for his years." Then she added:

[159]

"Freda's better, now, Mr. Mundstock, you were quite right. Time is the best healer."

The door opened and Freda came in, carrying the plates on a tray.

She didn't take long to make the oatmeal, he thought, but perhaps there was no longer any need to talk about her. His method had turned out to be effective.

It was oatmeal with a drop of milk poured over it. He did not ask where they had got the milk from. Simon licked his lips in a funny fashion and sat down properly to the table . . .

"Have you heard about the policeman stopping Simon in the street?"

He looked up in surprise.

"It was ages ago," said Simon, "in January."

"Yes, a long time ago," Grandmother agreed.

"He didn't stop me, either, he only told me to move on. There were soldiers marching along and singing."

"He was looking into the druggist's window in Armorers Lane," said Mrs. Stern.

"He just didn't want me hanging about when they went past."

"He wasn't rough about it, though?" he asked hastily.

"No, he wasn't nasty about it, he just said move along there, young man."

"He'd got three crowns to buy a piece of soap," Mrs. Stern suddenly started sobbing and they all lowered their eyes.

"And then he saw you going along the street with your cart all hung round with queer things, and people turning round to look at you, but you didn't notice him," Mrs. Stern sighed as she went on.

"What they really wanted to see was what you were going to do when you came up to the soldiers marching in the other direction. That was what they were curious about . . ." Simon blushed.

He lifted his head from the plate of porridge and asked:

"When was this?"

"Ages ago. In January." Simon waved his spoon in the air.

"Soldiers marching towards me when I was pushing my cart along? What happened then?"

"You managed it very cleverly," Simon said with admiration, and swallowed a spoonful of oatmeal. "You turned into Lily Street, don't you remember, and swept the pavement in front of the bookshop. But I knew it was only a trick, your cart was absolutely full and anyway the man who used to work at the Post Office sweeps Lily Street."

"Mr. Kalbfleisch . . ." Mrs. Stern supplied the name.

"Look at that, now," he said after a pause, smiling, his eyes gazing into the distance. And he thought to himself that was *that* day, that lucky Friday in Armorers Lane. I never even noticed those soldiers. He was still smiling as he asked:

"So you no longer believe it's going to be over by spring? You are still afraid you'll be sent away somewhere?"

Mrs. Stern suddenly banged her spoon down on the table.

"Yes, yes, we shall. The war's not over and spring has come. We're going to be sent to the concentration camp!"

Freda lifted her head and her eyes quivered.

"You're not!" he declared energetically. "You're not going to be sent away."

"Mr. Mundstock," Mrs. Stern's voice was strangely quiet now, as if waiting for a storm to break; "I can see without looking at the calendar that April is here. When we were children we learned that the first day of spring was March 21st, which falls in the month of Nisan, after which comes the month of Iyar . . ."

"Can't you drop the subject while we're having supper, at least?" Otto sounded rather irritable.

"You've got it all wrong," Grandmother commented.

"All right, so I'm crazy!" Mrs. Stern shouted and got to her feet. "All right, it isn't spring. It's January and the snow's still falling . . ." She was getting ready to scream and weep but Otto finally stood up and flung his spoon down on the table.

"In God's name," he shouted, "can't you be quiet at the table? When we've got a visitor here too? And then you talk about this place being like a concentration camp. You're driving me mad, I tell you!"

He saw it was time to be firm. Things could not go on like that.

"Pull yourself together," he said in a loud voice, but quite calmly. "This sort of thing won't do any good. You give way to despair and then everything looks black. In a little while you'll be looking at things differently again. Come back to the table and eat your supper quietly."

Mrs. Stern came back to the table and sat down, and went on eating between her sobs. Otto picked up his spoon again. He looked at Freda furtively; she was bent over her plate, her face hidden in her hair. He wondered whether she wasn't the best off of them all.

"It's wise," he said after a while, "to take everything into account; suppose, say, we were sent away a week before it ended. Would a week be long enough to kill us? That's what I say, take all eventualities into account. Take all the facts one by one, step by step, methodically, and prepare yourself for them all. That's what I'm doing, preparing myself for it all the time. The whole secret, you see, is not to have any illusions. If you go about with your eyes open there's nothing to be afraid of. Do I look as though I was afraid?"

The expressions on their faces were just what they had been when he came to join them just before five.

"Now it's time to light the candles . . ."

Simon lit the candle and squealed.

"That's what comes of your father not lighting it, the way it's done in proper families," Mrs. Stern commented. "Everything's upside down in this family, and then they say the sins of the fathers are not visited upon the children."

"Simon dear, run and do something about the burn," Grandmother urged him. "Freda, go with him and see he puts a drop of oil on it."

Simon only laughed. He started muttering and waving his hands back and forth over the flame.

"Monkey tricks," said Grandmother, and his mother said:

"You don't know what you'll be like when you're as old as Mr. Haus."

They took the cloth off and he spread out his thirty-two deceitful images, saying with a smile that this was a new method. In fact he dealt them this way so as to be able to choose which cards to interpret himself and not be dependent on what they drew. He picked all hearts, denoting joy, luck, love; clubs, for good news, cheerful tempers, good health; and diamonds, signifying wealth, property, money. The last was for Mrs. Stern; and that she was overtrusting with some people. "If only it were true," she commented. Freda drew hearts and an occasional club; he thought she was listening to him calmly enough this time. "She's got over it," he thought to himself. Grandmother was lucky too, all hearts and clubs. She was smiling happily in her white lace cap, reminding him of an aged nursemaid. "What you told us last time was monstrous," she said. Simon was still kneeling and bending over the table, turning every now and again to try and blow out the candle standing by the door. He never managed to do more than make it flicker. Suddenly he said:

"Tell my fortune too!"

They all laughed, except Freda who sighed. Otto muttered under his breath.

For a moment he hesitated before deciding on a card for Simon. He did not mind him gazing across the table with such devotion, although it prevented him from concentrating properly. He drew hearts and clubs.

"Now this means a good school report," he began, "and here we have fun, the theatre, animals, and so on . . . When are we going to the zoo again?" he asked.

"To look up the monkeys and the elephants," Simon nodded, "if they haven't all kicked the bucket."

"He was only a little boy, the last time you went," Mrs. Stern said with a sigh; "how long ago it seems!"

"We'll be going again before long," he answered, and pointed to another card: "That's love."

[163]

They all laughed out loud, except Freda, and Simon squealed.

"Time enough to be thinking about girls," Mrs. Stern exclaimed. "You're not sixteen yet, remember!"

"Why should it be time enough?" Grandmother sat upright in her plush chair. "Better a girl than listening to your nonsense. He's turned fifteen, you know."

Then she said suddenly in a cool voice:

"He could have had a girl long ago, like in any sensible family. He ought to go round and see Haus some time. There's that girl from the Community Office there. She's about his age."

At Grandmother's words Mrs. Stern caught her head in her hands. Simon went on kneeling on his chair, his chin resting in his hands; he was still smiling, but had blushed a little. He glanced at Otto, who turned his eyes up to the chandelier with a resigned air.

He said he would have to go.

True, he had not told them much. Although they thanked him as he said goodbye in the hall, and told him warmly to come again; although they grumbled that it would probably be another six months before he turned up again. He promised not to keep them waiting for so long next time, and their pleasure at the promise, meant to be taken seriously, was sincere. He playfully threatened Freda not to dare to leave him out when she invited her wedding guests after the war, and she smiled sadly, lowering her eyes. He took it as a sign of modesty. He told Simon not to hurry about going to see Mr. Haus, and he pulled a face, looking at his mother out of the corner of one eye. As he put on his coat he said uncertainly to Mrs. Stern and to the old lady peeping at him through her lace cap, but so that Simon could not hear him:

"We'll talk over Simon's future next time."

CHAPTER 16

He slowed down a little as he passed the name-plate on the street corner. Above was written: *Benediktiner Gasse* and below there was Benedict Street. The Germans can't even translate it properly, he thought, but thank goodness he was already in the street where Haus lived.

The house was terribly ramshackle. An incredibly filthy passage led into it, with cobwebs hanging from the ceiling and rubbish caked in the dried mud underfoot. The only living creature about was a mouse. It was fleeing into the yard at the back. In the yard the ash cans were on their sides by a pile of rubbish, and a rusty old bucket lay there . . . It was May, he thought, but there was not a trace of May to be seen out there . . . The two-story building was in the yard. The upper windows were broken and stopped up with planks and straw, and nobody seemed to be living there. Haus lived on the ground floor, with a door straight from the yard. He saw his own head mirrored in a windowpane . . . It is light for a long time in May, especially in Summer Time, he thought, but it's as dark as the grave inside there . . .

He went up to the door and knocked.

[165]

It was dead quiet inside.

He knocked again and again, but in vain. When he tried the knob the door would not yield. He stepped back and looked at the dirty window. He thought he saw a head moving behind it. It could have been an optical illusion, but he thought he ought to turn his face towards the window so that Haus could see who it was, or at least realize it was someone wearing a star. He turned that way, and in a little while he heard footsteps and a chain rattled. The door opened and he could step inside.

The footsteps dragged over to the window and the sound of a roll of blackout paper being let down was heard. The room became even darker than before. Then a match was struck, the tiny yellow flame threw a flickering shadow on the floor and a candle began to burn. One; a second was lit from that, and then a third. Then he saw a shadow move towards the corner, and the flames of the candles shot up.

A pale auburn-haired girl stood in the corner, staring at him as if he were a ghost. This is the girl, Simon, he said to himself.

"I am Theodore Mundstock," he said, "and I've come to see Mr. Moyshe Haus."

"Mr. Moyshe Haus is not here," the girl answered shyly.

"Where is Mr. Haus? Will he be back?"

"Mr. Haus will be back," the girl replied and retreated to the wall.

"What time will Mr. Haus be back?"

He put on a friendly tone of voice, and a smile appeared round his lips. He had probably frightened the girl.

"Mr. Haus comes at six o'clock," she replied.

He looked at his watch; it was half past five.

"Perhaps I ought to wait, then, if you don't mind," he said. The girl nodded.

For a while she stood silent, and then she motioned with her hand: "Here is a chair. Won't you sit down, sir?"

He thanked her and sat down in the wicker armchair. He looked round the room at the piles of old furniture and rubbish. In one corner stood a white statue.

"Haven't you got electric light in here?" he asked, seeing a lamp hanging from the ceiling.

"Yes, we have, only they've cut it off," she said shyly.

He noticed then that near him a row of candlesticks stood on a sort of chest, with half-burned-down candles in them. He said nothing. He remembered the washtub and looked around the room again, but could not see a washtub anywhere. There was not even a water tap in the place, or if there was it was not to be seen. How had the poor fellow tried to drown himself, he wondered. It occurred to him that the girl might tell him something.

"Have you got another room here?" he asked her.

She stood stock still, like a statue, her arms hanging limply by her sides.

"You're afraid of me, I suppose, but you needn't be. I've known Mr. Haus for a very long time. I won't hurt you. I know the Jewish Community Office sent you here."

The girl turned her head slightly and her hair glowed red in the gloomy candlelight.

"Is there more room here?" he repeated his question and smiled at her.

"There's a sort of glory-hole."

That must be where he keeps the washtub, he thought, and did not ask any more.

He began to wonder how old she was. She certainly would not be any older than Simon. She was more likely to be younger. If she was the same age as Simon she would look different. Girls always looked older than boys at that age. He wondered what Simon would say to the place. He could not imagine him coming here, being in this room. That idea of Grandmother's was sheer madness. How ever could she have thought of it?

There was silence once more. The girl stood dumbly in her corner and he sat still without speaking. It began to be embarrassing. To break the silence he said in a friendly voice:

"Why don't you sit down? There's another chair here."

"There are two, only you can't see them from here."

"Sit down, then," he pressed her.

The girl came shyly out of her corner and sat down.

There was more light on her face now. She was indeed ginger-haired, and very pale. In spite of her pallor, though, she was very beautiful. A remarkable Jewish type, with a regular mouth and large, beadlike eyes. In the candlelight he could not have said what color they were. She really could not be more than fifteen years old. But she seemed to him to be extremely dirty.

"Do you like it here?" he asked with a crabbed smile.

She nodded.

"Is Mr. Haus kind?"

Again she nodded and went on looking at him in silence.

"Is he rather sick?"

She shook her head.

"Does he sleep well?"

She shook her head again.

"Really not?"

"Only when I read to him," she returned.

"So he goes off to sleep nicely when you read to him," he said with a smile.

"No, he doesn't go to sleep, he sleeps well."

He felt a chill come over him. Not a chill of fear. It was a strange feeling.

"Where has he gone now?" he asked.

The girl moved her head in the direction of the ceiling.

"Where?"

"Far away . . ."

"And he'll be back at six, you said?"

She nodded.

"So we'll just have to wait," he said, looking at his watch. It was a quarter to the hour. He went on talking, to break the silence that had fallen again: "I came to ask what the news is from the Community Office. I'm very interested in what's going on."

[168]

He saw that she seemed to be smiling, a tart smile.

"Won't I be able to ask him?" he smiled back.

"Yes, but you really ought to have come during the daytime, sir, there won't be much time now."

"We wake up at half past six," she added in reply to his curious glance.

"I won't keep Mr. Haus long, don't worry. Fifteen minutes at the most. Will that be all right?"

She nodded.

Now he could feel something unnatural in the air. Something he could not find words to express. Something he had never come up against in his life before. He fidgetted a little on the chair, and then suddenly stared at the girl wildly.

"Why did you say you wake up at half past six? I'm not going to spend the night here, you know. I'm going away in a little while."

"I know that," the girl laughed; "before half past six."

"Not half past six in the morning, though . . . Now! In . . ." he consulted his watch . . . "in less than half an hour. Before eighteen-thirty. You won't be getting up then."

"Oh, yes, we will," the girl nodded. "That's just when we are on our way back."

"Way back where?" he gasped.

"Back home, of course, up there," and the girl pointed upwards.

He touched his forehead. It was wet. No, not from fear; it was a strange and unaccustomed feeling of anxiety. He tried not to show it. He ran his eyes round the room, and felt as though a shadow had started to hover round him. It might have been the way the candle flames began to flicker, a little way away from him.

"Can you tell me," he asked, "where Mr. Haus is now? Couldn't you explain things to me a bit?"

He stared fixedly at the pleasant pale face beneath the ginger hair. She began to smile. It looked as though she was growing bigger, sitting on the chair facing him, and he was growing smaller.

"It's all the same wherever he is. He's asleep in the next room."

"For heaven's sake, girl, he's here all the time? Couldn't you have told him I was here?"

She shook her head.

"He went to sleep so beautifully today."

"And you say he'll wake up at six and come in here?"

She gave a smile and a nod.

Lord in Heaven, I've never heard anything like this, he thought, it's really like being in a spirit world. She was looking him in the eye with the calmest smiling face he had ever seen. A pale, pleasant little face crowned by ginger hair. There could be no doubt about it.

The girl was crazy.

He began to lose patience. Looking at his watch he saw that it was five minutes to six. He wanted to get up and go, but then he thought he might as well wait for another five minutes. Everything he had heard at the Sterns' went crowding through his head. She must have gone mad after she came here, he thought, the Community Office wouldn't have sent her here to look after him if she'd been crazy; she must have gone mad from being with him. He tried not to think of it. He turned slightly and looked towards the corner where she had stood when he first came. There was a heap of rags there, and the thought flashed through his mind that she probably lay there to sleep. He shuddered slightly, thinking of Simon. Looking at the chair he was sitting on he seemed to see a shadow flickering round it. He kept a tight hold on himself.

"There are other ladies and gentlemen that come here," the girl volunteered. . . . "For lessons . . . Mr. Haus teaches them the letters and numbers, and when they know that they know what dreams are and it doesn't make them unhappy any more. Up there . . ." and she pointed upwards, "they feel happy."

Haus must have set up a spiritualist school, he thought.

[170]

"Are they Jews, the people who come here?" he asked uncertainly.

"Of course they are," she smiled. "The others don't need it, do they? They don't need to know the real truth . . ."

He wasn't listening any more. He called out suddenly: "It's six now, young lady!"

The girl got up from her chair and moved over to the candles. "I'm not a young lady, sir," she said softly.

"What's your name, then?" he asked.

"Khanina."

"My second name? . . . I'm not allowed to tell," she smiled.

Don't be silly, he thought to himself, I can find out from the Community Office if I want to know; you're known there, all right.

"I'm not allowed to tell at the Office, either," the girl seemed to be reading his thoughts. "All they know there is the name they dream about . . . That's not my real name. Come and join us and learn the letters and the numbers, too, and learn your real name. And you'll find out when you are really awake and when you are only dreaming . . ."

You bet, he thought to himself. That's right up my alley! Then a sort of joking curiosity took hold of him, and he decided to ask what the star was called that they were living on . . .

"It's not really a star," she replied, "it's a whole constellation, the Swan . . ."

An unending silence ensued. He was gazing fixedly at her pale face with the candle burning below it, and listening to the beating of his own heart. He saw her strange smile, but it might have been the play of the shadows. It was a horrifying smile.

"Where is Mr. Haus, I ask you, it's long past six. He's still asleep!"

"He's here," said the girl with the calmest smile he had ever seen on any face.

"What d'you mean, *here?*" he sprang up from his chair.

[171]

"Just here," and the girl made a vague gesture in the air. "Can't you see him?"

He realized then that she was quite mad, and this realization calmed him somewhat.

"Look here, young lady," he tried to speak in his gentlest voice; "I have really only come to see Mr. Haus for a few minutes. I don't want to bother either you or him. I wouldn't want to detain you on your journey to the constellation of the Serpent . . ."

"The Swan," she corrected him.

"All right, the Swan if you like. It doesn't make any difference," he shrugged off the interruption.

"Oh, yes, sir, it makes a big difference, you wouldn't be going in the right direction at all. It's not that way . . ."

"All right, all right, I'm sorry, I got them mixed up," he replied testily. "Mr. Otto Stern came to see you one day, and I promised him I'd come round too . . . Now just tell me whether I can see Mr. Haus or not." His voice had begun to tremble.

She looked at him, puzzled, and shook her head in surprise.

"I thought you wanted to talk to him, to ask him about something," she said.

"That's exactly what I did want," he retorted sharply.

"Why don't you speak to him, then? Look, he's standing over there," and the shadow of her hand fluttered on the back of a cupboard.

"I can't see him, in God's name I can't see him," cried Mr. Mundstock and leaped up again. He caught his head in his hands: "God Almighty, the salvation of our souls, show me, let me see him with my own eyes . . ." he groaned.

"Come this way, then, sir," the girl said, moving towards the wall.

There was a door in the wall which he had not noticed before.

She opened it.

"You can see him now, can't you? I'll give you a light."

She took a candlestick and carried it towards the open door.

"But you mustn't speak to him in here, sir," she said firmly; "this is where he sleeps."

He looked into the tiny place.

In a long wooden washtub lay Mr. Moyshe Haus.

"Eloi!" Mr. Mundstock cried out and the flame of the candle flickered. "He's dead!"

"You are wrong, sir," the girl answered, raising the candle high, "the spirit has carried him off. He is immortal."

He flung himself out through the door.

Calm, calm, calm, he muttered to himself as he sank on his own sofa; keep calm, keep calm. It'll pass, you've got over other things all right. Keep calm!

He knocked at the Cizeks' door.

"I'm afraid I feel ill," he whispered, his eyes bloodshot. They both hurried out to him.

"It'll pass, Mr. Mundstock," said Mrs. Cizek, helping him to turn his sofa into a bed. "Something must have upset you. I haven't seen you look like this for a long time. You've been looking so well lately."

"It'll pass, Mr. Mundstock," said Mr. Cizek, "wait a minute and I'll bring you something to help you calm down."

It really did pass off.

As he got up from his plank bed next morning he shook his head sadly. That's was not the way out, it really was not, not the way old Haus had taken. Had he escaped?

Poor old Haus, who had chosen to commune with the spirits instead of facing reality.

Why had he not gone to see him earlier, when he could still have told him of the way of salvation?

CHAPTER 17

The sun was rising in the east.

In May the rising sun is like a cherry the birds have been at. Sweet juice trickles from it. But when there is a war on the earth, it bleeds. Why do wars happen? Nobody has found the answer to that question yet, thought Mr. Mundstock as he got up from his plank bed. He went over to the window and saw the sun yellow across the house roofs visible from his fourth-floor window. Even so he had to lean out a little.

Far below him the street spread as supremely calm and empty as though the war had yet to begin. Not a leaf stirred on the trees, not a bird sang. The windows across the way were still asleep.

Mr. Mundstock smiled.

Then he suddenly felt there was something menacing quivering in the air.

Something menacing quivering in the air, he thought, that's strange, as though Nature had guessed what is going to happen to me today. Why did I choose this day? Because it is the day I don't sweep the streets, I've got bread and tea in, so I

[174]

don't need to stir from home. It will be as quiet indoors as it is outside now. That's why I chose today.

He turned away from the window with the smile of a man who has chosen the best time for what he has to do, and went out into the hall to get up strength for the coming day by drinking a glass of cold water.

With this water-breakfast inside him he returned to the room, turned the plank bed back into a sofa and sat down. He had plenty of time. His suitcase stood by the door, packed ready. He looked at it with a smile for some time, its brown sides rounded out like the belly of a well-fed horse. The locks were trembling with the strain. This horse had an excellent pedigree. He had bought it long ago at an Aryan shop. The miles I've traveled with it through Slovakia, he thought, I even had it with me by the River Vah . . . He turned back to the window. The dead quiet of the morning still bore in on him from the street. The sun had not yet sprung up above the roofs and everybody was still asleep. With the happy expression of a man who knows and accepts what fate has in store for him, he half-closed his eyes.

Today he was faced with the most terrible thing fate had forced on him, the final stage of his strictly systematic preparations. All he had to do was decide which time of the day would suit this last horror of all. Morning? Afternoon? It was a waste of time to consider it; he had chosen his time before he lay down on his bunk the night before. He knew he would be approaching his terrible end in the late hours of the evening. When his neighbors the Cizeks would be safely asleep and nobody was likely to knock at his door.

In the morning there were still a few minor details to be attended to, and one of these was the horse. He opened his eyes and smiled at the horse standing ready by the door of his room.

He knew that towards noon men in uniform would come and order him to weigh his horse in front of them. They would want to know whether it was not over fifty kilograms. If it were they could say he was a crook who had embezzled part of the contents of his own flat . . . He had therefore come to the conclusion that it would be better to leave with a horse of ten kilograms less weight. A delicate rosy light was flooding in through the window; the sun rose above the roof of the house opposite and laid a patch of color on the floor below his curtain. No, he said, looking at the rosy glow, forty wouldn't be right. It was written that he was allowed fifty. They might say, Mr. Mundstock, you're a crook. What have you done with those ten kilograms? Thrown it out on the way? Throwing things out on the way is just the same as embezzling Reich property . . . Maybe they were counting on his horse for a little private gain, and that would be another reason for making sure it wasn't under weight. Then they'd fall on him for a crook because he'd made off with their personal property. It was unfortunately a well-known fact that a Jewish citizen was always in the wrong, whatever he did. He decided that the only way to avoid being a crook was to pack exactly the weight allowed. His mind's eye saw Mrs. Civrna's scales. It was a special type of decimal scale which would weigh up to sixty kilograms and yet could be folded up and carried under your arm like a folding stool. Her sister had sent it to her from America before the war. The trouble was, it meant he would have to go and fetch it . . . The rosy glow under the window had disappeared; the sun had risen through the eastern sky. The hands on Mr. Mundstock's Swiss watch were slowly creeping onwards. It was unfortunate, but there it was. If he wanted to have done with the horse he had to slip down to the janitress at once.

This morning he felt particularly comfortable in the armchair, though. Perhaps the last few days had tired him a little. He half-closed his eyes, watching the rosy light spreading over the right side of his window frame, then half-closed his eyes again, and in the end he fell asleep.

He got up from the sofa to go downstairs much later, when it was nearly twelve, nearly twelve, when the men in uniform might knock at the door any minute.

As he was getting ready to go, though, someone really did knock. There was a chorus of women's voices coming from downstairs, and on the doorstep stood Mrs. Cizek.

Her news came as a mild surprise.

"I hope they got him," he said.

"Mr. Mundstock," said Mrs. Cizek, "you ought to come round for a glass of wine this evening, when my husband gets back."

"I don't know how I can ever repay you," he said with a sigh, sincerely touched. "You're always so kind to me." He would have liked to stroke the dear kind woman's hand.

"Agreed, then?"

"I think I could, towards evening," he stopped suddenly.

"That's agreed, then."

My little black horse, you've no idea what's happened, he said as he came back into the room and went straight towards the window.

The solemn tones of a funeral march came from the loud-speakers in the street and soared towards the roofs.

Beethoven, he said to himself, the funeral march from Beethoven. He's been called to meet his Maker and that's the end of his career. Yesterday he may have been marching down a double file of soldiers in his jack-boots with his hand raised in salute, and the oak leaves with their brilliants and the swords decorating his uniform jingling. Yesterday people may still have trembled before him. And look at him now! Before you knew what was happening he was no more than a heap of dust that could be lifted on a shovel and thrown into the river. A sad end for an SS general. A sad end indeed. Something of the same sort was awaiting him that evening.

And he suddenly remembered, good heavens, I've got to weigh that horse! Time flies and I dozed off and now I'm making matters worse by hanging about playing with foolish ideas. Maybe things will have quietened down, they can't stand about downstairs all morning, they have dinners to cook.

Things were far from quiet in the building.

Mrs. Civrna stood at her door in her brightly colored overalls, surrounded by many women. As they heard his footsteps on the first floor they fell silent and turned to look at the staircase. When they saw who it was Mrs. Civrna lifted her hands to heaven and the women round her exchanged significant smiles.

Beethoven's funeral march could be heard coming from the street, trombones, harps, and violas.

He smiled to himself, thinking of how he was going to weigh his horse.

Someone entered the house, the funeral march at his heels.

A leather coat came into the passage, hat pulled down over its face; the coat covered the gaunt figure of the Gestapo man Korka. Without saying a word he took off his hat and went up the stairs.

The funeral march soared and swelled solemnly.

"I've come to borrow your scale, Mrs. Civrna," he whispered. "Would you mind lending me it till the afternoon?"

"What for?" he answered playfully when they showered him with questions. "I'm going to weigh my horse. My bundle, you know."

"For God's sake, don't say you've had your summons?"

"No, no," he smiled at them. "I'm only getting ready for it. In case I had to go."

"In case you had to go?" said Mrs. Heycl, and waved her hand airily. "There's no need to bother about that now. They've shot him and everything'll fall to pieces. They're going to have other things to worry about than driving people off to concentration camps." The others agreed with her. "No need to bother about that at all," said Mrs. Bohac; "you won't have to go anywhere, it'll all be over now."

"It'll all be over," they all said at once and their eyes flashed and they set their lips firmly.

Grumbling, Mrs. Civrna brought out her scales.

"Here you are," she said, and her bright sleeve swept menacingly past his foot as she put the thing down.

He felt very relieved as he picked the scale up.

They followed him up to the first floor with compassionate glances.

In the hall he dragged the suitcase on to the scales and found it weighed fifty-one kilograms. He opened it and considered what to take out. He took out one pair of shoes, two books, replaced the bar of laundry soap by a cake of toilet soap, and wondered whether to leave the blanket in or not. Then he thought of Mr. Vorjarhen on his bunk, and decided to leave the blanket in.

With pleasurable curiosity he dragged the case back on to the scales; it was now exactly fifty kilograms.

Then he thought of a little board on wheels that he could put under his horse and draw it along like a handcart. For some time he had had the feeling that he would never manage to carry fifty kilograms in his hand, even with the help of his piece of flannel. Fifty kilograms in one hand would be too much even for Mr. Klokocnik. The piece of flannel was essential, but the board was equally essential, he had to admit, and that was a problem to be considered. The wheels would be difficult . . .

It was getting to be three o'clock in the afternoon. The sun was high above the housetops.

He ate some bread and drank some tea, and thought: now I will take the scale back to Mrs. Civrna. She's sure to have finished dinner, like me; just as he was ready to leave there came a knock at the door.

"Mr. Mundstock," it was Mrs. Cizek whispering to him on

the landing, "they've just announced martial law. Yes, really, martial law. Come in and listen, quick—or run and listen at the window. The loudspeakers are announcing it too."

What do they really mean by that? he wondered as he went back into the room.

"For approval of the attempt on the life. . . . For hiding persons not registered with the police. . . . For . . . the death penalty. Whoever . . . will be shot."

So that's what they mean by it, he shook his head sadly and came away from the window. He sat down for a while.

Martial law all over Bohemia and Moravia, he considered it, that's revenge. They're taking their revenge for one of their men shot. They think it's their right. . . . Mr. Mundstock shrugged his shoulders; he had long stopped being afraid of them, himself. He was indifferent to their existence now, but what shocked him was the thought that martial law meant the threat of death to many people. To the Sterns, perhaps . . . the name came to him, but he put it from him at once and sat with his head in his hand.

He suddenly realized he was sitting there thinking again instead of taking the scales back as he had set out to do. As he got up the thought crossed his mind that perhaps the final stage of his preparations, planned for that evening, was coming too late after all. Martial law meant the threat of sudden death for so many people, he thought, perhaps they'll shoot me like that, too!

He looked at the suitcase ready and weighed, with the piece of gray flannel lying on the handle; looking at his watch he saw the hands jerking forward. All those preparations, and then to be taken by surprise? Impossible! He shrugged, picked up the scale, and went down to Mrs. Civrna's.

Fortunately the women were no longer hanging about the passage. It was half past three by then. But bright-colored overalls were moving down by the cellar door. She came up and opened her front door, inviting him in.

"A reign of terror, Mr. Mundstock, that's what we're going

to have now," she said, shaking her fist, "but we'll stick it out."

He put the scale down by the wall and wondered whether he hadn't left it too late and what the Sterns thought about it.

"Watch that Korka, now," said the janitress, "he'll be on duty all round the clock. He's at home at the moment, but they'll be sending for him, I expect. He'll be lording it in a car."

He stood there saying nothing, his eyes fixed on the scale, and thinking about a board with wheels attached. Maybe Mrs. Civrna would know of something. He'd be able to push his horse along on wheels.

"Show no mercy," the janitress was speaking from inside the pantry, where she was putting the scale away. "Not human, I say. Just you wait till the word comes, and we'll send them packing all right!"

He turned away from the pantry and thought about his board. He'd ask Mrs. Civrna in the morning, but not today; today everybody was full of the evil being done.

"Wouldn't you like a bit of sugar, or some millet?"

He smiled sadly and bowed his head. Then he took his leave.

She shut the door behind him, frowning.

Climbing up to the fourth floor again he thought his visit to the Cizeks' that evening might hold up his plans quite a bit. Oughtn't he to excuse himself and say he'd come tomorrow instead?

He had not even looked at his watch when Mrs. Cizek knocked for the third time that day.

He opened the door with a sigh.

"They got him, Mr. Mundstock," she told him in a low voice. "They expect him to die soon."

So that's that, he thought, he'll be dead, and his gaze was fixed on the balustrade behind her. He noticed that the black paint was peeling off.

"Come round this evening after my husband gets home.

We'll have a glass of wine for a treat. Now I've got to slip round to the druggist's for an aspirin, Charlie's got a cold."

"Charlie's got a cold," he tore his eyes away from the balustrade. "How did he manage that now, at the end of May?"

"It's hay fever," she said, "I used to have it at his age, too. He needs to keep warm and sweat it out, and have a good sleep . . ."

A thought struck him.

"If you're going to the druggist's, Mrs. Cizek, would you mind bringing me a sleeping tablet?"

Poor thing, he thought as she went down the stairs, she probably thinks I'm terribly upset and only just managing to keep myself in hand. I don't want the tablet for tonight, though, I'll slip it into the suitcase.

Come round this evening after my husband comes home, he thought it over, but when will that be? At six? Seven? Should he start before the visit? He rejected that idea at once. They might come to ask him over when he was right in the middle of his preparations. Or, God forbid, when he was right in the middle of the thing itself, and that would be a catastrophe. He would have to wait for Mr. Cizek to come home, or else he would have to refuse the invitation outright. He could not carry out his plan until he was sure the Cizeks would not come to knock at his door.

He looked at the suitcase, weighed and ready, with the piece of gray flannel on the handle.

You're all right, he said as though he was talking to his horse, you're the least of my problems. The worst is still to come. If only it was over; things were not looking too good.

He went over to the window; the hot air of a May day was there, but he could no longer see the sun, which was sailing somewhere in the southern sky. There was music of sorts coming from the loudspeakers down in the street again. Suddenly he heard the squeal of brakes in front of the house, and leaning out of his fourth floor window he saw the roof of a

German car. From beneath it there emerged two pairs of shoulders clad in leather coats, and two heads. From where he was they looked like gray ants. To the music of harps and trombones they disappeared somewhere under the wall, where his eyes could not follow them. He assumed they had come into the building.

Stepping back from the window he looked round the room with indifference. It occurred to him with a jolt that they might be coming to search his flat.

Let them come, he thought, he had nothing in the place that mattered . . .

His old smile came back.

Going into the hall, he took down from its hook a jacket with the yellow six-pointed star sewn on it, put it on and arranged it neatly, straightening his shirt collar at the neck; then he turned to face the door.

Now they can come, he said to himself.

Still the thought that what he was going to do that evening should have been done the day before kept returning.

If they came now, it would be the only mistake he had made in his calculations. If they came, that was the only thing he had not yet been through.

As he stood facing the door and waiting for them to ring the bell, his gaze fell on the letter box. He had had it for nearly thirty years, and up to a short while ago he had been in the habit of hurrying to it every day, but it was only now that he noticed how the lower part was pierced with narrow slits, ending in squares and circles. Behind them was the gray air of the empty box. He thought it must be terribly hot for the Gestapo men in those leather coats in May. They must perspire terribly by the time they got up to the fourth floor. How did they cut that metal, he wondered, it must be done by machine, by hand it would be an expensive business. They'd have a conveyor belt, the tin plate would be cut to pattern and then folded into shape. He remembered the way they learned to make paper accordions in the primary school. Folding a piece of paper like a fan and then bending it over four times. Then every fold was bent separately, in different directions alternately, and then the whole thing was joined together and that was the most difficult operation of all. Would he still be able to do it? Probably not. The Sterns had a letter box, too, but it looked different. A pattern of stars, perhaps. He hoped they wouldn't go out on the streets unnecessarily. Especially Simon. Had he made a mistake not to do today's business yesterday? If they came . . .

Though he stood there a long, long time looking at the letter box, nobody came. Five minutes passed and then ten, and still nothing happened. The landing outside was as silent as at midnight and the flat was quiet too, except for the low moan of the music coming up from the street outside.

A smile flitted over his face.

He took off his jacket with the Star of David and hung it carefully on a clothes hanger where it belonged. He was smiling as he went back into the room.

He reached the window just as a car door slammed down below and the roof of the German car moved off to the sound of flutes and violins.

Who knows what they came for, he thought, and went to sit in his armchair.

The last step, today, would be terrible and a chill would shudder down his spine; he thought it over, concealing nothing, pretending nothing, looking at it objectively, but all the time he felt there was a degree of conflict in his mind. If his practical method proved its worth, as his preparatory exercises ought to show, then this last step would never happen and his preparations for it were unnecessary. On the other hand, if he were properly prepared for it, there would be not the shadow of a doubt in his mind even if it appeared to be a threat. It was very well thought out and it could not be avoided. Even the single crack disappeared, although it was self-contradictory. All he needed now was for evening to come. For everything to be quiet. Before it happened he would go and drink to the attempt on that man's life. Who would have thought it? *Die Gläsern werden dazu klingen,* he remembered a German march he had often heard coming from the loudspeakers, *die Gläsern werden klingen* . . . No, he really ought to excuse himself and not go to the Cizeks' tonight, but he had to decide which excuse to make. The loudspeakers in the street below were silent now, and the street quiet. He began to feel time drag . . .

Mrs. Cizek knocked at the door.

She handed him the sleeping tablets. Her face was strained, and she no longer looked as happy as she had earlier.

"The Gestapo's just been here, Mr. Mundstock. They came to fetch Korka. I had to have the bad luck to run into them. He'd got his hands in his pockets and didn't even say good afternoon. Mrs. Civrna says we'd better be on the watch. She was unlucky, like me, she was just standing in the passage . . ."

Heavens, what a day, he thought, did you have to swallow the tablets with a glass of water, like those Swiss pills? He asked automatically:

"Do you think he'd been spying on us here in the building?"

"It's quite possible. He just used to pass us by with a good morning, but he might have seen everything that went on. I'm a bit afraid now. He could go and tell them all he knows."

"Don't worry, Mrs. Cizek," he said after a moment's thought whether he ought not to get some iodine as well as the tablets. "As far as I know there was nobody in the place he could have any cause to inform on. All very respectable people. He'd have to invent things."

Back in his room he wondered whether he ought not to pack some cotton as well; he could do that next morning, cotton weighs nothing. If only night would come. Time seemed to be dragging even more slowly. He thought of the Sterns, and then again of Mrs. Civrna offering him millet. He made up his mind that if Mrs. Cizek knocked for the fifth time he would say he was too tired and would she excuse him.

At six Mrs. Cizek came running across; he had never seen her look like that before.

"Whatever is happening," he exclaimed, "are things never going to settle down?"

"Mr. Mundstock, the radio has just announced the first victims of the martial law," she said breathlessly, leaning against the doorpost. "They're beginning to shoot people."

It was so unexpected he could not think of his excuses.

It was eight o'clock and he had just gone out on to the landing to make sure his door closed properly, when someone ran out of the Cizeks' flat opposite. He had only just disappeared down the stairs when Mrs. Cizek came out with a piece of paper in her hand. Her husband had written briefly and hastily that he would not be spending the night at home. He looked at Mrs. Cizek uncomprehendingly.

"It means my husband's got too much work in the factory and will have to stay overtime," she said as though it was the most usual thing in the world, but she had to catch hold of the doorpost for support. "I'm afraid our little evening will have to wait, Mr. Mundstock . . ."

"And how is Charlie feeling now?" he asked.

She made an effort to smile, and said he was perspiring nicely. In a little while she'd change his pyjamas and put him to sleep with his sister.

"We'll leave our glass of wine for tomorrow, after my husband gets back, shall we?" she said again, as her smile faded, and Mr. Mundstock agreed willingly.

"It really will be better tomorrow," he said. "It's been such a queer day today."

He wished her goodnight and then locked his door with a feeling of embarrassment.

In May the sun is the same in the west as in the east, like a ripe cherry. In wartime it reminds you of blood. The sun had long since set, but Mr. Mundstock had not watched it, for his window was to the east. Apart from the land of his fathers somewhat further to the south, it was the only thing he had to the east. He was looking at his watch, but even so he felt he could sense the blood of the setting sun. He was not afraid for himself. He just shrugged his shoulders over his own fate. Perhaps everything will be quiet now, he thought. My terrible day is just going to begin.

Then he decided to wait a few more hours for safety's sake.

CHAPTER 18

He was standing facing the wall. His hands were tied behind his back and his eyes blindfolded. Behind him he could hear the monotonous clicking of heels and snapping of rifle barrels. Heels clicking and rifles being loaded . . .

The words of a philospher he had once read came to his mind: "If we exist, there is no death; if death exists, we do not." If these words were true, he thought, death would be easy. How simple! How amazingly convinced! He did so want to believe them. He tried to master his feelings by assuring himself there was no need for fear. But the click with which the simplicity of death should appear to him did not come. Behind him they were walking about and reloading their rifles, perhaps they were even aiming, but they did not press the trigger. They were doing it on purpose to make him nervous, and had no idea they were playing his game. At least he had time to think! It was a miracle that he could, at such a tumultuous moment, but perhaps it was because of the training he had put himself through. If we exist, there is no death; if death exists, we do not . . .

It occurred to him that death is a landmark at which people

come to a stop. As long as they are alive people stop at far less momentous landmarks, like the end of a holiday, a change of job, a rise in wages, or the day they get married . . . But when they take leave of themselves, of the self they have spent their whole lives with . . . Now he can complete his leave-taking, although the men with their rifles behind his back have no idea of it. Let them go on walking about. Death is a landmark at which people come to a stop . . .

It occurred to him . . .

Oh, yes.

His settling of accounts with life was a more humdrum affair than the accounts he used to do in the string and rope business.

They had been bad times he had lived through since the Nazis had invaded his country. When they poured in they ruined the lives of millions of people. Ruining people's lives, that was something the law was not ready for; that was politics. In those evil days he lived as one among millions, but perhaps he had suffered from it more than others. It ran counter to his Jewish way of thinking. His Jewish mind rose in protest against it. His intelligence refused to accept it. His brain seemed to hold the pain of the whole of Europe.

The loss of his country's independence overwhelmed him, but in that misfortune he felt he was one of millions. In their own misfortune he felt alone. He knew that it was the most terrible persecution they had suffered in all the six thousand years of their proven existence. Before the war there had been people who accused them of being the richest and most powerful people in the world; poor, helpless Jews appeared on the Nazi posters, sitting on their sacks of gold; and behold, everything was far more complicated than that. To discover the difference between the posters and the truth the world had to sink deep into the darkness, and even so people did not see it.

What if he had not been born in Europe? In America they were not persecuted. Nor had the savage claws stretched out to Africa or Australia. But here he was, and he had to resign himself to it. Resign himself? Of course he had to. In his case any suggestion that he could do anything about it was nonsensical. He was an elderly, worn-out man. There was no point in saying he had no arms to take out and fight in the street with. He had no need to excuse or defend himself before anyone, not even before Steiner and Knapp, the two young Jews who had got away to Slovakia to join the partisans; he was indeed an elderly, worn-out man. The question then arose whether it did not call for more courage for a worn-out elderly man like himself to resign himself to his Jewish fate than to run away from the Nazi Mizraim.

Then he stopped following these thoughts.

He was standing facing the wall with his hands tied and his eyes blindfolded and fatigue was getting the better of him. He kicked the wall.

It was the movement of a man asking for death.

Asking them to do something, to press the trigger at last.

They went on clicking their heels and snapping their rifle barrels; minutes in which a man would reject the whole of his life and wish he had never been born. In the torment he was going through it occurred to him to cry out, and as he opened his mouth . . .

He felt his mouth firmly closed, his teeth clenched on something between his lips that tasted like metal. Of course. Now he knew they would shoot him at last. He formed his last farewell and pressed on the tin frog.

The frog clicked once, and then again, as his teeth released their grip.

Mr. Mundstock fell to the ground.

Then he quickly pulled the rope from his hands and with his hands free tore the scarf from his eyes. Then he quickly got to his feet, for he knew this death was not enough. There could be another death, a far stranger one. Could there really be? He hesitated for a moment, as though in horror of something, then his old determination was restored. It would be so, he confirmed his own thoughts, and I must not give in. I am almost at my goal! Beasts like the Nazis would find incredible things to do. He had heard that in concentration camps people were shut up in cells without windows and left to die of suffocation.

Yet there could certainly be even worse things than suffocation for want of air. They could turn gas on in cells like that, for they were indeed beasts who would think of things no normal person would do. He tested the rubber pipe attached to the gas tap and felt under the burner for the matches . . .

His thoughts went to Mr. Vorjahren, the Backers, the Radnitzers, the Grünwalds, Mrs. Heksch, Kolb.

Then to poor old Haus . . .

Then the whole of the Stern family, including Simon in whose future he had always believed and hoped. Whom he had wanted to do his little bit to help . . .

Then the unhappy Ruth Kraus . . .

Here he felt he must spend a longer time.

All through the Nazi occupation he had tried to think of Ruth Kraus as little as possible. He had suppressed his memories of her, as though she had only been a slight episode on the periphery of his life. Thoughts of her came upon him from time to time, not often; once when he had had millet porridge for supper, and again when he had been hurrying to visit the Sterns; at the Sterns, then that day when he had sought refuge in the miserable rope; then at Hanukkah, when he reread her last letter . . . No, his thoughts of her had not been frequent, as if she had only been a slight episode on the periphery of his life, and he knew this had been deliberate and necessary, simply to prevent himself going mad. And just as during the occupation he had thought of her as little as possible, he had never gone to visit her, terrified that he might find her flat locked and empty, that she had gone. That she had gone and ended in the only place in the world where there is peace and quiet, where her poor father lay. . . . When he had finally rid himself of fear and torment, and was capable of facing this part of reality, too, when he was able to think of Ruth Kraus again and even to go and visit her, it was too late. One day he had learned, as he suddenly admitted to himself at that moment, that Ruth Kraus had been deported. Yes, Ruth Kraus had gone with a transport at the beginning of spring that year . . . he admitted it to himself now, and his brow and temples were damp and his dry lips whispered: I wasted the whole of my bitter life with Ruth . . . I wasted the whole of my life with Ruth . . . *Eine unverheiratete jüdische Sau* . . . all alone . . . and he touched the very bottom of his brain.

Not until then did he realize he was fainting, beginning to lose consciousness . . .

He asked quickly for the gas to be turned off. . . . Indeed, he did turn the tap and the gas no longer poured from the burner. Exhausted, he dragged himself to the window and opened it, and the gas slowly disappeared from the little hall into the street. Then he went back to face the wall, and at last. . . .

The last flash of consciousness passed through his mind and Mr. Mundstock fell to the ground once more, for the last time. As he fell he knocked against the wall and smelt the lime in the distemper and the dust. He was lying on the floor now, and round his mouth . . .

Round his mouth a happy smile was playing, the smile of a man who has put his earthly life behind him and reached his last goal. The last reality, the real thing waiting for him in the concentration camp, had been experienced too. The most terrible fate in store for him had been fulfilled. Death had revealed its simplicity to him.

It was two in the morning.

And still!

Still it was not over, as he realized with surprise a little later.

He suddenly felt he was being dragged up from the floor. He was frightened but immediately felt grateful. All right, there was no reason to refuse a short sequel. Where was it written

that this brought his preparations to an end? As you like . . .
But before he could finish the thought a blow in the face
brought him to himself. As you like. His false teeth shot out
like lightning. What next? Pushing him about? As you like.
Anything else?

One of them was standing by his bed; the other by the
desk.

"What are these letters for?" he shouted and Mr. Mundstock
saw he was wearing a leather coat. "Vofjahren, Stern, Ruth
Kraus, Kraus, *eine reine Sau, nicht wahr? Aber das ist un-
glaublich. Das ist doch eine ganze Packung!*" The papers were
flung about on the floor, it looked as though the desk was
spouting papers, he smiled to himself.

"What's this board for?" the one by the bed shouted and
Mr. Mundstock saw he was wearing a leather coat too. "What's
this nonsense? You got children?" and he kicked at the tin frog
until it hopped under the desk. Let them rave, he smiled, it
doesn't surprise me. It doesn't matter to me any more at all,
I've finished my epilogue. This is mere playing around com-
pared to what I've just been through. . . . They were in the
hall now, throwing things out of the cupboard, all the rope
and bits of string.

"*Was ist das für Stricke?*" yelled the one of them, "*habt ihr
wohl Seilerei gehabt? Oder wollt ihr euch damit hängen?*"

"What about this gas?" the other was yelling, "*hier strömt
immerfort Gas aus. Ihr habt euch wegmachen wollen, ihr
Schweinhund!*"

So he wanted to do himself in, did he, the swine of a dog, he
smiled and said nothing, they really were just ordinary madmen. They were taking it out of him for spoiling their rifle-
loading exercise. For having come into the world at all. His
smile was tinged with scorn.

The first dashed back into the room and kicked the lamp
over, with the ship of Columbus's day sailing round the shade.
The lamp crashed and went out.

It was the end.

They went out and banged the door of his bachelor flat behind them, the door they had kicked open to get in.

So that's that, Mr. Mundstock breathed a sigh of relief and began to pick up his false teeth, with a little smile. That's really enough systematic preparation for one day. In fact, there was much more of it than I had planned.

Mrs. Cizek ran across, pale, in her bathrobe.

"Nothing has happened to me, Mrs. Cizek, really not, what are you worrying about? It was only a little rehearsal, that's all. Can I get the door to shut? That's a trifle. But now I'm really going to bed."

"I think it was the same two that came here with Korka this afternoon, Mr. Mundstock. Thank God it was no worse! I'll go and get you a locksmith first thing in the morning."

Mr. Mundstock smiled anxiously, but said nothing, being by nature tactful. Mrs. Cizek, on the other hand, deathly pale, was full of admiration for Mr. Mundstock. How calm and courageous he was, how firm and with a smile, just as though nobody had been going through his flat, searching it, at all.

CHAPTER 19

June 8th, 1942.

Dear Mr. Mundstock,

We send you our greetings; we are done for. Mr. Mundstock, our death warrant has just come.

We are going to Terezin.

Simon is the only one who is not going. Simon will be staying here, Mr. Mundstock. They are separating us. They told us he would go with the next lot.

We are terribly anxious about the poor boy. Otto says thank God, because it'll all be over before the next transport leaves. Do you believe that, too? You don't! It isn't true! The next transport is leaving in a few days and going somewhere else, and we shall never see each other again. The idea of it is sending me out of my mind. Has it happened to other people? Has it ever happened to parents, Mr. Mundstock, to have their children torn from them and then to be driven to their deaths, each on his own? Has what is happening to us ever happened to anyone in the world before . . . ?

We are all weeping, Mr. Mundstock, and I am at the

end of my tether. I am going blind and deaf and paralyzed. I don't know whether I shall live long enough to see that day. Otto tries to comfort me, but he is wrong as usual, poor Otto . . .

Freda is bearing up the best of all. Just imagine it, Mr. Mundstock, our Freda! Do you remember what she was like? Now she doesn't speak, but walks about the flat singing softly to herself, strange songs they are, and every now and again she smiles. Imagine it, she smiles! Mr. Mundstock, that's the only thing that is keeping us going at all. We can't help admiring her . . .

Otto packed three cases for us, but he doesn't know where he put the shoe cream, the brush, and a little nail file we used to have. You can't buy the things for love or money and I don't know what we're going to look like when we get there, I shall be ashamed to show my face . . .

Grandmother speaks nothing but Hebrew, and it's terrible. We can't understand her. Mr. Mundstock, we don't understand a word she says! Yesterday she was trying to teach me to write the letter em, it stands for mother and you write it differently at the end and at the beginning or in the middle of a word, she just says she's forgotten all her Czech, and she won't speak German. I'm not surprised, God knows, but I don't know why I'm writing all this to you. I don't even know what . . .

Mr. Mundstock, we shall not be coming back. Not us, for sure . . .

But we beg you, and I go on my knees to you, keep an eye on Simon for us. Do you remember him? Our son. He used to collect the stamps you gave him and stick them in an album. You were always like God to him, he believed everything you said and he trusted you. Mr. Mundstock, we're leaving the poor boy a little green suitcase, I bought it at an Aryan shop before the war, it cost me fifty crowns although Goldstein had the same thing for forty-

five, it's on the couch in the kitchen. He'd better take two pairs of pants and all the warm underwear. It's all packed in the case along with his shoes. We left him a thousand crowns for the poor boy to live on, and they may come and ask him to pay something, but the rent is paid up to the end of the quarter, so don't let the poor boy pay it again, the receipt's in the purse. Oh, God, Mr. Mundstock, the underwear he's got was all expensive, bought at Aryan shops, I had to waste money so he wouldn't go the way I had . . .

I don't think we shall ever meet again, Mr. Mundstock. Unless it's in Heaven, if the Lord has mercy on our souls and does not send us to perdition. In Abraham's bosom . . .

Keep well, Mr. Mundstock, you did not manage to get round to see us again. Forgive us if we have ever done anything to hurt you, but I don't think we did. With sincerest greetings from your friends the Sterns, who hope you will come out of all this better than they have done.

Klara, née Taub, Otto my husband, Grandmother my mother, Freda our daughter, Simon our son . . .

His hands dropped to his sides.

He came to himself after he did not know how long.

She had written with her last scrap of strength, at the end of her tether both bodily and mentally. Her pen had jerked about on the page and scratched the paper, and some of the lines were barely legible. But he read in them that she did not believe the war would soon be over, she did not even believe they would survive. At last he saw the crushing truth: she had never believed his words, his promises, the things he thought up for her, however probable they may have seemed, however well he had meant it; this realization brought with it a vast, infinite sadness, and he had to sit down. Then he remembered Freda. Freda was singing and smiling! He had helped Freda!

He felt such a happy excitement burst on him that he would have liked to sink to the ground like at New Year in the prayer Aleyn, and thank the Heavens for this almost incredible miracle, but. . . . The thought came faster than his knees could bend. Simon! Keep an eye on Simon! He believes in you. He trusts you. You were always like God to him. We beg you, and I go on my knees to you . . .

Once again his eyes flitted over the lines and in his fevered chase through the stumbling words he suddenly became aware of the fundamental fact at the bottom of it all: that they were being deported. That all the Sterns were being sent to Terezin, to the concentration camp of Terezin. The Sterns he had known for thirty years. Mrs. Stern, Klara, with whom he had failed; Otto, the former draper who had perhaps believed what he said; their daughter, once a bride-to-be, whom he had helped; their eighty-year-old grandmother; all of them. All of them, except for Simon their son, who believed in him like God . . . He suddenly realized that Simon was going to be left on his own, standing alone like a tree in the storm, waiting for him to come and see him, or perhaps he would come round himself, before the thunderbolt fell, before the next transport left, and he would be taken off to another concentration camp, nobody knew where, nor what it was called . . . And as he realized all this, horror overwhelmed him.

It was not the horror of martial law. It was not the horror of Gestapo men in their gray leather coats. It was not the horror of the concentration camps and the cells with gas in them. It was not horror of anything that had or would come with that dark age of criminal misery and barbarity they were living in, that hell of inhumanity, torture and sorrow. It was the immeasurable horror of his realization that for this boy who put so much trust in him he had done nothing of any use all his life . . .

For the first time in weeks Mr. Mundstock sat in his chair with his head sunk in his hands. For the first time in weeks Mr. Mundstock told himself his life had been wasted, useless and vain. For the first time in weeks tears of pity, of self-disillusionment, filled his eyes and were ready to spill over on his shocked face—but they did not. Suddenly everything soared within him and he awoke from his grim dream, his dark, nonsensical fantasy . . . Getting abruptly to his feet he picked up the Sterns's letter which had fallen to the floor. I am a fool, he cried, standing by the desk, a fool, for God's sake don't I know all is not yet lost? Don't I know we're not going to die? Who said the transport was a misfortune that had to end in death? What ever made me think that? It's not too late at all. There's still time to do everything.

I am not a messiah, he said, turned towards the window, the Lord has not allowed me to help his people Israel. But you, you He will not take from me. All that I wanted to do for you remained nothing more than a lovely rosy dream. But now the moment has come when I shall help you.

I shall teach you my methods and my way of doing things. I shall teach you to look the facts in the face so as to be able to stand up to them . . . And then, when we come back from the concentration camp . . .

Mr. Mundstock went back to his armchair and half-closed his eyes. He saw himself walking through to Havel Street, Mr. Vorjahren was sitting at the first table; he saw the park, and met Mrs. Hobzek there, who told him Mr. Kolb had come back and the next day they were all going out to his country place in Klanovice; he saw the Botanical Gardens with everything in bloom, he was sitting there with Ruth, who had just come back, looking at the palms in the glass-houses, and in a little while it would be time to go to the pictures. And he saw Simon with a birthday bunch of roses, his dear happy Simon with great glowing eyes and a smile on his lips. So here we are, my boy, he said, you see we've come through it all. You are here and so am I. And now all that matters is for your first steps in this new life to be good and happy, good and happy, the way I always wanted it for you. It doesn't matter about me, I'm getting old, as you can see, gray-haired and ready for the end, so to speak, but you are at the start. All I believed and hoped in the old days was just prejudice, the way a man with neither wife nor children of his own dreams, just rosy dreams. There is no time for that now. Now I have to put them into practice. My life was not useless and vain, no, it was not, and nothing was lost, then, nothing . . . As he sat in the armchair with half-closed eyes, seeing and hearing all this, a good, happy smile appeared round his lips, and in his eyes beneath their half-closed lids was a pure gleam, like two rosy Hanukkah lights . . .

CHAPTER 20

It was a Sunday evening, a late Sunday evening in June, so late it was almost night. There was drizzling rain outside.

The radio was playing an intermezzo, perhaps from *Cavalleria Rusticana,* perhaps from *I Pagliacci,* perhaps from some other opera. No, it was not an intermezzo. It was the overture to Verdi's *Forza del destino.* Mr. Theodore Mundstock was not listening to the overture from *La Forza del destino,* because it was a long time since he had owned a radio.

He was sitting in his room by the light of his repaired lamp, and on the lampshade the sailing ship of Christopher Columbus rocked on the waves of an endless sea; he was quietly finishing off a slice of bread sprinkled with salt. He was just going to drink his ersatz coffee when the bell rang. Mr. Mundstock put down his mug, got up and went to open the door. Quickly and calmly, although he knew from the ring that it must be a stranger, for whom the janitress had had to open the front door. He turned on the light in the hall, a bulb hung on the wall, and a single thought raced through his mind. All the people he knew had already been sent away, almost to a man. There was practically nobody left. Not even the Sterns, except for the youngest . . . No, it was not possible that his turn would not come, also. It was not possible that he should stay where he was, left behind, left to his fate. It must be the messenger.

Mr. Mundstock opened the door.

A man stood at the door.

Although it was dark on the landing, lit only by the strip of yellowish light from his hallway, Mr. Mundstock could see well. At the door stood a young man of about twenty-three with a crumpled green tie and a pale face. On his chest a big six-pointed yellow star stood out. Mr. Mundstock noticed that the young man was clutching an envelope in one hand. He nodded in silence and held out his hand. He opened the envelope and read the message.

No more than fifty kilograms; mustering point: the Trade Fair; to leave by transport.

Mr. Mundstock looked at the young man with a smile.

It was the smile of an elderly, slightly gray gentleman long, long past twenty-three, past almost the whole of his life; a calm smile, kind, serene; a smile of infinite, boundless indulgence and an imperceptible hint of some gentle, fading sorrow . . .

The young man opened his mouth and gaped with surprise, unable to find words. For a year he had been delivering these summonses, but this was something he had never yet come up against. He seemed to see a halo round the head in front of him, but it was only the silhouette against the pale light of one bulb in the little hall. He turned and fled.

It was Sunday evening, a late Sunday evening in June, so late it was almost night, and the radio was playing the overture to *La Forza del destino*, which Mr. Theodore Mundstock could not listen to. A millimeter further along the dial the first notes of one of Beethoven's symphonies sounded. He did not know which, for he could not hear that either.

Columbus's ship sailed calmly on round the lampshade, nearer and nearer to its goal.

It was nearing morning.

The lamp on the desk was still burning, and Columbus's ship was sailing round the lampshade.

Mr. Theodore Mundstock was finishing his job of tidying the flat.

He had nothing there that had been borrowed and not returned. Everything in the place was his own, everything— except for the Hanukkah menorah and one or two other things that had been his grandmother's—bought for his honest earnings over thirty years with the firm of Löwy and Rezmovitch, String and Rope. The bookcase, the table and chairs, the sofa that could be turned into a bed, the mirror, the desk, the lamp. . . . Under the lamp the black casket with letters and postcards in it . . . He took them out, went over to the Hanukkah candlestick and lit the *shammash*.

"God the everlasting and almighty, whose power is infinite, worketh great and inimitable wonders in heaven and earth," said Mr. Theodore Mundstock and thought to himself over the lighted *shammash*; "strange and wondrous are His works, as we have learned from time immemorial . . ." said Mr. Mundstock, holding the letters and postcards in the flame of the candle until the paper caught fire and burned and shrank in a moment to a handful of crumbling black ashes. Then he snuffed the candle.

Mr. Theodore Mundstock had finished the job of tidying his flat.

It was nearing morning.

The lamp on the desk was still burning, and the ship on the lampshade was sailing calmly on, nearer and nearer to its goal.

It was raining softly outside.

CHAPTER 21

The street.

Early morning.

The dust which had collected on the pavement during the recent dry weather had not yet risen into the air.

A solitary figure walking alone is the only live creature moving.

Fresh, pink-cheeked, the gentleman was smiling gently.

The corner of the house was a landmark.

He could still turn round, give a little smile, wave his hand. The corner of the house moved forward and hid the figures of the sad, shocked women at the door. Now he had to pass strange things . . .

He looked with an indulgent smile at the tradesman's sign. It was snow-white, with shining red lettering. Over the shop the butchers' square dance. He would have stopped for a while if he had not been in a hurry, but he was in a hurry. And then: he thought he caught sight of a giant head behind the ground-floor window, a face with menacing bristling mustaches, and beneath it two great paws resting on the glass counter. An enormous St. Bernard. He had better grip his piece of dove-gray flannel in his hand, and jerk his suitcase along, to get out of sight of those eyes, and then he would turn round with a kind smile. Patience, he whispered, our turn will come and then you'll see. I'll repay everything. Just you hang on courageously. But the kind ogre was not in his window, he was still snoring in bed, with no suspicion who would be passing by so early; that was one hurdle safely overcome. Jacob Pazourek, Baker? No, he had to smile here. There was not the slightest threat. He had said farewell to the baker the evening before, when he bought his last bit of bread; one piece carefully measured off was ready in his pocket.

In fact, his path did not lie that way. It lay by the park.

The city park—that was a magic place so early in the morning.

> The fresh June green of the trees, still unsullied by the dust
>   of the streets,
> the green of the grass and the bushes,
> Godspeed on your journey, a safe arrival and a safe return,
>   sir,

He smiled and nodded, it was so delightful that he could not resist. His counting of his steps slowed down, his flapping of his hands, his gait. A question was whisked towards him out of the park, touching him:

> Where are you off to,
> surely not to a spa,
> you're as sound as a pippin, with that complexion, those
>   eyes,
> what would you be doing there,
> you must be going on holiday, surely,
> but aren't you going too soon, too soon,
> June is too soon, you should try July,
> or wait till the beginning of August . . .

That's true, he replied, I ought to, not deceiving himself with his own answer, but you know, park, I decided to go on this Friday in June. Perhaps it was foolish of me, a voice spoke within him . . .

He went along cheerfully with his suitcase, counting every step his feet took; he had his star, if he had had wings as well he would have soared above the street.

He felt, indeed, as though he was being wafted along.

The case?

He did not feel its weight at all, as though something was bearing them along. In the belly of his earthly horse without a board or wheels there were not fifty nor even forty kilograms, but a mere fifteen, the outcome of belated but wise consideration.

He tripped to the corner of the park, where the policeman's helmet had gleamed that day, and dropped his eyes to the ground. Search as he would, he could see nothing but dust, no trace of what had happened in the street that day; yet all at once he thought he heard the sound of bells . . . That's an illusion, he whispered and smiled, that was long ago, long ago, that it happened. And he hurried on.

The ancient Jewish Town Hall has something in common with the angels, but since it faces to the west it was gloomy at that hour of the morning, as gloomy as the synagogue next to it, dark both with shadow and with mediaeval age, but beyond the sun was rising . . .

From the center of the golden-red crown of the sun rose the baroque spire with the ancient Hebrew clock on its side. The Hebrew clock on the little spire looked as though it was on the sun.

His glance passed to the steps by the side of the synagogue, leading up to the broad busy street.

This was the way he used to go to Havel Street.

He would not go there today, not today, it would delay him too much. When he returned . . . he would find the building and go up the wooden stairs to the first floor . . . He seemed to hear the hollow sound of his own footsteps, like drum-beats . . . His smiling eyes, reflecting the steps and the paving of the road beyond, grew more serious and quivered a little . . . The sun rose a little higher behind the synagogue and the Town

Hall, as though it wanted to get a look at him. But only the hands of the iron Hebrew clock moved forward a fraction. He turned the corner quickly . . .

Counting his steps, changing hands and agitating his fingers, agitating his fingers, changing hands and counting his steps, in his dark blue coat, on his breast the bright yellow six-pointed star gleaming like a streaming celestial body in the dark depths of the universe, he was carried on past an Old Town house with narrow arched windows, pinnacles and spires, with long-necked gargoyles; a sad smile passed over his features.

He was smiling at his own delusions of the past, the foolishness he had long since put aside.

What was he doing, he wondered.

He was sitting behind his desk meditating, perhaps about the feast of Shevuoth which was just over; perhaps he was standing facing the wall in prayer, perhaps saying the Yoser or the Ofan or the Ahava or the Zulat, perhaps the Av Harakhamim. Perhaps he was no longer there at all.

He dropped his eyes hastily to the ground and whispered, *auf wiedersehen, auf wiedersehen,* but he knew the Chief Rabbi was too old a man for there to be any certainty he would live to see the end, and so it was his duty to commend him to the mercies of God.

For all the good he has done may the Most Holy receive him into Heaven.

And he mechanically whispered *Yisgadal veyiskadash shme rabbo* . . .

The prayer for the dead. . . .

Bent heads and yellow lights seemed to be passing by. He tried to smile again, and was round the corner in another street, ten steps and he changed hands, agitated his fingers, and soon there was another street corner and another, and then round one corner . . .

A school, a sports shop, the high wall of a church ahead.

A cinema.

[207]

A highly colored woman's face.

It was not her.

A glimpse long since swept away, a faint shadow of a smile . . .

The pavement!

Here he looked round with proprietary pride.

Although he was in a hurry, he had to look round and make sure. Over there he saw a match box, there a burned-out match, and plenty of dust everywhere. He was sad to see it. But the street did its best to comfort him. Something white, as light as a feather, fluttered to his feet. As he agitated his fingers they held a discarded tram ticket. A friendly greeting from Saltpetre Street.

Nor was it the only one.

His street was grateful to him.

As he moved towards the church he stopped in his tracks. Someone was singing, so early in the morning. The song came from an open window above his head, borne on the morning breeze, a lovely plaintive melody as though an angel were singing, soaring up on high. The voice was a high tenor, clear and sweet, as though an opera singer or a teacher of singing lived there, it was strange he had never heard the voice all the time he swept that street. With a smile as gentle as the breeze playing with the plaintive melody he looked up at the window; the singer was hidden behind a curtain and could not be seen, but seemed to be singing for him, because he knew he would be passing that way. On his way . . . The plaintive melody grew fainter and fell silent, and from the window came the deep solemn sound of a chord on the piano . . . He trembled. He would have to hurry. Yes, hurry. It was high time he got there. After all . . .

Yes, he had known it and had been thinking of it.

He knew who would be there too.

Whom he would meet there.

With whom he would be traveling.

This was the first "next" transport.

I helped him pack the little green case they left ready when they went, he said to himself as he hurried towards the church. We packed five shirts, shoes for warm weather, the fawn pullover in case it gets cool, all his warm underwear and two pairs of pants. Did we put all the underwear in? I wonder if he'll have enough socks. We shut the case without even counting them, but perhaps there were two pairs . . . I hope he dressed properly for the journey today. Not to be too hot, and I hope his trousers won't be too tight, he's grown out of them a bit these two years of war . . . I hope he's got a cap, though, in case it rains in the afternoon . . .

He passed the corner by the church wall, a little patch of pavement in between high black walls, the place where he used to rest. This was where he used to pretend to be cleaning his broom and doing all kinds of things to it to mend it, a corner not yet hidden in shadow for the sun had not yet got so far. He could not hang about here today, but when he returned he would stand here as he used to with his broom, oh, dear, would he still remember how? and he would reminisce. Now he had to make up for lost time, though. The poor boy was certainly there waiting for him by now . . .

A tram was pounding along to the stop nearby, empty at this time of day, and going in his direction towards the Trade Fair. But he was not allowed to get in and ride there, although it was empty and he held a used ticket in his hand, from Saltpetre Street. Never mind. He was getting along all right. He had his piece of flannel, counted his steps, changed hands, agitated his fingers . . .

The tram rang its bell and moved off, and he hurried along after it, the poor boy was certainly there waiting for him, he changed hands, counted his steps, agitated his fingers, and to pass the time more quickly he kept his eyes on the ground.

The streets were paved in all kinds of ways, old and new, rough and smooth, sometimes fairly clean and elsewhere scattered with rubbish, but one thing they all had in common: the thick dust that had accumulated in the recent dry days. His feet stirred the dust up and the sun rose slowly behind his back, until he felt like an angel in a picture. Then he slowed down for the last time . . .

As he gazed at the street he was being wafted along . . .

The narrow patches of brown earth between the rounded cobble stones, the rounded cobbles he was treading, set in curved lines, sunken irregularly, jutting up here and there. A paving which was indelibly engraved on his memory.

His eyes and his pink cheeks glowed for a moment like the six and thirty candles of the menorah.

As if he would not recognize it!

If he were to lift his head he would see the druggist's shop where the old hose-pipe had lain that day, and over there would be the biggest house in the street, where the pile of rubble from the dismantled stove had stood.

The spot at which his salvation had been born.

Not only his salvation, not only his.

The holy, blessed paving of Armorers Lane.

He knew he ought to stop and kneel down as if it were Aleyn, and kiss it. That wonderful, delightful paving.

A flash of realization!

Was it not Friday again, the same as that day in January which he had marked in his calendar afterwards, only this was a June Friday? Was it not exactly half a year?

His blessed methods and ways of going about things.

If only he could kiss them symbolically too. But methods and ways of doing things could not be picked up and kissed like cobble stones, they were in his own mind, in that half year of practical preparation, in everything he did and thought, and they were in that good suitcase, the piece of grey flannel, his hands, the piece of bread ready in his pocket, in the counting, changing hands, agitating fingers, they were . . .

Yes, he knew very well where they were too: in the fact that there was no shadow running along by his side, the shadow that had been his inseparable companion before, the shadow that would come when its name was called, the shadow of his own self, of that sorry, hounded, exhausted, torn individual; it was such a long time ago that he'd been like that, an eternity ago, almost; now he need fear and tremble at nothing, and so he no longer needed to call upon his shadow, and what was more: he would never need to call upon it again.

He gazed down at the paving of Armorers Lane and his thoughts turned to the boy again. His own salvation had been born here, but had he had time to prepare the boy for everything during those three days? Had they really been through all the preparations in those three days? Did I not forget to tell him, he wondered, not to laugh too much in case it annoyed them, because the poor boy hasn't got false teeth like I have? And not to leave scraps of food on his plate, he'd better have a paper bag with him to carry the scraps away in, because if he couldn't finish what they gave him then they might give him less next time. And he shouldn't wear sunglasses there, in case they thought he imagined he was on holiday at the seaside and sent him to work underground somewhere . . . Didn't I forget anything, and has he really understood? I ought to have started training him earlier, he thought, I hope to God it doesn't fail . . . He took another quick look round and hastened his pace. He was almost running now. It was time he was there. At the mustering point. At the Trade Fair . . .

At last he was there.

Before Mr. Mundstock there opened the broad street, already busy at that early hour, and on the other side of it a gray concrete colossus, many stories of broad plate-glass windows.

He felt flushed and hot.

Here, then, should be the crowning success of his life, he thought with a little shiver, what a blessing his counting and changing hands had been, he hardly felt he had had anything to carry at all. But his senses were not deceived.

He had arrived. . . .

In front of the Trade Fair the broad paved space was

crowded with hundreds and hundreds of men, women, children, old men and old women, with suitcases and traveling baskets, rucksacks and bundles, and all wearing the yellow star as he was, Mr. Theodore Mundstock.

So I'll be traveling with all those people, he smiled in pity. All those people.

Their silent despair, their helplessness, their suppressed terror came to him in a wave of feeling across the wide busy street, like a rock whose weight pressed on his own spirit too.

The burden of Israel, the timeless, the immortal.

The poor creatures, it was still in waiting for them, he thought to himself, they did not know what to expect. But he knew; he had been through it all, and nothing could take him by surprise, he reassured himself . . .

His eyes wandered restlessly over the paved space, jumping about from one group to another, leaping from one yellow star to another as though they were stepping stones on which he could ford the river below the walls of Jericho. At last his eyes found what they were searching for.

He saw him.

He saw him standing a little aside from the rest, on his own, the boy with great dark eyes and a little green case. Yes, it was him. Simon.

"I've found you," he whispered, "you are the only one the Lord has not taken from me. I have been able to help you, you at least. I've taught you my blessed methods, my ways of doing things. Count your steps and change hands, every ten steps, every five, and you'll come through. . . . Oh God, let it work . . ."

As he saw Simon standing alone among those crowds, their despair, helplessness and terror coming to him across the wide busy street, he suddenly wondered whether there was any point in it at all for Simon. The thought flashed through his mind that perhaps there were things you could not prepare for . . . That's one thing I forgot to practice with him, it struck him, just that very thing, not to stand aside by himself in the crowd; he ought to try to look like the others, and I forgot to tell him that . . .

With his suitcase and his piece of gray flannel Mr. Theodore Mundstock stepped hastily out into the street to join the poor creatures there in front of the Trade Fair, given over to death, and to join the boy standing there so alone among them, the boy to whom he owed so much; he gazed before him at the pavement on the other side, at those poor creatures given over to death, at Simon standing so alone, poor boy, it was him, but he had not yet seen who was coming, but he could not call out; he smiled uncertainly, his cheeks throbbing with pity, his whole soul in that strange day.

At that moment, in the middle of the street, he realized: for Heaven's sake, be careful!

I'm in the middle of the street, I'm approaching my goal!

I ought not to be counting up to ten, now, I ought only to be counting up to five! I must keep strictly to my method, or it would not work.

And stopping with a jerk in the middle of the road he changed hands after five paces, according to his celestial plan. . . .

He heard a horrible noise. Glancing round he saw an enormous military truck bearing down on him. Everything went dark, some vast force tore his case from his hand, and he realized he had fallen into some dreadful trap . . . My God, what has happened? he heard the words shriek in his head; what were we doing, just practising, we couldn't prepare ourselves for everything, it was all some terrible mistake I made, I must have made an awful mistake . . . he felt as though a star was falling, a star that was a part of him, down, down, and it flashed through his mind, Heavens, could the boy see, would he understand, oh God, the poor boy . . . and at that moment he cried out in helpless terror. The cry was torn from him, his last cry: Mon, Mon!

He felt stone against his cheek and the last thing he recognized was the paving of that broad busy street, covered with dust . . .

People hurried up, a policeman in a helmet.

Mr. Theodore Mundstock lay beneath the giant wheel of a German truck and there was a pool of blood there.

When the truck moved and they turned Mr. Mundstock over on to his back, the policeman, although he was no doctor, saw that this man who had so suddenly stopped still in the middle of the road would never get to the other side.

It was a thin man with a graying face and motionless eyes, eyes turned beseechingly somewhere towards Heaven. The yellow Jewish star on his dark blue coat was covered in dust, but strange to say there was not a speck of blood on it. A hand in the crowd bending over him dusted it as though to suggest they might learn the identity of the dead man, and an almost inaudible voice whispered *Yisgadal veyiskadash shme rabbo* . . .

Someone might have noticed the scrap of flannel in the crushed palm. You could not tell what color it had been. It was covered with blood. But nobody noticed the little shadow trembling terrified on the paved street by the dead man.

It was cast by a weeping boy with a star and a little green case, who had run out the moment he heard someone on the other side of the road call his name . . .

Algren, Nelson.
The Man With The Golden Arm
pb: $9.95
Never Come Morning
pb: $8.95
The Neon Wilderness
pb: $8.95

Anderson, Sherwood.
The Triumph of the Egg
pb: $8.95

Boetie, Dugmore.
Familiarity Is the Kingdom of the Lost
pb: $6.95

Brodsky, Michael.
Dyad
cl: $23.95, pb: $11.95
Three Goat Songs
cl: $18.95, pb: $9.95
X in Paris
pb: $9.95
Xman
cl: $21.95, pb: $11.95

Codrescu, Andrei, ed.
American Poetry Since 1970 : Up Late
2nd ed. cl: $25.95, pb: $14.95

Ernaux, Annie.
A Woman's Story
cl: $15.95

Grimes, Tom.
A Stone of the Heart
pb: $15.95

Kalberkamp, Peter.
Mea Culpa
pb: $10.95

Martin, Augustine, ed.
Forgiveness: Ireland's Best Contemporary Short Stories
cl: $25.95, pb: $12.95

Oakes, John G.H., ed.
In the Realms of the Unreal: "Insane" Writings
cl: $24.95, pb: $12.95

Perdue, Tito.
Lee
cl: $17.95

Rabon, Israel.
The Street
pb: $9.95

Rivera, Oswald.
Fire and Rain
pb: $17.95

Santos, Rosario, ed.
And We Sold the Rain: Contemporary Fiction from Central America
cl: $18.95, pb: $9.9.5

Sokolov, Sasha.
A School for Fools
pb: $9.95

Vassilikos, Vassilis.
Z
pb: $11.95

fiction
Four Walls Eight Windows

Bachmann, Stephen, ed.
Preach Liberty: Selections from the Bible for Progressives
pb: $10.95

Beuys, Joseph.
Energy Plan for the Western Man: Joseph Beuys in America
cl: $18.95

David, Kati.
A Child's War: WW II Through the Eyes of Children
cl: $17.95

Dubuffet, Jean.
Asphyxiating Culture and Other Writings
cl: $17.95

Fried, Ronald K.
Corner Men: Great Boxing Trainers
cl: $21.95

Gould, Jay M., and Goldman, Benjamin.
Deadly Deceit: Low-Level Radiation, High-Level Cover-up
cl:$19.95, pb: $10.95

Hoffman, Abbie.
The Best of Abbie Hoffman: Selections from "Revolution for the Hell of It," "Woodstock Nation", "Steal This Book" and new writings
cl: $21.95, pb: $14.95

Howard-Howard, Margo (with Abbe Michaels).
I Was a White Slave in Harlem
pb: $12.95

Johnson, Phyllis, and Martin, David, eds.
Frontline Southern Africa: Destructive Engagement
cl: $23.95, pb: $14.95

Jones, E.P.
Where Is Home? Living Through Foster Care
cl: $17.95, pb: $9.95

Null, Gary.
The Complete Guide to Sensible Eating
pb:$14.95

Null, Gary, and Robins, Howard, D.P.M.
How to Keep Your Feet and Legs Healthy for a Lifetime: The Complete Guide to Foot and Leg Care
pb: $12.95

Ridgeway, James.
Cast a Cold Eye: The Best Columns of 1990-91
cl: $18.95, pb: $9.95

Ridgeway, James.
The March to War
pb: $10.95

Wasserman, Harvey.
Harvey Wasserman's History of the United States
pb: $8.95

Zerden, Sheldon.
The Best of Health
cl: $28.95, pb: $14.95

Four Walls Eight Windows
non-fiction

To order directly from the publisher, please complete the order form below and send with check or money order to:

Four Walls Eight Windows
PO Box 548, Village Station
New York, NY 10014
or Call 1-800-835-2246 (ext.123)
to order with an American
Express® Card

Qty.	Title	Price

Name

Address (no PO Boxes)

City/State/Zip

Prices valid through 12/31/92.

Subtotal	
Postage	$2.5
TOTAL	

☐ Send me a free catalogue